LORD KELVIN'S MACHINE

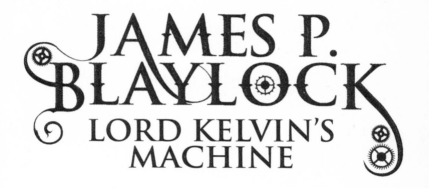

JAMES P. BLAYLOCK

LORD KELVIN'S MACHINE

TITAN BOOKS

Lord Kelvin's Machine
Print edition ISBN: 9780857689849
E-book edition ISBN: 9780857689856

Published by Titan Books
A division of Titan Publishing Group Ltd
144 Southwark Street, London SE1 0UP

First edition: March 2013

1 3 5 7 9 10 8 6 4 2

James P. Blaylock asserts the moral right to be identified as the author of this work.

A CIP catalogue record for this title is available from the British Library.

Printed and bound in the United States.

Did you enjoy this book? We love to hear from our readers.
Please email us at readerfeedback@titanemail.com or write to us at
Reader Feedback at the above address.

To receive advance information, news, competitions, and exclusive offers online,
please sign up for the Titan newsletter on our website.

WWW.TITANBOOKS.COM

This book is for Viki

And for Mark Duncan, Dennis Meyer, and Bob Martin.
The best is in the blood, there's no coincidence about it.

...And we cannot even regard ourselves as a constant; in this flux of things, our identity itself seems in a perpetual variation; and not infrequently we find our own disguise the strangest in the masquerade.

ROBERT LOUIS STEVENSON
"Crabbed Age and Youth"

PROLOGUE
MURDER IN THE SEVEN DIALS

Rain had been falling for hours, and the North Road was a muddy ribbon in the darkness. The coach slewed from side to side, bouncing and rocking, and yet Langdon St. Ives was loath to slow the pace. He held the reins tightly, looking out from under the brim of his hat, which dripped rainwater in a steady stream. They were two miles outside Crick, where they could find fresh horses—if by then it was fresh horses that they needed.

Clouds hid the moon, and the night was fearfully dark. St. Ives strained to see through the darkness, watching for a coach driving along the road ahead. There was the chance that they would overtake it before they got into Crick, and if they did, then fresh horses wouldn't matter; a coffin for a dead man would suffice.

His mind wandered, and he knew he was tired and was fueled now by hatred and fear. He forced himself to concentrate on the road ahead. Taking both the reins in his left hand, he wiped rainwater out of his face and shook his head, trying to clear it. He was foggy, though. He felt drugged. He squeezed his eyes shut and shook his head again, nearly tumbling off the seat when a wave of dizziness hit him. What was this? Was he sick? Briefly, he considered reining up and letting Hasbro, his gentleman's gentleman, drive the coach. Maybe he ought to give it up for the rest of the night, get inside and try to sleep.

His hands suddenly were without strength. The reins seemed to slip straight through them, tumbling down across his knees, and the horses, given their head, galloped along, jerking the coach behind them as it rocked on its springs. Something was terribly wrong with him—more than mere sickness—and he tried to shout to his friends, but as if in a dream his voice was airy and weak. He tried to pluck one of the reins up, but it was no use. He was made of rubber, of mist…

Someone—a man in a hat—loomed up ahead of the coach, running out of an open field, up the bank toward the road. The man was waving his hands, shouting something into the night. He might as well have been talking to the wind. Hazily, it occurred to St. Ives that the man might be trouble. What if this were some sort of ambush? He flopped helplessly on the seat, trying to hold on, his muscles gone to pudding. If that's what it was, then it was too damned bad, because there was nothing on earth that St. Ives could do to save them.

The coach drove straight down at the man, who held up a scrap of paper—a note, perhaps. Rainwater whipped into St. Ives's face as he slumped sideways, rallying his last few remnants of strength, shoving out his hand to pluck up the note. And in that moment, just before all consciousness left him, he looked straight into the stranger's face and saw that it wasn't a stranger at all. It was himself who stood at the roadside, clutching the note. And with the image of his own frightened face in his mind, St. Ives fell away into darkness and knew no more.

* * *

They had traveled almost sixteen miles since four that afternoon, but now it was beginning to seem that continuing would be futile. The black night was cold, and the rain still beat down, thumping onto the top of the coach and flooding the street six inches deep in a river that flowed down High Holborn into the Seven Dials. The pair of horses stood with their heads bowed, streaming rainwater and standing nearly to their fetlocks in the flood. The streets and storefronts were empty and dark, and as Langdon St. Ives let the drumming of raindrops fill his head with noise, he dreamed that he was a tiny man helplessly buried in a coal scuttle and that a fresh load of coal was tumbling pell-mell down the chute...

He jerked awake. It was two in the morning, and his clothes were muddy and cold. On his lap lay a loaded revolver, which he meant to use before the night was through. The coach overturning outside Crick had cost them precious hours. What that had meant—seeing the ghost of himself on the road—St. Ives couldn't say. Most likely it meant that he was falling apart. Desperation took a heavy toll. He might have been sick, of course, or tired to the point of hallucination, except that the fit had come over him so quickly, and then passed away entirely, and he had awakened to find himself lying in the mud of a ditch along the roadway, wondering how on earth he had gotten here. It was curious, but even more than curious, it was unsettling.

Long hours had gone by since, and during those hours Ignacio Narbondo might easily have spirited Alice away. He might have... He stared out into the darkness, shutting the thought out of his mind. The chase had led them to the Seven Dials, and now the faithful Bill Kraken, whose arm had been broken when the carriage overturned, was searching through a lodging house. Narbondo *would* be there, and Alice with him. St. Ives told himself that, and heedlessly rubbed the cold metal of the pistol, his mind filled with thoughts even darker than the night outside.

Generally, he was the last man on earth to be thinking about "meting out justice," but there in the rainy Seven Dials street he felt very much like that proverbial last man, even though Hasbro, his gentleman's gentleman, sat opposite him on the seat, sleeping heavily, wrapped in a greatcoat and carrying a revolver of his own.

And it wasn't so much a desire for justice that St. Ives felt; it was cold, dark murder. He hadn't spoken in three hours. There was nothing left to say, and it was too late at night, and St. Ives was too full of his black thoughts to make conversation; he was empty by now of anything save the contradictory thoughts of murder and of Alice, and he could find words for neither of those. If only they knew for certain where she was, where he had taken her...The Seven Dials was a mystery to him, though—such a tangle of streets and alleys and cramped houses that there was no sorting it out even in daylight, let alone on a night like this. They were close to him, though. Kraken would root him out. St. Ives fancied that he could feel Narbondo's presence in the darkness around him.

He watched the street past the wet curtain. Behind them a mist-shrouded lamp shone in a second-story window. There would be more lamps lit as the night drew on into morning, and for the first time the thought sprang into St. Ives's head that he had no desire to see that morning. Morning was insupportable without Alice. To hell with Narbondo's death. The gun on St. Ives's lap was a pitiful thing. Killing Narbondo would yield the satisfaction of killing an insect—almost none at all. It was life that mattered, Alice's life. The life of the London streets on an April morning was a phantasm. Her life alone had color and substance.

He wondered if he was bound, ultimately, for a madhouse,

following in the sad footsteps of his father. Alice was his sanity. He knew that now. A year ago such a thought would have puzzled him. Life had largely been a thing of beakers and calipers and numbers. Things change, though, and one became resigned to that.

There was a whistle. St. Ives sat up, closed his fingers over the revolver handle, and listened through the rain. He shoved half out through the door, the coach rocking gently on its springs and the sodden horses shaking themselves in anticipation, as if finally they would be moving—somewhere, anywhere out of the flood. A sudden shout rang out from ahead, followed by the sound of running footsteps. Another shout, and Bill Kraken, looking nearly drowned, materialized through the curtain of water, running hard and pointing wildly back over his shoulder.

"There!" he shouted. "There! It's him!"

St. Ives leaped into the street and slogged after Kraken, running heavily, the rain nearly blinding him.

"The coach!" Kraken yelled, out of breath. He turned abruptly and grabbed for St. Ives's arm. There was the rattling sound of another coach in the street and the clop of horse's hooves. Out of the darkness plunged a teetering old cabriolet drawn by its single horse, the driver exposed to the weather and the passenger half hidden by the curtain fixed across the narrow, coffin-shaped side chamber. The cab slewed around into the flood, the horse throwing streamers of water from its hooves, and the driver—Ignacio Narbondo—whipping the reins furiously, his feet jammed against the apron to keep himself from flying out.

St. Ives leaped into the street, lunging for the horse's neck and shouting futilely into the rain. The fingers of his right hand closed over a tangle of streaming mane, and he held on as he was yanked off his feet, waving the pistol in his left hand, his heels dragging on the wet road as the horse and cab brushed past him and tore away, slamming him backward into the water. He fired the already-cocked pistol straight into the air, rolled onto his side as he cocked it again, and fired once more at the hurtling shadow of the cab.

A hand clutched his arm. "The coach!" Kraken yelled again, and St. Ives hauled himself heavily out of the water-filled gutter and lunged after him.

Hasbro tossed at the reins even as St. Ives and Kraken clambered in, and the pair of horses lurched off down the narrow street, following the diminishing cab, which swayed and pitched and flung its way toward Holborn. As soon as St. Ives was in and had caught his balance, he threw the coach door open again and leaned out, squinting through the ribbons of water that flew up from the wheels and from the horses' hooves. The coach banged along, tossing him from side to side, and he aimed his pistol in a thousand directions, never fixing it on his target long enough for him to be able to squeeze the trigger.

They had Narbondo, though. The man was desperate. Too desperate, maybe. Their haste was forcing him into recklessness. And yet if they didn't pursue him closely they would lose him again. An awful sense of destiny swarmed over St. Ives. He held on and gritted his teeth as the dark houses flew past. Soon, he thought. Soon it'll be over, come what will. And no sooner had he thought this than the cabriolet, charging along a hundred yards ahead now, banged down into a water-filled hole in the street.

Its horse stumbled and fell forward, its knees buckling. The tiny cab spun like a slowly revolving top as Narbondo threw up the reins and held on to the apron, sliding half out, his legs kicking the air. The cab tore itself nearly in two, and the sodden curtain across the passenger chamber flew out as if in a heavy wind. A woman—

Alice—tumbled helplessly into the street, her hands bound, and the cabriolet crashed down atop her, pinning her underneath. Narbondo was up almost at once, scrambling for a footing in the mire and staggering toward where Alice lay unmoving.

St. Ives screamed into the night, weighed down by the heavy dreamlike horror of what he saw, of Alice coming to herself, suddenly struggling, trapped beneath the overturned cabriolet. Hasbro reined in the horses, but for St. Ives, even a moment's waiting was too much waiting, and he threw himself through the open door of the moving coach and into the road, rolling up onto his feet and pushing himself forward into the onslaught of rain. Twenty yards in front of him, Narbondo crawled across the wreckage of the cab as the fallen horse twitched in the street, trying and failing to stand up, its leg twisted back at a nearly impossible angle.

St. Ives pointed the pistol and fired at Narbondo, but the bullet flew wide, and it was the horse that whinnied and bucked. Desperately, St. Ives smeared rainwater out of his face with his coat sleeve, staggering forward, shooting wildly again when he saw suddenly that Narbondo also had a pistol in his hand and that he now crouched over the trapped woman. He supported Alice's shoulders with his left arm, the pistol aimed at her temple.

Horrified, St. Ives fired instantly, but he heard the crack of the other man's pistol before he was deafened by his own, and through the haze of rain he saw its awful result just as Narbondo was flung around sideways with the force of St. Ives's bullet slamming into his shoulder. Narbondo managed to stagger to his feet, laughing a hoarse seal's laugh, before he collapsed across the ruined cab that still trapped Alice's body.

St. Ives dropped the pistol into the flood and fell to his knees. Finishing Narbondo meant nothing to him anymore.

PART I

IN THE DAYS OF THE COMET

# THE PERUVIAN ANDES

ONE YEAR LATER

L angdon St. Ives, scientist and explorer, clutched a heavy alpaca blanket about his shoulders and stared out over countless miles of rocky plateaus and jagged volcanic peaks. The tight weave of ivory-colored wool clipped off a dry, chill wind that blew across the fifty miles of Antarctic-spawned Peruvian Current, up from the Gulf of Guayaquil and across the Pacific slope of the Peruvian Andes. A wide and sluggish river, gray-green beneath the lowering sky, crept through broad grasslands behind and below him. Moored like an alien vessel amid the bunch grasses and tola bush was a tiny dirigible, silver in the afternoon sun and flying the Union Jack from a jury-rigged mast.

At St. Ives's feet the scree-strewn rim of a volcanic cone, Mount Cotopaxi, fell two thousand feet toward steamy open fissures, the crater glowing like the bowl of an enormous pipe. St. Ives waved ponderously to his companion Hasbro, who crouched some hundred yards down the slope on the interior of the cone, working the compression mechanism of a Rawls-Hibbing

Mechanical Bladder. Coils of India-rubber hose snaked away from the pulsating device, disappearing into cracks in the igneous skin of the mountainside.

A cloud of fierce sulphur-laced steam whirled suddenly up and out of the crater in a wild sighing rush, and the red glow of the twisted fissures dwindled and winked, here and there dying away into cold and misty darkness. St. Ives nodded and consulted a pocket watch. His left shoulder, recently grazed by a bullet, throbbed tiredly. It was late afternoon. The shadows cast by distant peaks obscured the hillsides around him. On the heels of the shadows would come nightfall.

The man below ceased his furious manipulations of the contrivance and signaled to St. Ives, whereupon the scientist turned and repeated the signal—a broad windmill gesture, visible to the several thousand Indians massed on the plain below. "Sharp's the word, Jacky," muttered St. Ives under his breath. And straightaway, thin and sailing on the knife-edged wind, came a half-dozen faint syllables, first in English, then repeated in Quechua, then giving way to the resonant cadence of almost five thousand people marching in step. He could feel the rhythmic reverberations beneath his feet. He turned, bent over, and, mouthing a quick silent prayer, depressed the plunger of a tubular detonator.

He threw himself flat and pressed an ear to the cold ground. The rumble of marching feet rolled through the hillsides like the rushing cataract of a subterranean river. Then, abruptly, a deep and vast explosion, muffled by the crust of the earth itself, heaved at the ground in a tumultuous wave, and it appeared to St. Ives from his aerie atop the volcano as if the grassland below were a giant carpet and that the gods were shaking the dust from it. The marching horde pitched higgledy-piggledy into one another, strewn over the ground like dominoes. The stars in the eastern sky seemed to dance briefly, as if the earth had been jiggled from her course. Then, slowly, the ground ceased to shake.

St. Ives smiled for the first time in nearly a week, although it was the bitter smile of a man who had won a war, perhaps, but had lost far too many battles. It was over for the moment, though, and he could rest. He very nearly thought of Alice, who had been gone these twelve months now, but he screamed any such thoughts out of his mind before he became lost among them and couldn't find his way back. He couldn't let that happen to him again, ever—not if he valued his sanity.

Hasbro labored up the hillside toward him carrying the Rawls-Hibbing apparatus, and together they watched the sky deepen from blue to purple, cut by the pale radiance of the Milky Way. On the horizon glowed a misty semicircle of light, like a lantern hooded with muslin—the first faint glimmer of an ascending comet.

DOVER

LONG WEEKS EARLIER

The tumbled rocks of Castle Jetty loomed black and wet in the fog. Below, where the gray tide of the North Sea fell inch by inch away, green tufts of waterweed danced and then collapsed across barnacled stone, where brown penny-crabs scuttled through dark crevices as if their sidewise scramble would render them invisible to the men who stood above. Langdon St. Ives, wrapped in a greatcoat and shod in hip boots, cocked a spyglass to his eye and squinted north toward the Eastern Docks.

Heavy mist swirled and flew in the wind off the ocean, nearly obscuring the sea and sky like a gray muslin curtain. Just visible through the murk some hundred-fifty yards distant, the steamer H.M.S. *Ramsgate* heaved on the ground swell, its handful of paying passengers having hours since wended their way shoreward toward one of the inns along Castle Hill Road—all the passengers, that is, but one. St. Ives felt as if he'd stood atop the rocks for a lifetime, watching nothing at all but an empty ship.

He lowered the glass and gazed into the sea. It took an act of will to believe that beyond the Strait lay Belgium and that behind him, a bowshot distant, lay the city of Dover. He was overcome suddenly with the uncanny certainty that the jetty was moving, that he stood on the bow of a sailing vessel plying the waters of a phantom sea. The rushing tide below him bent and swirled around the edges of thrusting rocks, and for a perilous second he felt himself falling forward.

A firm hand grasped his shoulder. He caught himself, straightened, and wiped beaded moisture from his forehead with the sleeve of his coat. "Thank you." He shook his head to clear it. "I'm tired out."

"Certainly, sir. Steady on, sir."

"I've reached the limits of my patience, Hasbro," said St. Ives to the man beside him. "I'm convinced we're watching an empty ship. Our man has given us the slip, and I'd sooner have a look at the inside of a glass of ale than another look at that damned steamer."

"Patience is its own reward, sir," replied St. Ives's manservant.

St. Ives gave him a look. "My patience must be thinner than yours." He pulled a pouch from the pocket of his greatcoat, extracting a bent bulldog pipe and a quantity of tobacco. "Do you suppose Kraken has given up?" He pressed curly black tobacco into the pipe bowl with his thumb and struck a match, the flame hissing and sputtering in the misty evening air.

"Not Kraken, sir, if I'm any judge. If our man went ashore along the docks, then Kraken followed him. A disguise wouldn't answer, not with that hump. And it's an even bet that Narbondo wouldn't be away to London, not this late in the evening. For my money he's in a public house and Kraken's in the street outside. If he made away north, then Jack's got him, and the outcome is the same. The best..."

"Hark!"

Silence fell, interrupted only by the sighing of wavelets splashing against the stones of the jetty and by the hushed clatter of distant activity along the docks. The two men stood barely breathing, smoke from St. Ives's pipe rising invisibly into the fog. "There!" whispered St. Ives, holding up his left hand.

Softly, too rhythmically to be mistaken for the natural cadence of the ocean, came the muted dipping of oars and the creak of shafts in oarlocks. St. Ives stepped gingerly across to an adjacent rock and clambered down into a little crab-infested grotto. He could just discern, through a sort of triangular window, the thin gray line where the sky met the sea. And there, pulling into view, was a long rowboat in which sat two men, one plying the oars and the other crouched on a thwart and wrapped in a dark blanket. A frazzle of black hair drooped in moist curls around his shoulders.

"It's him," whispered Hasbro into St. Ives's ear.

"That it is. And up to no good at all. He's bound for Hargreaves's, or I'm a fool. We were right about this one. That eruption in Narvik was no eruption at all. It was a detonation. And now the task is unspeakably complicated. I'm half inclined to let the monster have a go at it, Hasbro. I'm altogether weary of this world. Why not let him blow it to smithereens?"

St. Ives stood up tiredly, the rowboat having disappeared into the fog. He found that he was shocked by what he had said—not only because Narbondo was very nearly capable of doing just that, but also because St. Ives had meant it. He didn't care. He put one foot in front of the other these days out of what?—duty? revenge?

"There's the matter of the ale glass," said Hasbro wisely, grasping St. Ives by the elbow. "That and a kidney pie, unless I'm mistaken, would answer most questions on the subject of futility.

We'll fetch in Bill Kraken and Jack on the way. We've time enough to stroll round to Hargreaves's after supper."

St. Ives squinted at Hasbro. "Of course we do," he said. "I might send you lads out tonight alone, though. I need about ten hours' sleep to bring me around. These damned dreams…In the morning I'll wrestle with these demons again."

"There's the ticket, sir," said the stalwart Hasbro, and through the gathering gloom the two men picked their way from rock to rock toward the warm lights of Dover.

"I can't imagine I've ever been this hungry before," said Jack Owlesby, spearing up a pair of rashers from a passing platter. His features were set in a hearty smile, as if he were making a strong effort to efface having revealed himself too thoroughly the night before. "Any more eggs?"

"Heaps," said Bill Kraken through a mouthful of cold toast, and he reached for another platter at his elbow. "Full of the right sorts of humors, sir, is eggs. It's the unctuous secretions of the yolk that fetches the home stake, if you follow me. Loaded up with all manners of fluids."

Owlesby paused, a forkful of egg halfway to his mouth. He gave Kraken a look that seemed to suggest he was unhappy with talk of fluids and secretions.

"Sorry, lad. There's no stopping me when I'm swept off by the scientific. I've forgot that you ain't partial to the talk of fluids over breakfast. Not that it matters a bit about fluids or any of the rest of it, what with that comet sailing in to smash us to flinders…"

St. Ives coughed, seeming to choke, his fit drowning the last few words of Kraken's observation. "Lower your voice, man!"

"Sorry, Professor. I don't think sometimes. You know me. This coffee tastes like rat poison, don't it? And not high-toned rat poison either, but something mixed up by your man with the hump."

"I haven't tasted it," said St. Ives, raising his cup. He peered into the depths of the dark stuff and was reminded instantly of the murky water in the night-shrouded tide pool he'd slipped into on his way back from the tip of the jetty last night. He didn't need to taste the coffee; the thin mineral-spirits smell of it was enough. "Any of the tablets?" he asked Hasbro.

"I brought several of each, sir. It doesn't pay to go abroad without them. One would think that the art of brewing coffee would have traveled the few miles from the Normandy coast to the British Isles, sir, but we all know it hasn't." He reached into the pocket of his coat and pulled out a little vial of jellybean-like pills. "Mocha Java, sir?"

"If you would," said St. Ives. "'All ye men drink java,' as the saying goes."

Hasbro dropped one into the upheld cup, and in an instant the room was filled with the astonishing heavy aroma of real coffee, the chemical smell of the pallid facsimile in the rest of their cups retreating before it. St. Ives seemed to reel with the smell of it, as if for the moment he was revitalized.

"By God!" whispered Kraken. "What else have you got there?"

"A tolerable Wiener Melange, sir, and a Brazilian brew that I can vouch for. There's an espresso too, but it's untried as yet."

"Then I'm your man to test it!" cried the enthusiastic Kraken, and he held out his hand for the little pill. "There's money in these," he said, plopping it into his full cup and watching the result as if mystified. "Millions of pounds."

"Art for art's sake," said St. Ives, dipping the end of a white kerchief into his cup and studying the stained corner of it in the sunlight shining through the casement. He nodded, satisfied, then tasted the coffee, nodding again. Over the previous year, since the episode in the Seven Dials, he had worked on nothing but these tiny white pills, all of his scientific instincts and skills given over to the business of coffee. It was a frivolous expenditure of energy and intellect, but until last week he could see nothing in the wide world that was any more compelling.

He bent over his plate and addressed Bill Kraken, although his words, clearly, were intended for the assembled company. "We mustn't, Bill, give in to fears about this... this... heavenly visitation, to lapse into metaphysical language. I woke up fresh this morning. A new man. And the solution, I discovered, was in front of my face. I had been given it by the very villain we pursue. Our only real enemy now is time, gentlemen, time and the excesses of our own fears."

St. Ives paused to have another go at the coffee, then stared into his cup for a moment before resuming his speech. "The single greatest catastrophe now would be for the news to leak to the general public. The man in the street would dissolve into chaos if he knew what confronted him. He couldn't face the idea of the earth smashed to atoms. It would be too much for him. We can't afford to underestimate his susceptibility to panic, his capacity for running amok and tearing his hair whenever it would pay him in dividends not to."

St. Ives stroked his chin, staring at the debris on his plate. He bent forward, and in a low voice he said, "I'm certain that science will save us this time, gentlemen, if it doesn't kill us first. The thing will be close, though, and if the public gets wind of the threat from this comet, great damage will come of it." He smiled into the befuddled faces of his three companions. Kraken wiped a dribble of egg from the edge of his mouth. Jack pursed his lips.

"I'll need to know about Hargreaves," continued St. Ives, "and you'll want to know what I'm blathering about. But this isn't the place. Let's adjourn to the street, shall we?" And with that the men arose, Kraken tossing off the last of his coffee. Then, seeing that Jack was leaving half a cup, he drank Jack's off too and mumbled something about waste and starvation as he followed the rest of them toward the hotel door.

D r. Ignacio Narbondo grinned over his tea. He watched the back of Hargreaves's head as it nodded above a great sheet of paper covered with lines, numbers, and notations. Why oxygen allowed itself to flow in and out of Hargreaves's lungs Narbondo couldn't at all say; the man seemed to be animated by a living hatred, an indiscriminate loathing for the most innocent things. He gladly built bombs for idiotic anarchist deviltry, not out of any particular regard for causes, but simply to create mayhem, to blow things to bits. If he could have built a device sufficiently large to obliterate the Dover cliffs and the sun rising beyond them, there would have been no satisfying him until it was done. He loathed tea. He loathed eggs. He loathed brandy. He loathed the daylight, and he loathed the nighttime. He loathed the very art of constructing infernal devices.

Narbondo looked round him at the barren room, the lumpy pallet on the ground where Hargreaves allowed himself a few hours' miserable sleep, as often as not to lurch awake at night, a shriek half uttered in his throat, as if he had peered into a mirror and seen the face of a beetle staring back. Narbondo whistled merrily all of a sudden, watching Hargreaves stiffen, loathing the melody that had broken in upon the discordant mumblings of his brain.

Hargreaves turned, his bearded face set in a rictus of twisted rage, his dark eyes blank as eclipsed moons. He breathed heavily. Narbondo waited with raised eyebrows, as if surprised at the man's reaction. "Damn a man that whistles," said Hargreaves slowly, running the back of his hand across his mouth. He looked at his hand, expecting to find heaven knew what, and turned slowly back to his bench top. Narbondo grinned and poured himself another cup of tea. All in all it was a glorious day. Hargreaves had agreed to help him destroy the earth without so much as a second thought. He had agreed with uncharacteristic relish, as if it was the first really useful task he had undertaken in years. Why he didn't just slit his own throat and be done with life for good and all was one of the great mysteries.

He wouldn't have been half so agreeable if he knew that Narbondo had no intention of destroying anything, that his motivation was greed—greed and revenge. His threat to cast the earth forcibly into the path of the approaching comet wouldn't be taken lightly. There were those in the Royal Academy who knew he could do it, who supposed, no doubt, that he might quite likely do it. They were as shortsighted as Hargreaves and every bit as useful. Narbondo had worked devilishly hard over the years at making himself feared, loathed, and, ultimately, respected.

The surprising internal eruption of Mount Hjarstaad would throw the fear into them. They'd be quaking over their breakfasts at that very moment, the lot of them wondering and gaping. Beards would be wagging. Dark suspicions would be mouthed. Where was Narbondo? Had he been seen in London? Not for months. He had threatened this very thing, hadn't he?—an eruption above the Arctic Circle, just to demonstrate the seriousness of his intent, the degree to which he held the fate of the world in his hands.

Very soon—within days—the comet would pass close enough to the earth to provide a spectacular display for the masses— foolish creatures. The iron core of the thing might easily be pulled so solidly by the earth's magnetic field that the comet would hurtle groundward, slamming the poor old earth into atoms and all the gaping multitudes with it. What if, Narbondo had suggested, what if a man were to give the earth a push, to propel it even closer to the approaching star and so turn a long shot into a dead cert, as a blade of the turf might put it? And with that, the art of extortion had been elevated to a new plane.

Well, Dr. Ignacio Narbondo was that man. Could he do it? Narbondo grinned. His advertisement of two weeks past had drawn a sneer from the Royal Academy, but Mount Hjarstaad would wipe the sneers from their faces. They would wax grave. Their grins would set like plaster of Paris. What had the poet said about that sort of thing? "Gravity was a mysterious carriage of the body to cover the defects of the mind." That was it. Gravity would answer for a day or two, but when it faded into futility they would pay, and pay well. Narbondo set in to whistle again, this time out of the innocence of good cheer, but the effect on Hargreaves was so immediately consumptive and maddening that Narbondo gave it off abruptly. There was no use baiting the man into ruination before the job was done.

He thought suddenly of Langdon St. Ives. St. Ives was nearly unavoidable. For the fiftieth time Narbondo regretted killing the woman on that rainy London morning one year past. He hadn't meant to. He had meant to bargain with her life. It was desperation had made him sloppy and wild. It seemed to him that he could count his mistakes on the fingers of one hand. When he made them, though, they weren't subtle mistakes. The best he could hope for was that St. Ives had sensed the desperation in him, that St. Ives lived day-to-day with the knowledge that if he had only eased up, if he hadn't pushed Narbondo so closely, hadn't forced his hand, the woman might be alive today, and the two of them, St. Ives and her, living blissfully together, pottering in the turnip garden. Narbondo watched the back of Hargreaves's head. If it was a just world, then St. Ives would blame himself. He was precisely the man for such a job as that—a martyr of the suffering type.

The very thought of St. Ives made him scowl, though. Narbondo had been careful, but somehow the Dover air seemed to whisper "St. Ives" to him at every turning. He pushed his suspicions out of his mind, reached for his coat, and stepped silently from the room, carrying his teacup with him. On the morning street outside he smiled grimly at the orange sun that burned through the evaporating fog, then he threw the dregs of his tea, cup and all, over a vine-draped stone wall and strode away east up Archcliffe Road, composing in his mind a letter to the Royal Academy.

"**D**amn me!" mumbled Bill Kraken through the fingers mashed against his mouth. He wiped away furiously at the tea leaves and tea that ran down his neck and collar. The cup that had hit him on the ear had fallen and broken on the stones of the garden.

He peered up over the wall at Narbondo's diminishing figure and added this last unintended insult to the list of villainies he had suffered over the years at Narbondo's hands.

He would have his turn yet. Why St. Ives hadn't given him leave merely to beat the stuffing out of this devil Hargreaves Kraken couldn't at all fathom. The man was a monster; there was no gainsaying it. They could easily set off one of his own devices— hoist him on his own filthy petard, so to speak. His remains would be found amid the wreckage of infernal machines, built with his own hands. The world would have owed Bill Kraken a debt.

But Narbondo, St. Ives had insisted, would have found another willing accomplice. Hargreaves was only a pawn, and pawns could be dealt with easily enough when the time came. St. Ives couldn't afford to tip his hand, nor would he settle for anything less than fair play and lawful justice. That was the crux of it. St. Ives had developed a passion for keeping the blinders on his motivations. He would be driven by law and reason and not fuddle things up with the odd emotion. Sometimes the man was scarcely human.

Kraken crouched out from behind the wall and slipped away in Narbondo's wake, keeping to the other side of the road when the hunchback entered a stationer's, then circling round to the back when Narbondo went in at the post office door. Kraken stepped through a dark, arched rear entry, a ready lie on his lips in case he was confronted. He found himself in a small deserted room, where he slid behind a convenient heap of crates, peeping through slats at an enormously fat, stooped man who lumbered in and tossed Narbondo's letter into a wooden bin before lumbering back out. Kraken snatched up the letter, tucked it into his coat, and in a moment was back in the sunlight, prying at the sealing wax with his index finger. Ten minutes later he was at the front door of the post office, grinning into the wide face of the postman and mailing Narbondo's missive for the second time that morning.

"Surely it's a bluff," said Jack Owlesby, scowling at Langdon St. Ives. The four of them sat on lawn chairs in the Gardens, listening with half an ear to the lackluster tootings of a tired orchestra. "What would it profit him to alert the *Times*? There'd be mayhem. If it's extortion he's up to, this won't further his aim by an inch."

"The threat of it might," replied St. Ives. "If his promise to pitch the earth into the path of the comet weren't taken seriously, the mere suggestion that the public be apprised of the magnetic affinity of the comet and the earth might be. Extortion on top of extortion. The one is pale alongside the other one. I grant you that. But there could be a panic if an ably stated message were to reach the right sort of journalist—or the wrong sort, rather." St. Ives paused and shook his head, as if such panic wasn't to be contemplated. "What was the name of that scoundrel who leaked the news of the threatened epidemic four years ago?"

"Beezer, sir," said Hasbro. "He's still in the employ of the *Times*, and, we must suppose, no less likely to be in communication with the doctor today than he was then. He would be your man, sir, if you wanted to wave the bloody shirt."

"I rather believe," said St. Ives, grimacing at the raucous climax of an unidentifiable bit of orchestration, "that we should pay this man Beezer a visit. We can't do a thing sitting around

Dover. Narbondo has agreed to wait four days for a reply from the Academy. There's no reason to believe that he won't keep his word—he's got nothing to gain by haste. The comet, after all, is ten days off. We've got to suppose that he means just what he claims. Evil begets idiocy, gentlemen, and there is no earthly way to tell how far down the path into degeneration our doctor has trod. The next train to London, Hasbro?"

"Two-forty-five, sir."

"We'll be aboard her."

⇜ LONDON AND HARROGATE ⇝

The Bayswater Club, owned by the Royal Academy of Sciences, sat across from Kensington Gardens, commanding a view of trimmed lawns and roses and cleverly pruned trees. St. Ives peered out the window on the second floor of the club, satisfied with what he saw. The sun loomed like an immense orange just below the zenith, and the radiant heat glancing through the geminate windows of the club felt almost alive. The April weather was so altogether pleasant that it came near to making up for the fearful lunch that would at any moment arrive to stare at St. Ives from a china plate. He had attempted a bit of cheerful banter with the stony-faced waiter, ordering dirt cutlets and beer as a joke, but the man hadn't seen the humor in it. What he *had* seen had been evident on his face.

St. Ives sighed and wished heartily that he was taking the sun along with the multitudes in the park, but the thought that a week hence there mightn't be any park at all—or any multitudes, either—sobered him, and he drained the bottom half of a glass of claret. He regarded the man seated across from him. Parsons, the ancient secretary of the Royal Academy, spooned up broth with an enthusiasm that left St. Ives tired. Floating on the surface of the broth were what appeared to be twisted little bugs, but must have been some sort of Oriental mushroom, sprinkled on by a chef with a sense of humor. Parsons chased them with his spoon.

"So you've nothing at all to fear," said Parsons, dabbing at his chin with a napkin. He grimaced at St. Ives in a satisfied way, like a proud doggy who had fetched in the slippers without tearing holes in them. "The greatest minds in the scientific world are at work on the problem. The comet will sail past us with no commotion whatsoever. It's a matter of electromagnetic forces, really. The comet might easily be drawn to the earth, as you say, with disastrous consequences. Unless, let's imagine, if we can push ourselves so far, the earth's magnetic field were to be forcibly suspended."

"Suspended?"

"Shut off. Current interruptus." Parsons winked.

"Shut off? Lunacy," St. Ives said. "Sheer lunacy."

"It's not unknown to have happened. Common knowledge has it that the magnetic poles have reversed themselves any number of times, and that during the interim between the establishing of new poles, the earth was blessedly free of any electromagnetic field whatsoever. I'm surprised that a physicist such as yourself has to be informed of such a thing." Parsons peered at St. Ives over the top of his pince-nez, then fished up out of his broth a tendril of vegetable. St. Ives gaped at it. "Kelp," said the secretary, slathering the dripping weed into his mouth.

St. Ives nodded, a shiver running up along his spine. The pink chicken breast that lay beneath wilted lettuce on his plate began, suddenly, to fill him with a curious sort of dread. His lunches with Parsons at the Bayswater Club invariably went so. The secretary was always one up on him, simply because of the food. "So what, exactly, do you intend? To *hope* such an event into existence?"

"Not at all," said Parsons smugly. "We're building a device."

"A *device*?"

"To reverse the polarity of the earth, thereby negating any natural affinity the earth might have for the comet and vice versa."

"Impossible," said St. Ives, a kernel of doubt and fear beginning to sprout within him.

"Hardly." Parsons waved his fork with an air of gaiety, then scratched the end of his nose with it. "No less a personage than Lord Kelvin himself is at work on it, although the theoretical basis of the thing was entirely a product of James Clerk Maxwell. Maxwell's sixteen equations in tensor calculus demonstrated a good bit beyond the idea that gravity is merely a form of electromagnetism. But his conclusions, taken altogether, had such terrible and far-reaching side implications that they were never published. Lord Kelvin, of course, has access to them. And I think that we have little to fear that in such benevolent hands, Maxwell's discoveries will lead to nothing but scientific advancement. To more, actually—to the temporary reversal of the poles, as I said, and the switching off, as it were, of any currents that would attract our comet. Trust us, sir. This threat, as you call it, is a threat no more. You're entirely free to apply your manifold talents to more pressing matters."

St. Ives sat silently for a moment, wondering if any objections would penetrate Parsons's head past the crunching of vegetation. Quite likely not, but St. Ives hadn't any choice but try. Two days earlier, when he had assured his friends in Dover that they would easily thwart Ignacio Narbondo, he hadn't bargained on this. Was it possible that the clever contrivances of Lord Kelvin and the

Royal Academy would constitute a graver threat than that posed by the doctor? It wasn't to be thought of. Yet here was Parsons, full of talk about reversing the polarity of the earth. St. Ives was duty-bound to speak. He seemed to find himself continually at odds with his peers.

"This... device," St. Ives said. "This is something that's been cobbled together in the past few weeks, is it?"

Parsons looked stupefied. "It's not something that's been *cobbled* together at all. But since you ask, no. I think I can safely tell you that it is the culmination of Lord Kelvin's lifelong work. All the rest of his forays into electricity are elementary, pranks, gewgaws. It's this engine, sir, on which his genius has been expended."

"So he's had the lifelong ambition of reversing the polarity of the earth? To what end? Or are you telling me that he's *anticipated* the comet for the past forty years?"

"I'm not telling you either of those, am I? If I chose to tell you the truth about the matter, which I clearly don't choose to do, you wouldn't believe it anyway. It would confound you. Suffice it to say that the man is willing to sacrifice ambition for the good of humanity."

St. Ives nodded, giving his chicken a desultory poke with the end of his finger. It might easily have been some sort of pale tide-pool creature shifting in a saline broth on the plate. Ambition... He had his own share of ambition. He had long suspected the nature of the device that Lord Kelvin tinkered with in his barn in Harrogate. Parsons was telling him the truth, or at least part of it. And what the truth meant was that St. Ives, somehow, must possess himself of this fabulous machine.

Except that the idea of doing so was contemptible. There were winds in this world that blew a man into uncharted seas. But while they changed the course of his action, they ought not to change the course of his soul. Take a lesson from Robinson Crusoe, he told himself. He thought about Alice then, and of the brief time they had spent together. Suddenly he determined to hack the weeds out of her vegetable garden, and the thought buoyed him up. Then, just as suddenly, he was depressed beyond words, and he found himself staring at the mess on his plate. Parsons was looking contentedly out the window, picking at his teeth with a fingernail.

First things first, St. Ives said to himself. Reverse the polarity of the earth! "Have you read the works of young Rutherford?" he asked Parsons.

"Pinwinnie Rutherford of Edinburgh?"

"Ernest Rutherford. Of New Zealand. I ran across him in Canada. He's done some interesting work in the area of light rays, if you can call them that." St. Ives wiggled loose a thread of chicken, carried the morsel halfway to his mouth, looked at it and changed his mind. "There's some indication that alpha and beta rays from the sun slide away along the earth's magnetic field, arriving harmlessly at the poles. It seems likely, at a hasty glance, that without the field they'd sail in straightaway—we'd be bathed in radioactivity. The most frightful mutations might occur. It has been my pet theory, in fact, that the dinosaurs were laid low in precisely that same fashion—that their demise was a consequence of the reversal of the poles and the inherent cessation of the magnetic field."

Parsons shrugged. "All of this *is* theory, of course. But the comet is eight days away, and *that's* not at all theory. It's not a brontosaurus, my dear fellow, it's an enormous chunk of iron that threatens to smash us into jelly. From your chair across the table it's easy enough to fly in the face of the science of mechanics, but

I'm afraid, sir, that Lord Kelvin will get along very well without you—he has in the past."

"There's a better way," said St. Ives simply. It was useless to lose his temper over Parsons's practiced stubbornness.

"Oh?" said the secretary.

"Ignacio Narbondo, I believe, has showed it to us."

Parsons dropped his spoon onto his lap and launched into a choking fit. St. Ives held up a constraining hand. "I'm very much aware of his threats, I assure you. And they're not idle threats, either. Do you propose to pay him?"

"I'm constrained from discussing it."

"He'll do what he claims. He's taken the first steps already."

"I realize, my dear fellow, that you and the doctor are sworn enemies. He ought to have danced his last jig on the gallows a long time ago. If it were in my power to bring him to justice, I would, but I have no earthly idea where he is, quite frankly, and I'll warn you, with no beating about the bush, that this business of the comet must not become a personal matter with you. I believe you take my meaning. Lord Kelvin sets us all an example."

St. Ives counted to ten very slowly. Somewhere between seven and eight, he discovered that Parsons was very nearly right. What he said was beside the point, though. "Let me repeat," St. Ives said evenly, "that I believe there's a better way."

"And what does a lunatic like Narbondo have to do with this 'better way'?"

"He intends, if I read him aright, to effect the stoppage of certain very active volcanoes in arctic Scandinavia via the introduction of petrifactive catalysts into open fissures and dykes. The subsequent detonation of an explosive charge would lead to the eruption of a chain of volcanic mountains that rise above the jungles of Amazonian Peru. The entrapped energy expended by such an upheaval would, he hopes, cast us like a Chinese rocket into the course of the comet."

"Given the structure of the interior of the earth," said Parsons, grinning into his mineral water, "it seems a dubious undertaking at best. Perhaps…"

"Are you familiar with hollow-earth theory?"

Parsons blinked at St. Ives. The corners of his mouth twitched.

"Specifically with that of McClung-Jones of the Quebec Geological Mechanics Institute? The 'thin-crust phenomenon'?"

Parsons shook his head tiredly.

"It's possible," said St. Ives, "that Narbondo's detonation will effect a series of eruptions in volcanoes residing in the hollow core of the earth. The stupendous inner-earth pressures would themselves trigger an eruption at Jones's thin-crust point."

"Thin-crust point?" asked Parsons in a plonking tone.

"The very Peruvian mountains toward which our man Narbondo has cast the glad eye!"

"That's an interesting notion," muttered Parsons, coughing into his napkin. "Turn the earth into a Chinese rocket." He stared out the window, blinking his eyes ponderously, as if satisfied that St. Ives had concluded his speech.

"What I propose," said St. Ives, pressing on, "is to thwart Narbondo, and then effect the same thing, only in reverse—to propel the earth temporarily out of her orbit in a long arc that would put the comet beyond her grasp. If the calculations were fined down sufficiently—and I can assure you that they have been—we'd simply slide back into orbit some few thousand miles farther along our ellipse, a pittance in the eyes of the incalculable distances of our journeying through the void."

St. Ives sat back and fished in his coat for a cigar. Here was the Royal Academy, unutterably fearful of the machinations of Ignacio Narbondo—certain, that is, that the doctor was not merely talking through his hat. If they could trust to Narbondo to destroy the earth through volcanic manipulation, then they could quite clearly trust St. Ives to save it by the same means. What was good for the goose, after all. St. Ives took a breath and continued. "There's been some study of the disastrous effects of in-step marching on bridges and platforms—military study mostly. My own theory, which abets Narbondo's, would make use of such study, of the resonant energy expended by a troop of synchronized marchers…"

Parsons grimaced and shook his head slowly. He wasn't prepared to admit anything about the doings of the nefarious doctor. And St. Ives's theories, although fascinating, were of little use to them here. What St. Ives wanted, perhaps, was to speak to the minister of parades…

Then there was this man Jones. Hadn't McClung-Jones been involved in certain ghastly lizard experiments in the forests of New Hampshire? "Very ugly incident, that one," Parsons muttered sadly. "One of your hollow-earth men, wasn't he? Had a lot of Mesozoic reptiles dummied up at a waxworks in Boston, as I recall, and insisted he'd found them sporting in some bottomless cavern or another." Parsons squinted shrewdly at St. Ives. It was *real* science that they would order up here. Humanity cried out for it, didn't they? Wasn't Lord Kelvin at that very moment riveting together the carcass of the device that Parsons had described? Hadn't St. Ives been listening? Parsons shrugged. Discussions with St. Ives were always—how should one put it?—revealing. But St. Ives had gotten in out of his depth this time, and Parsons's advice was to strike out at once for shore—a hearty breaststroke so as not to tire himself unduly. He patted St. Ives on the sleeve, waving the wine decanter at him.

St. Ives nodded and watched the secretary fill his glass nearly to the top. There was no arguing with the man. And it wasn't argument that was wanted now, anyway. It was action, and that was a commodity, apparently, that he would have to take with his own hands.

St. Ives's manor house and laboratory sat some three quarters of a mile from the summerhouse of William Thomson, Lord Kelvin. The River Nidd ran placid and slow between, slicing neatly in two the broad meadow that separated the grounds of the manor from the grounds of the summerhouse. The willows that lined the banks of the Nidd effected a rolling green cloudbank that almost obscured each house from the view of the other, but from St. Ives's attic window, Lord Kelvin's broad low barn was just visible atop a grassy knoll. Into and out of that barn trooped a platoon of white-coated scientists and grimed machinists. Covered wagons scoured along the High Road from Kirk Hammerton, bearing enigmatic mechanical apparatus, and were met at the gates by an ever-suspicious man in a military uniform.

St. Ives watched their comings and goings through his spyglass. He turned a grim eye on Hasbro, who stood silently behind him. "I've come to a difficult decision, Hasbro."

"Yes, sir."

"I've decided that we must play the role of saboteur, and nothing less. I shrink from such deviltry, but far more is at stake here than honor. We must ruin, somehow, Lord Kelvin's machine."

"Very good, sir."

"The mystifying thing is that I thought it was something else that he was constructing in that barn. But Parsons couldn't have lied so utterly well. He isn't capable of it. We've got to suppose that Lord Kelvin will do just what he says he will do."

"No one will deny it, sir."

"Our sabotaging his machine, of course, necessitates not only carrying out the plan to manipulate the volcanoes, but implies utter faith in that plan. Here we are setting in to thwart the effort of one of the greatest living practical scientists and to substitute our own feeble designs in its stead—an act of monumental egotism."

"As you say, sir."

"But the stakes are high, Hasbro. We *must* have our hand in. It's nothing more nor less than the salvation of the earth, secularly speaking, that we engage in."

"Shall we want lunch first, sir?"

"Kippers and gherkins, thank you. And bring up two bottles of Double Diamond to go along with it—and a bottle or two for yourself, of course."

"Thank you, sir," Hasbro said. "You're most generous, sir."

"Very well," mumbled St. Ives, striding back and forth beneath the exposed roof rafters. He paused and squinted out into the sunlight, watching another wagon rattle along into the open door of Lord Kelvin's barn. Disguise would avail them nothing. It would be an easy thing to fill a wagon with unidentifiable scientific trash—heaven knew he had any amount of it lying about—and to dress up in threadbare pants and coat and merely drive the stuff in at the gate. The guard would have no inkling of who he was. But Lord Kelvin, of course, would. A putty nose and false chin whiskers would be dangerous things. If any members of the Academy saw through them they'd clap him in irons, accuse him very rightly of intended sabotage.

He could argue his case well enough in the courts, to be sure. He could depend on Rutherford, at least, to support him. But in the meantime the earth would have been beat to pieces. That wouldn't answer. And if Lord Kelvin's machine was put into operation and was successful, then he'd quite possibly face a jury of mutants—two-headed men and a judge with a third eye. They'd be sympathetic, under the circumstances, but still…

The vast interior of Lord Kelvin's barn was awash with activity—a sort of carnival of strange debris, of coiled copper and tubs of bubbling fluids and rubber-wrapped cable thick as a man's wrist hanging from overhead joists like jungle creepers. At the heart of it all lay a plain brass box, studded with rivets and with a halo of wires running out of the top. This, then, was the machine itself, the culmination of Lord Kelvin's life's work, the boon that he was giving over to the salvation of mankind.

The machine was compact, to be sure—small enough to motivate a dogcart, if a man wanted to use it for such a frivolous end. St. Ives turned the notion over in his mind, wondering where a man might travel in such a dogcart and thinking that he would gladly give up his entire fortune to be left alone with the machine for an hour and a half. First things first, he reminded himself, just as three men began to piece together over the top of it a copper pyramid the size of a large doghouse. Lord Kelvin himself, talking through his beard and clad in a white smock and Leibnitz cap, pointed and shouted and squinted with a calculating eye at the device that piece by piece took shape in the lamplight. Parsons stood beside him, leaning on a brass-shod cane.

At the sight of Langdon St. Ives standing outside the open door, Parsons's chin dropped. St. Ives glanced at Jack Owlesby and Hasbro. Bill Kraken had disappeared. Parsons raised an exhorting finger, widening his eyes with the curious effect of making the bulk of his forehead disappear into his thin gray hair.

"Dr. Parsons!" cried St. Ives, getting in before him. "Your man at the gate is a disgrace. We sauntered in past him mumbling nonsense about the Atlantic cable and showed him a worthless letter signed by the Prince of Wales. He tried to shake our hands. You've *got* to do better than that, Parsons. We might have been anyone, mightn't we?—any class of villain. And here we are, trooping in like so many ants. It's the great good fortune of the Commonwealth that we're friendly ants. In a word, we've come to offer our skills, such as they are."

St. Ives paused for breath when he saw that Parsons had begun to sputter like the burning fuse of a fizz bomb, and for one dangerous moment St. Ives was fearful that the old man would explode, would pitch over from apoplexy and that the sum of their efforts would turn out to be merely the murder of poor Parsons. But the fit passed. The secretary snatched his quivering face back into shape and gave the three of them an appraising look, stepping across so as to stand between St. Ives and the machine, as if his gaunt frame, pinched by years of a weedy vegetarian diet, would somehow hide the thing from view.

"*Persona non grata,* is it?" asked St. Ives, giving Parsons a look in return, then instantly regretting the action. There was nothing to be gained by being antagonistic.

"I haven't any idea how you swindled the officer at the gate," said Parsons evenly, holding his ground, "but this operation has been commissioned by Her Majesty the Queen and is undertaken by the collected members of the Royal Academy of Sciences, an organization, if I remember aright, which does not count you among its members. In short, we thank you for your kind offer of assistance and very humbly ask you to leave, along with your ruffians."

He turned to solicit Lord Kelvin's agreement, but the great man was sighting down the length of a brass tube, tugging on it in order, apparently, to align it with an identical tube that hung suspended from the ceiling fifteen feet away. "My lord," said Parsons, clearing his throat meaningfully, but he got no response at all, and gave off his efforts when St. Ives seemed intent on strolling around to the opposite side of the machine.

"*Must* we make an issue of this?" Parsons demanded of St. Ives, stepping across in an effort to cut him off and casting worried looks at Hasbro and Jack Owlesby, as if fearful that the two of them might produce some heinous device of their own with which to blow up the barn and exterminate the lot of them.

St. Ives stopped and shrugged when he saw Bill Kraken, grimed with oil and wearing the clothes of a workman, step out from behind a heap of broken crates and straw stuffing. Without so much as a sideways glance at his employer, Kraken hurried to where Lord Kelvin fiddled with the brass tube. Kraken grasped the opposite end of it and in a moment was wrestling with the thing, hauling it this way and that to the apparent approval of his lordship, and managing to tip St. Ives a broad wink in the process.

"Well, well," said St. Ives in a defeated tone, "I'm saddened by this, Parsons. Saddened. I'd hoped to lend a hand."

Parsons seemed mightily relieved all of a sudden. He cast St. Ives a wide smile. "We thank you, sir," he said, limping toward the scientist, his hand outstretched. "If this project were in the developmental stages, I assure you we'd welcome your expertise. But it's really a matter of nuts and bolts now, isn't it? And your genius, I'm afraid, would be wasted." He ushered the three of them out into the sunlight, smiling hospitably now and watching until he was certain the threat had passed and the three were beyond the gate. Then he called round to have the gate guard relieved. He couldn't, he supposed, have the man flogged, but he could see to it that he spent an enterprising year patrolling the thoroughfares of Dublin.

LONDON AND HARROGATE AGAIN

It was late evening along Fleet Street, and the London night was clear and unseasonably warm, as if the moon that swam in the purple sky beyond the dome of St. Paul's were radiating a thin white heat. The very luminosity of the moon paled the surrounding stars, but as the night deepened farther away into space, the stars were bright and thick enough to remind St. Ives that the universe wasn't an empty place after all. And out there among the planets, hurtling toward earth, was the vast comet, its curved tail comprising a hundred million miles of showering ice, blown by solar wind along the uncharted byways of the void. Tomorrow or the next day the man in the street, peering skyward to admire the stars, would see it there. Would it be a thing of startling beauty, a wash of fire across the canvas of heaven? Or would it send a thrill of fear through a populace still veined with the superstitious dread of the medieval church?

The shuffle of footsteps behind him brought St. Ives to himself. He wrinkled his face up, feeling the gluey pull of the horsehair eyebrows and beard, which, along with a putty nose and monk's wig, made up a very suitable disguise. Coming along toward him was Beezer the journalist, talking animatedly to a man in shirtsleeves. Beezer chewed the end of a tiny cigar and waved his arms to illustrate a story that he told with particular venom. He seemed unnaturally excited, although St. Ives had to remind himself that he was almost entirely unfamiliar with the man— perhaps he always gestured and railed so.

St. Ives fell in behind the two, making no effort to conceal himself. Hasbro and Jack Owlesby stood in the shadows two blocks farther along, in an alley past Whitefriars. There was precious little time to waste. Occasional strollers passed; the abduction would have to be quick and subtle. "Excuse me," St. Ives said at the man's back. "Mr. Beezer is it, the journalist?"

The two men stopped, looking back at St. Ives. Beezer's hands fell to his side. "'At's right, Pappy," came the reply. Beezer squinted at him, as if ready to doubt the existence of such a wild figure on the evening street.

"My name, actually, is Penrod," said St. Ives. "Jules Penrod. You've apparently mistaken me for someone else. I have one of the twelve common faces."

Beezer's companion burst into abrupt laughter at the idea. Beezer, however, seemed impatient at the interruption. "Face like yours is a pity," he said, nudging his companion in the abdomen with his elbow. "Suits a beggar, though. I haven't got a thing for you, Pappy. Go scrub yourself with a sponge." And with that the two of them turned and made away, the second man laughing again and Beezer gesturing.

"One moment, sir!" cried St. Ives, pursuing the pair. "We've got a mutual friend."

Beezer turned and scowled, chewing his cigar slowly and thoughtfully now. He stared carefully at St. Ives's unlikely visage and shook his head. "No, we don't," he said, "unless it's the devil. Any other friend of yours would've hung himself by now out of regret. Why don't you disappear into the night, Pappy, before I show you the shine on my boot?"

"You're right, as far as it goes," said St. Ives, grinning inwardly. "I'm a friend of Dr. Ignacio Narbondo, in fact. He's sent me round with another communication."

Beezer squinted at him. The word *another* hadn't jarred him.

"Is that right?" he said.

St. Ives bowed, clapping a hand hastily onto the top of his head to hold his wig on.

"Bugger off, will you, Clyde?" Beezer said to his friend.

"That drink…" came the reply.

"Stow your drink. I'll see you tomorrow. We'll drink two. Now get along."

The man turned away regretfully, despondent over the lost drink perhaps, and St. Ives waited to speak until he had crossed Whitefriars and his footsteps faded. Then he nodded to the still-scowling Beezer and set out on the sidewalk again, looking up and down the street as if to discern anything suspicious or threatening. Beezer fell in beside him. "It's about the money," said St. Ives.

"The money?"

"Narbondo fears that he promised you too much of it."

"He's a filthy cheat!" cried Beezer, eliminating any doubts that St. Ives might have had about Beezer's having received Narbondo's message, mailed days past from Dover.

"He's discovered," continued St. Ives, "that there are any of a number of journalists who will sell out the people of London for half the sum. Peabody at the *Herald*, for instance, has agreed to cooperate."

"The filthy scum-sucking cheat!" Beezer shouted, waving a fist at St. Ives's nose. "Peabody!"

"Tut, tut," admonished St. Ives, noting with a surge of anxious anticipation the darkened mouth of the alley some thirty feet distant. "We haven't contracted with Peabody yet. It was merely a matter of feeling out the temperature of the water, so to speak. You understand. You're a businessman yourself in a way." St. Ives gestured broadly with his left hand as if to signify that a man like Beezer could be expected to take the long view. With his right he reached across and snatched the lapels of Beezer's coat, yanking him sideways. Simultaneously he whipped his left hand around and slammed the startled journalist square in the back, catapulting him into the ill-lit alley.

"Hey!" shouted Beezer, tripping forward into the waiting arms of Jack Owlesby, who leaped in to pinion the man's wrists. Hasbro, waving an enormous burlap bag, appeared from the shadows and flung the bag like a gill net over Beezer's head, St. Ives yanking it down across the man's back and pushing him forward off his feet. Hasbro snatched at the drawrope, grasped Beezer's shoulders, and hissed through the canvas, "Cry out and you're a dead man!"

The struggling Beezer collapsed like a sprung balloon, having an antipathy, apparently, to being a dead man. Jack clambered up onto the bed of a wagon, hauled open the lid of a steamer trunk, and, along with St. Ives and Hasbro, yanked and shoved and grappled the feebly struggling journalist into the wood and leather prison. He banged ineffectively a half-dozen times at the sides of the trunk, mewling miserably, then fell silent as the wagon rattled and bounced along the alley, exiting on Salisbury Court and making away south toward the Thames.

A half hour later the wagon had doubled back through Soho, St. Ives having set such a course toward Chingford that Beezer couldn't begin to guess it out from within his trunk. Hasbro, always prepared, had uncorked a bottle of whiskey, and each of the three men held a glass, lost in his own thoughts about the warm April night and the dangers of their mission. "Sorry to bring you in on this, Jack," said St. Ives. "There might quite likely be the devil to pay before we're through. No telling what sort of a row our man Beezer might set up."

"I'm not complaining," Jack said.

"It was Dorothy I was thinking about, actually. We're only weeks finished with the pig incident, and I've hauled you away again. There she sits in Kensington wondering what sort of nonsense I've drummed up now. She's a stout woman, if you don't mistake my meaning."

Jack nodded, glancing sideways at St. Ives, whose voice had gotten heavy with the sound of regret. St. Ives seemed always to be on the edge of a precipice, standing with his back to it and pretending he couldn't see that it was there, waiting for him to take an innocent step backward. Work furiously—that had become the byword for St. Ives, and it was a better thing, perhaps, than to go to pieces, except that there was something overwound about St. Ives sometimes that made Jack wonder if it wouldn't be better for him to try to see into the depths of that pit that stretched out behind him, to let his eyes adjust to the darkness so that he might make out the shadows down there.

But then Jack was settled in Kensington with Dorothy, living out what must look to St. Ives like a sort of storybook existence. The professor couldn't help but see that Dorothy and Alice had been a lot alike, and Jack's happiness must have magnified St.

Ives's sorrow. If Dorothy knew, in fact, what sort of business they pursued this time, she probably would have insisted on coming along. Jack thought of her fondly. "Do you know…" he began, reminiscing, but the sound of Beezer pummeling the sides of the trunk cut him off.

"Tell the hunchback!" shrieked a muffled voice, "that I'll have him horsewhipped! He'll be sulking in Newgate Prison again by the end of the week, by God! There's nothing about him I don't know!"

St. Ives shrugged at Hasbro. Here, perhaps, was a stroke of luck. If Beezer could be convinced that they actually *were* agents of Narbondo, it would go no little way toward throwing the man off their scent when the affair was over, especially if he went to the authorities with his tale. Beezer hadn't, after all, committed any crime, nor did he contemplate one—no crime, that is, beyond the crime against humanity, against human decency. "Narbondo has authorized us to eliminate you if we see fit," said St. Ives, hunching over the trunk. "If you play along here you'll be well paid; if you struggle, you'll find yourself counting fishes in the rocks off Southend Pier." The journalist fell silent.

Early in the predawn morning the wagon rattled into Chingford and made for the hills beyond, where lay the cottage of Sam Langley, son of St. Ives's longtime cook. The cottage was dark, but a lamp burned through the slats in the locked shutters of a low window in an unused silo fifty yards off. St. Ives reined in the horses, clambering out of the wagon at once, and with the help of his two companions, hauled the steamer trunk off the tailgate and into the unfastened door of the silo. Jack Owlesby and Hasbro hastened back out into the night, and for a moment through the briefly open door, St. Ives could see Sam Langley stepping off his kitchen porch, pulling on a coat. The door shut, and St. Ives was alone in the feebly lit room with the trunk and scattered pieces of furniture.

"I'm going to unlock the trunk…" St. Ives began.

"You sons of…" Beezer started to shout, but St. Ives rapped against the lid with his knuckles to silence him.

"I'm either going to unlock the trunk or set it afire," said St. Ives with great deliberation. "The choice is yours." The trunk was silent. "Once the trunk is unlocked, you can quite easily extricate yourself. The bag isn't knotted. You've probably already discovered that. My advice to you is to stay absolutely still for ten minutes. Then you can thrash and shriek and stamp about until you collapse. No one will hear you. You'll be happy to know that a sum of money will be advanced to your account, and that you'll have a far easier time spending it if you're not shot full of holes. Don't, then, get impatient. You've ridden out the night in the trunk; you can stand ten minutes more." Beezer, it seemed, had seen reason, for as St. Ives crouched out into the night, shook hands hastily with Langley, leaped into the wagon, and took up the reins, nothing but silence emanated from the stones of the silo.

Two evenings earlier, on the night that St. Ives had waylaid Beezer the journalist, the comet had appeared in the eastern sky, ghostly and round like the moon reflected on a frosty window—just a circular patch of faint luminous cloud. But now it seemed fearfully close, as if it would drop out of the heavens toward the earth like a plumb bob toward a melon. St. Ives's telescope, with its mirror of speculum metal, had been a gift from Lord Rosse himself, and he peered into the eyepiece now, tracking the flight of the comet for no other reason, really, than to while away the dawn hours. He slept only fitfully these days, and his dreams weren't pleasant.

There was nothing to calculate; work of that nature had been accomplished weeks past by astronomers whose knowledge of astral mathematics was sufficient to satisfy both the Royal Academy and Dr. Ignacio Narbondo. St. Ives wouldn't dispute their figures. That the comet would spin dangerously close to the earth was the single point that all of them agreed upon. His desire in watching the icy planetoid, beyond a simple fascination with the mystery and wonder of the thing, was to have a look at the face of what might easily be his last great nemesis, a vast leviathan swimming toward them through a dark sea. He wondered if it was oblivion that was revealed by the turning earth.

Hasbro packed their bags in the manor. Their train left Kirk Hammerton Station at six. Dr. Narbondo, St. Ives had to assume, would discover that same morning that he had been foiled, that Beezer, somehow, had failed him. The morning *Times* would rattle in on the Dover train, ignorant of pending doom. The doctor would try to contact the nefarious Beezer, but Beezer wouldn't be found. He's taken ill, they would say on Fleet Street, repeating the substance of the letter St. Ives had sent off to Beezer's employers. Beezer, they'd assure Narbondo, had been ordered south on holiday—to the coast of Spain. Narbondo's forehead would wrinkle with suspicion, and the wrinkling would engender horrible curses and the gnashing of teeth. St. Ives almost smiled. The doctor would know who had thwarted him.

But the result would be, quite likely, the immediate removal of Narbondo and Hargreaves to the environs of northwestern Scandinavia. The chase, thought St. Ives tiredly, would be on. The comet loomed only a few days away, barely enough time for them to accomplish their task.

A door slammed in the manor. St. Ives slipped from his stool and looked out through the west-facing window of his observatory, waving to Hasbro who, in the roseate light of an early dawn, dangled a pocket watch from a chain and nodded to his employer. In a half hour they were away, scouring along the highroad toward the station in Kirk Hammerton, where St. Ives, Hasbro, and Jack Owlesby would leave for Ramsgate and the dirigible that would transport them to the ice and tundra of arctic Norway. If the labors of Bill Kraken were unsuccessful, if he couldn't sabotage Lord Kelvin's frightful machine, they would all know about it, along with the rest of suffering humanity, two days hence.

Bill Kraken crouched in the willows along the River Nidd, watching through the lacy tendrils the dark bulk of Lord Kelvin's barn. The device had been finished two days earlier, the ironic result, to a degree, of his own labor—labor he wouldn't be paid for. But money wasn't of particular consequence anymore, not like it had been in the days of his squid merchanting or when he'd been rescued from the life of a lowly peapod man by the charitable Langdon St. Ives.

Kraken sighed. Poor St. Ives. There was suffering and there was suffering. Kraken had never found a wife, had never fathered children. He had been cracked on the head more often than he could remember, but so what? That kind of damage could be borne. The sort of blow that had struck St. Ives, though—that was a different thing, and Kraken feared sometimes that it would take a heavy toll on the great man before they all won through. Kraken wanted for nothing now, not really, beyond seeing St. Ives put right again.

In a cloth bag beside him wriggled a dozen snakes, collected from the high grass beyond the manor house. In a wire-screen cage beneath the snakes was a score of mice, hungry, as were the snakes, from days of neglect. A leather bellows dangled from his belt, and a hooded lantern from his right hand. No one else was on the meadow.

The Royal Academy had been glad to be quit of Ignacio Narbondo, who had taken ship for Oslo to effect his preposterous machinations. That was the rumor around Lord Kelvin's barn. The Academy would reduce his threats to drivel now that the machine was built. Why Narbondo hadn't followed through with his plan to alert the press no one could say, but it seemed to Secretary Parsons to be evidence that his threats were mere bluff. And that crackpot St. Ives had given up, too, thank God. All this had lightened the atmosphere considerably. A sort of holiday air had sprung up around what had been a business fraught with suspicion and doubt. Now the Academy was free to act without impediment…

Kraken bent out from under the willows and set out across the meadow carrying his bundles. It would do no good to run. He was too old to be cutting capers on a meadow in the dead of night, and if he tripped and dropped his mice or knocked his lantern against a stone, his plan would be foiled utterly. In an hour both the moon and the comet would have appeared on the horizon and the meadow would be bathed in light. If he was sensible, he'd be asleep in his bed by then.

The dark bulk of the barn loomed before him, the pale stones of its foundation contrasting with the weathered oak battens above.

Kraken ducked along the wall toward a tiny mullioned window beneath which extended the last six inches of the final section of brass pipe—the very pipe that Kraken himself had wrestled through a hole augered into the barn wall on that first day he'd helped Lord Kelvin align the things.

What, exactly, the pipe was intended to accomplish, Kraken couldn't say, but somehow it was the focal point of the workings of the device. Beyond, some twenty feet from the barn and elevated on a stone slab, sat a black monolith, smooth as polished marble. Kraken had been amazed when, late the previous afternoon, Lord Kelvin had flung a ballpeen hammer end over end at the monolith, and the collected workmen and scientists had gasped in wonder when the hammer had been soundlessly reflected with such force that it had sailed out of sight in the general direction of York. That the hammer had fallen to earth again, not a man of them could say. The reversal of the poles was to be accomplished, then, by emanating toward this monolith the collected magnetic rays developed in Lord Kelvin's machine, thus both exciting and deflecting them in a circuitous pattern, and sending them off, as it were, astride a penny whirligig. It was too much for Kraken to fathom, but Lord Kelvin and his peers were the giants of electricity and mechanics. A job like this had been child's play to them. Their heads weren't like the heads of other men.

Kraken squinted through the darkness at the monolith, doubly black against the purple of the starry night sky, and wondered at the remarkable perspicacity of great scientists. Here sat the impossible machine, primed for acceleration on the morrow. Could Kraken, a man of admittedly low intellect, scuttle the marvelous device? Kraken shook his head, suddenly full of doubt. He had been entrusted with little else than the material salvation of humanity...

Well, Kraken was just a small man with a small way of doing things. He had seen low times in his life, had mucked through sewers with murderers, and so he would have to trust to low means here. That was the best he could do.

He quit breathing and cocked an ear. Nothing but silence and the distant hooting of an owl greeted him on the night air. He untied the bellows from his belt and shook them by his ear. Grain and broken biscuits rattled within. He shoved the mouth of the bellows into the end of the brass tube and pumped furiously, listening to the debris clatter away, down the tilted pipe. Long after the last of the grain had been blown clear of the bellows, Kraken continued to manipulate his instrument, desperate to send the bulk of it deep into the bowels of the apparatus. Haste would avail him nothing here.

Finally satisfied, he tied the bellows once again to his belt and picked up the mouse cage. The beasts were tumultuous with excitement, stimulated, perhaps, by the evening constitutional, or sensing somehow that they were on the brink of an adventure of powerful magnitude. Kraken pressed the cage front against the end of the tube and pulled open its little door. The mice scurried around in apparent amazement, casting wild glances here and there, curious about a heap of shredded newspaper or the pink ear of a neighbor. Then, one by one, they filed away down the tube like cattle down a hill, sniffing the air, intent suddenly on biscuits and grain.

The snakes were a comparatively easy case. A round dozen of the beasts slithered away down the tube in the wake of the mice, anxious to be quit of their sack. Kraken wondered if he hadn't ought to wad the sack up and shove it into the tube, too, in order to make absolutely sure that the beasts remained trapped inside.

But the dangers of doing that were manifold. Lord Kelvin or some particularly watchful guard might easily discover the stopper before Kraken had a chance to remove it. They mustn't, said St. Ives, discover that the sabotage had been the work of men—thus the mice and snakes. It might easily seem that the natural residents of the barn had merely taken up lodgings there, and thus the hand of Langdon St. Ives would go undetected.

It was very nearly within the hour that Bill Kraken climbed into bed. But his dreams were filled that night with visions of mice and snakes dribbling from the end of the tube and racing away into the darkness, having consumed the grain and leaving nothing behind sufficient to foul the workings of the dread machine. What could he do, though, save trust to providence? The shame of his failure—if failure it should be—would likely be as nothing next to the horrors that would beset them after Lord Kelvin's success. God bless the man, thought Kraken philosophically. He pictured the aging lord, laboring night and day to complete his engine, certain that he was contributing his greatest gift yet to humankind. His disappointment would be monumental. It seemed almost worth the promised trouble to let the poor man have a try at it. But that, sadly, wouldn't do. The world was certainly a sorrowful and contradictory place.

# NORWAY

The bright April weather had turned stormy and dark by the time St. Ives and Hasbro had chuffed into Dover, and the North Sea was a tumult of wind-tossed waves and driving rain. St. Ives huddled now aboard the Ostende ferry, out of the rain beneath an overhanging deck ledge and wrapped in an oilcloth, legs spread to counter the heaving swell. His pipe burned like a chimney, and as he peered out at the roiling black of the heavens, equally cloudy thoughts drew his eyes into a squint and made him oblivious to the cold and wet. Had this sudden turn of arctic weather anything to do with the experimentation of the Royal Academy? Had they effected the reversal of the poles prematurely and driven the weather suddenly mad? Had Kraken failed? He watched a gray swell loom overhead, threatening to slam the ferry apart, only to sink suddenly into nothing as if having changed its mind, and then tower up once again overhead, sheets of flying foam torn from its crest and rendered into spindrift by the wind.

His plans seemed to be fast going wrong. The dirigible he

had counted upon for transport had been "inoperable." The fate of the earth itself hung in the balance, and the filthy dirigible was "inoperable." They would all be inoperable by the end of the week. Jack Owlesby had stayed on in Ramsgate where a crew of nitwits fiddled with the craft, and so yet another variable, as the mathematician would say, had been cast into the muddled stew. Could the dirigible be made operable in time? Would Jack, along with the flea-brained pilot, find them in the cold wastes of arctic Norway? It didn't bear thinking about. One thing at a time, St. Ives reminded himself. They had left Jack with a handshake and a compass and had raced south intending to follow Narbondo overland, trusting to Jack to take care of himself.

But where was Ignacio Narbondo? He must have set sail from Dover with Hargreaves hours earlier, apparently under a false name—except that the ticket agent could find no record of his having boarded the Ostende ferry. St. Ives had described him vividly: the hump, the tangle of oily hair, the cloak. No one could remember having seen him board. He might have got on unseen in the early morning, of course.

It was conceivable, just barely, that St. Ives had made a monumental error, or that Narbondo had tricked the lot of them, had been one up on them all along. He might at that moment be bound, say, for Reykjavik, intent on working his deviltry on the volcanic wastes of the interior of Iceland. He might be sitting in a comfortable chair in London, laughing into his hat. What would St. Ives do then? Keep going, like a windup tin soldier on the march. He could imagine himself simply ambling away into Scandinavian forests, circling aimlessly through the trees like a dying reindeer.

But then in Ostende the rain let up and the wind fell off, and the solid ground beneath his feet once again lent him a steadiness of purpose. In the cold station, a woman stirred a caldron of mussels, dumping in handfuls of shallots and lumps of butter. Aromatic steam swirled out of the iron pot in such a way as to make St. Ives lightheaded. "Mussels and beer," he said to Hasbro, "would revive a body."

"That they would, sir. And a loaf of bread, I might add, to provide bulk."

"A sound suggestion," said St. Ives, striding toward the woman and removing his hat. He liked the look of her immediately. She was stooped and heavy and wore a dress like a tent, and it seemed as if all the comets in the starry heavens couldn't knock her off her pins. She dumped mussels, black and dripping, into a cleverly folded newspaper basket, heaping up the shells until they threatened to cascade to the floor. She winked at St. Ives, fished an enormous mussel from the pot, slid her thumbs into the hiatus of its open shell, and in a single swift movement pulled the mollusk open, shoved one of her thumbs under the orange flesh, and flipped the morsel into her open mouth. "Some don't chew them," she said, speaking English, "but I do. What's the use of eating at all if you don't chew them? Might as well swallow a toad."

"Indubitably," said St. Ives, happy enough to make small talk. "It's the same way with oysters. I never could stand simply to allow the creatures to slide down my throat. I fly in the face of custom there."

"Aye," she said. "Can you imagine a man's stomach, full of beasts such as these, whole, mind you, and sloshin' like smelts in a bucket?" She dipped again into the caldron, picked out another mussel, and ate it with relish, then grimaced and rooted in her mouth with a finger. "Mussel pearl," she said, holding up between thumb and forefinger a tiny opalescent sphere twice the size of a pinhead. She slid open a little drawer in the cart on which sat the caldron of mussels, and dropped the pearl in among what must have been thousands of the tiny orbs. "Can't stand debris," she said, grimacing.

The entire display rather took the edge off St. Ives's appetite, and the heap of mussels in his basket, reclining beneath a coating of congealing butter and bits of garlic and shallot, began to remind him of certain unfortunate suppers he'd consumed at the Bayswater Club. He grinned weakly at the woman and looked around at the hurrying crowds, wondering if he and Hasbro hadn't ought to join them.

"Man in here this afternoon ate one shell and all," she said, shaking her head. "Imagine the debris involved. Must have given his throat bones some trouble, I daresay."

"Shell and all?" asked St. Ives.

"That's the exact case. Crunched away at the thing like it was a marzipan crust, didn't he? Then he took another, chewed it up about halfway, saw what he was about, and spit the filthy thing against the wall there. You can see bits of it still, can't you, despite the birds swarming round. There's the smear of it against the stones. Do you see it there?—bit of brown paste is all it amounts to now."

St. Ives stared at the woman. "Big man?"

"Who?"

"This fellow who ate the shells. Big, was he, and with a beard? Seemed ready to fly into a rage?"

"That's your man, gents. Cursed vilely, he did, but not at the shells. It was at the poor birds, wasn't it, when they come round to eat up what your man spit onto the wall there. You can see it there, can't you? I never…"

"Was he in the company of a hunchback?"

"Aye," said the woman, giving her pot a perfunctory stirring. "Greasy little man with a grin. Seemed to think the world is a lark. But it ain't no lark, gentlemen. Here you've been, wasting my time this quarter hour, and not another living soul has bought a shell. You've frightened the lot of them off, is what I think, and you haven't paid me a penny." She glowered at St. Ives, then glowered at Hasbro.

"What time this afternoon?" asked St. Ives.

"Three hours past, say, or four. Might have been five. Or less."

"Thank you." St. Ives reached into his pocket for a coin. He dumped a half crown into her outstretched hand and left her blinking, he and Hasbro racing through the terminal toward the distant exit, each of them clutching a bag in one hand and a paper satchel of mussels in the other. The streets were wet outside, but the clouds were broken overhead and taking flight in the gray dusk, and the wind had simmered down to a billowy breeze. A bent man shambled past in trousers meant for a behemoth, clutching at a buttonless coat. St. Ives thrust his mussels at the man, meaning to do him a good turn, but his gesture was mistaken. The man cast him a look of mingled surprise and loathing, fetching the basket a swipe with his hand that sent the entire affair into the gutter. St. Ives hurried on without a word, marveling at misunderstood humanity and at how little space existed between apparent madness and the best of intentions.

In a half hour they were aboard a train once again, in a sleeping car bound for Amsterdam, Hamburg, and finally, to Hjørring, where on the Denmark ferry they'd once again set sail across the North Sea, up the Oslofjord into Norway.

St. Ives was determined to remain awake, to have a look at the comet when it sailed in over the horizon sometime after midnight. But the sleepless nights he had spent in the observatory and the long hours of travel since had worn him thin, and after a tolerable meal in the dining car, and what might likely turn out to be, on the morrow, a regrettable lot of brandy, he dropped away at once into a deep sleep, and the comet rose in the sky and fell again without him, slanting past the captive earth.

In Oslo Hargreaves had beaten a man half senseless with the man's own cane. In Trondheim, two hours before the arrival of St. Ives and Hasbro on the express, he had run mad and threatened to explode a greengrocer's cart, kicking the spokes out of one of the wheels before Narbondo had hauled him away and explained to the authorities that his companion was a lunatic bound for a sanitorium in Narvik.

St. Ives itched to be after them, but here he sat, becalmed in a small brick railway station. He stared impatiently out the window at the nearly empty station. A delay of a minute seemed an eternity, and each sighing release of steam from the waiting train carried upon it the suggestion of the final, fateful explosion. Hasbro, St. Ives could see, was equally uneasy at their motionless state, for he sat hunched forward on his seat as if trying to compel the train into flight. Finally, amid tooting and whooshing and three false starts, they were away again, St. Ives praying that the engineer had understood his translated request that they make an unscheduled stop on the deserted tundra adjacent to Mount Hjarstaad. Surely he would; he had accepted the little bag of assorted coffee tablets readily enough. What could he have understood them to be but payment?

Darkness had long since fallen, and with it had fled the last of the scattered rain showers. Ragged clouds pursued by arctic wind capered across the sky, and the stars shone thick and bright between. The train developed steam after puffing along lazily up a steepening grade, and within a score of minutes was hurtling through the mountainous countryside.

St. Ives was gripped once more with the excitement and peril of the chase. He removed his pocket watch at intervals, putting it back without so much as glancing at it, then loosening his already-loosened collar, peering out across the rocky landscape at the distant swerve of track ahead when the train lurched into a curve, as if the engine they pursued must surely be visible a half mile farther on.

The slow labored climb of steep hills was almost instantly maddening and filled him again with the fear that their efforts would prove futile, that from the vantage point of the next peak they would witness the detonation of half of Scandinavia: crumbling mountainsides, hurtling rocks. But then they would creep, finally, to another summit void of trees, where the track was wafered onto ledges along unimaginable precipices. And the train would plunge away again in a startling rush of steam and clatter.

They thundered through shrieking tunnels, the starry sky going momentarily black and then reappearing in an instant only to be dashed again into darkness. And when the train burst each time into the cold Norwegian night, both St. Ives and Hasbro were pressed against the window, peering skyward, relieved to see the last scattered clouds fleeing before the wind. Then all at once, as if waved into existence by a magic wand, the lights of the aurora borealis swept across the sky in lacy showers of green and red and blue, like a semitransparent Christmas tapestry hung across the wash of stars.

"Yes!" cried St. Ives, leaping to his feet and nearly pitching into the aisle as they rushed howling into another tunnel. "He's done it! Kraken has done it!"

"Indeed, sir?"

"Absolutely," said St. Ives, his voice animated. "Without the shadow of a doubt. The northern lights, my good fellow, are a consequence of the earth's electromagnetic field. It's a simple matter—no field, no lights. Had Lord Kelvin's machine done its work, the display you see before us would have been postponed for heaven knows how many woeful years. But here it is, isn't it? Good old Bill!" And on this last cheerful note, they emerged once again into the aurora-lit night, hurtling along beside a broad cataract that tumbled down through a boulder-strewn gorge.

Another hour's worth of tunnels, however, began to make it seem finally as if there were no end to their journey, as if, perhaps, their train labored around and around a clever circular track, that they had been monumentally hoaxed one last fateful time by Dr. Ignacio Narbondo. Then, in an effort of steam, the train crested yet another treeless summit, and away to the west, far below them, moonlight shimmered on the rippled surface of a fjord, stretching out to the distant Norwegian Sea. Tumbling down out of the rocky precipices to their right rushed the wild river they had followed for what seemed an age, the torrent wrapping round the edge of Mount Hjarstaad and disappearing into shadow where it cascaded, finally, into the vast emptiness of an abyss. A trestle spanned the cataract and gave out onto a tundra-covered plain, scattered with the angular moon shadows of tilted stones.

Ahead of them, some ten yards from the track and clearly visible in the moonlight, lay a strange and alien object—an empty steamer trunk, its lid thrown back and its contents removed. Beyond that, a hundred yards farther along, lay another, also empty and yanked over onto its side. The train raced past both before howling to a steam-shrieking stop that made St. Ives wince. So much for subtlety, he thought, as Hasbro pitched their bags onto the icy plain and the two leaped out after them, the train almost immediately setting forth again, north, toward Hammerfest, leaving the world and the two marooned men to their collective fate.

St. Ives hurried across the plain toward the slope of Mount Hjarstaad. A footpath wound upward along the edge of the precipice through which the river thundered and roiled. The air was full of cold mist and the booming of water. "I'm afraid we've announced our arrival through a megaphone," St. Ives shouted over his shoulder.

"Perhaps the roar of the falls…" said Hasbro at St. Ives's back. But the rest of his words was lost in the watery tumult as the two men hurried up the steepening hill, keeping to the edge of the trail and the deep shadows of the steep rocky cliffs.

St. Ives patted his coat, feeling beneath it the hard foreign outline of his revolver. He realized that he was cold, almost numbed, but that the cold wasn't only a result of the wet arctic air. He was struck with the overwhelming feeling that he was replaying his most common and fearful nightmare, and the misty water of the falls seemed to him suddenly to be the rain out of a London sky. He could hear in the echoing crash the sound of horse's hooves on paving stones and the crack of pistols fired in deadly haste.

The revolver in his waistband suddenly was almost repulsive to him, as if it were a poisonous reptile and not a thing built of brass and steel. The notion of shooting it at any living human being seemed both an utter impossibility and an utter necessity. His faith in the rational and the logical had been replaced by a mass of writhing contradictions and half-understood notions of revenge and salvation that were as confused as the unfathomable roar of the maelstrom in the chasm.

There was a shout behind him. A crack like a pistol shot followed, and St. Ives was pushed from behind. He rolled against a carriage-sized boulder, throwing his hands over his head as a hail of stones showered down around him, and an enormous rock, big as a cartwheel, bounded over his head, soaring away into the misty depths of the abyss.

He pushed himself to his knees, feeling Hasbro's grip on his elbow, and he peered up into the shadowy gloom above. There, leaping from perch to rocky perch, was a man with wild hair and beard—Hargreaves, there could be little doubt. Hasbro drew his revolver, steadied his forearm along the top of a rock, and fired twice at the retreating figure. His bullets pinged off rocks twenty feet short of their mark, but the effect on the anarchist was startling—as if he had been turned suddenly into a mountain sheep. He disappeared on the instant, hidden by boulders.

St. Ives forced himself to his feet, pressing himself against the stony wall of the path. Hasbro tapped his shoulder and gestured first at himself and then at the mountainside. St. Ives nodded as his friend angled away up a rocky defile, climbing slowly and solidly upward. He watched Hasbro disappear among the granite boulders, and for a moment he felt the urge to sit down right there in the dirt and wait for him.

He couldn't do that, though. There was too much at stake. And there was Alice to think of. Always there was Alice to think of. If revenge was the compelling motive for him now, so what? He had to call upon something to move him up the path; it might as well be raw hatred.

He sidled along carefully, grimly imagining himself following the course of the rock that had plummeted over his head moments ago. Icy dirt crunched underfoot, and the hillside opened up briefly on his right to reveal a wide, steep depression in the rock—a sort of conical hole at the bottom of which lay a black, silent tarn. The water of the tarn brimmed with reflected stars that were washed with the blue-red light of the aurora. It was a scene of unearthly beauty, and it reminded him of the alluring darkness of pure sleep.

Abruptly he jerked himself away and climbed farther up the trail, rounding a sharp bend. He could see high above him the mouth of the smoking crater. Perched on the rim and hauling on the coils of a mechanical bladder was the venomous Dr. Narbondo, the steamy reek of boiling mud swirling about his head and shoulders. Hargreaves capered like a lunatic beside him, dancing from one foot to the other like a man treading on hot pavement.

They were too distant to shoot at, but St. Ives compelled himself to take the pistol out of his waistband anyway. Calmly and with a will, he began to sing "God Save the Queen" in a low voice. It didn't matter what song—what he needed was a melody and a set of verses with which to sweep his mind clear of rubble. Narbondo worked furiously, looking back over his shoulder, scanning the rocky mountainside. There was nothing for St. Ives to do but step out into the open and rush up the path toward the two of them. It might be futile, exposing himself like that... He sang louder, but the thought that Hargreaves would simply kill him caused him to scramble the words, and for a moment he considered going back down to where Hasbro had cut off into the rocks, maybe following his friend's trail. But that would be a retreat, and he couldn't allow that.

He cocked his pistol and stepped forward in a crouch. Hargreaves grappled now with a carpetbag, pulling out unidentifiable bits and pieces of mechanical debris, which he fumbled with, trying to assemble them. His curses reached St. Ives on the wind. Narbondo raged beside him, turning once again to survey the rocks behind and below him. He looked straight down into St. Ives's face. Despite the distance, his expression was clear in the moonlight; hatred and fear and passion played across his features, and for a moment he stood stock-still, as if he had seen his fate standing there below him.

A pistol shot rang out, echoing away somewhere among the rocks, and Narbondo spun half around, grabbing his shoulder and shouting a curse. He worked his arm up and down as if testing it, and then pushed Hargreaves aside, tearing at the contents of the bag himself and shouting orders. Hargreaves immediately disappeared behind a tumble of rocks, and St. Ives scrambled for cover as the anarchist popped up almost at once to shoot wildly down at him. Another shot followed close on, and for an instant St. Ives saw Hasbro leaping across a granite slope, only to disappear again when Hargreaves spun around and fired at him.

St. Ives stood and darted up the path, breathing heavily in the thin air. There was the sound of another gunshot just as a spatter of granite chips sprayed into his face, nearly blinding him. He blinked and spit, creeping along until he could see Hargreaves above him, looking down. Hargreaves dropped like a stone, then stood up at once and fired again twice, the bullets pinging off the rocks beside St. Ives's head.

St. Ives yanked himself down, the smell of powdered granite in his nose. He smiled grimly, wiping at his watering eyes, the sudden danger surging over him like a sea wave, washing away his muddled doubts. He stood up to draw Hargreaves's fire, ducking immediately and hearing two shots, one after another, from Hargreaves and Hasbro both. He stood again, resting his forearm across the cold stone and setting up to fire carefully now. Hargreaves set out at a run, down and across the rocks. But he was too far away and moving too fast, and St. Ives was no kind of marksman. He waited too long, and his man again disappeared.

St. Ives stepped at once out onto the path, half expecting a bullet and half expecting Hasbro to provide covering fire. There sounded two more shots, from roughly the same direction, but St. Ives forced himself to ignore them, intent now on Narbondo, who worked madly, casting futile glances down at him and bellowing for Hargreaves, the roar of the falls drowning his words before they reached St. Ives, who ran straight up the path, leveling his pistol. He hadn't bothered to reload after the last couple of shots, but somehow it didn't matter to him. What he wanted now was to put his hands on Narbondo's throat. He had failed once before; he wouldn't fail again.

There was a warning shout, though—Hasbro's voice—and St. Ives turned to see Hargreaves scrambling toward him, ignoring Hasbro, who stood like a statue, his pistol raised and pointed at Hargreaves's back. Narbondo was oblivious to them all, as if he would cheerfully die rather than give up his loathsome dream. He peered suddenly skyward, though, his forearm thrown across his brow as if to shade his eyes from moonlight. St. Ives followed Narbondo's gaze, and there, below the moon, dropping past the pale blue wash of the aurora, drifted the dark ovoid silhouette of a descending dirigible.

St. Ives bolted forward, as if the sight of it had brought the world to him once again, had reminded him that he wasn't a solitary man facing a solitary villain, but that there was such a thing as duty and honor… He heard the crack of Hargreaves's pistol almost at the same time that the bullet struck him in the shoulder. He cried out and dropped to his knees, his revolver spinning away into the void on the opposite side of the path as he scuttled like a crab down again into the shelter of the rocks.

A shriek followed, and St. Ives looked up to see Hargreaves dancing next to Narbondo now, the two of them shouting and cursing. Hasbro stepped determinedly toward them as Narbondo furiously worked a mechanical detonator. It was too late for him, though, and he knew it. He hadn't had enough time. St. Ives was full of something like happiness, although it was cold and cheerless, and he stepped out onto the path again, gripping his bleeding shoulder.

Hargreaves raised his hand to shoot at Hasbro. But there was no sound at all, even though the man continued to pull the trigger. He pitched the gun away from him in disgust, picking up the carpetbag as if he would fling it into Hasbro's face. He turned with it, though, and slammed Narbondo in the back, roaring nonsense at him. Hasbro stood still twenty feet below them, his arm upraised, and shot Hargreaves carefully and steadily.

The anarchist lurched round, teetered for a moment on the edge of the crater, and then toppled off, disappearing into the mouth of the volcano as Narbondo made one last futile grab at the bag clutched in Hargreaves's flailing hand.

There was an instant when no one moved, all of them waiting, and then a thunderous explosion that rocked the mountainside— the volatile contents of the bag having been detonated by the fires of Mount Hjarstaad. The three men pitched to the ground as the explosion echoed away, replaced by the low roar of rocks tumbling toward the plain below. Hasbro was up at once, stepping toward the crater's edge, leveling his pistol at Narbondo, who stood still now, hangdog, his head bowed like that of a man defeated at the very moment of success. He raised his hands in resignation.

Then, without so much as a backward glance, he bolted down the footpath toward St. Ives, gathering momentum, running headlong at the surprised scientist. Hasbro spun around and tracked him with the pistol.

"Shoot!" St. Ives shouted, but a shot was out of the question unless he himself backed away, out of the line of fire. He scrambled back down the path toward the bend in the trail as Narbondo leaped along in great springing strides behind him, wild to escape, his face contorted now with fear and wonderment as he hurtled uncontrollably toward St. Ives. The scientist stopped to face him, but saw at once that Narbondo would run him down like an express train.

St. Ives turned and hurried downward, hearing Narbondo's footsteps slamming along and knowing he would be overtaken in seconds. The path widened just then, but turned sharply at the edge of the cliff, and St. Ives saw below him the waters of the starlit tarn, deadly still in the moonlight. In an instant he took it all in—Narbondo was moving too quickly. He would plummet off the edge of the path where it turned, hurtling into the abyss below. There was no hope for him.

And good riddance, St. Ives thought. But then, almost instinctively, he braced himself against two rocks, and as Narbondo raged past, St. Ives reached out to pull him down. He bulled past like a runaway express, though, and St. Ives, meaning to grab him by the arm, was slammed sideways instead, back into the rocks, managing only to knock Narbondo off-balance. His feet stuttered as he tried to stop himself, and then with a shriek he catapulted forward, away from the abyss, head over heels, caroming against a rock and then somersaulting like a circus acrobat across the steep scree-slippery slope until he plunged into the black waters of the tarn. The reflection of the moon and stars on the surface of the water disintegrated, the bits and pieces dancing wildly. But by the time Hasbro had made his way down to where St. Ives stood staring into the depths of the pool, the surface was lapping itself placid once again.

"He's gone," said St. Ives simply.

"Will he float surfaceward, sir?"

"Not necessarily," replied the scientist. "The fall must have knocked the wind from him. It might have killed him outright. He'll stay down until he bloats with gasses—until he begins to rot. And the water, I fear, is cold enough to slow the process substantially, perhaps indefinitely. We could wait a bit, just to be certain, but I very much fear that I've done too much waiting in my life."

Hasbro was silent.

"I might have saved him, there at the last," St. Ives said.

"Very doubtful, sir. I would cheerfully have shot him. And there'd be no use in saving him for the gallows. He wouldn't escape Newgate Prison a second time."

"What I wanted was to grab his arm, pull him down. But it seems I gave him a shove instead."

"And a very propitious shove, to my mind."

St. Ives looked at him tiredly. "I'm not sure I understand any of it," he said. "But it's over now. This part is." And with that St. Ives nodded at the horizon where glowed a great arc of white fire. As the two men watched, the flaming orb of the comet crept skyward, enormous now, as if it were soaring in to swallow the puny earth at a gulp.

Hasbro nodded quietly. "Shall we fetch their equipment, sir?"

"We'll want the lot of it," said St. Ives. "And to all appearances, we'll want it quickly. We've a long and wearisome journey ahead of us before we see the mountains of Peru." He sighed deeply. His shoulder began suddenly to ache. He turned one last time toward the tarn in which Narbondo had found an icy grave. His confrontation with Narbondo had rushed upon him, the work of a confused second, and had found him utterly unprepared, his actions futile.

It almost seemed choreographed by some chaotic higher authority who meant to show him a thing or two about confusion and regret and what most often happened to man's best-laid plans.

Hasbro stood in silence, waiting, perhaps, for St. Ives to come once again to life. Finally he set off up the path toward the summit, to fetch Narbondo's apparatus and leaving St. Ives to welcome Jack Owlesby, whose hurried footfalls scuffed up the trail behind them.

LONDON

Bill Kraken leaned against the parapet on Waterloo Bridge and grinned into the Thames. Four pints of Bass Ale had banked and stoked the fires of good cheer within him. Tomorrow would see the return of his companions; tonight would see the ascent of the diminishing comet. It was nearing midnight as he finished reading the last half paragraph in his ruined copy of Ashbless's *Account of London Scientists,* happy to note that although the Royal Academy had never publicly recognized the genius of his benefactor, Ashbless had devoted the better half of his book to accounts of St. Ives's successes and adventures.

Kraken closed and pocketed the book. The adventure of Lord Kelvin's machine had ended nicely, if strangely, three afternoons past. The mice and snakes that had rained on Leeds like a Biblical plague had mystified the populace, from the unbelieving Lord Kelvin to the man in the street, taking flight in wondering speculation. The newspapers had been full of it. Every reporter with, perhaps, the exception of Beezer had set out to investigate the incident, but the Royal Academy had put the cap on it—had hushed it up, had hauled away the clogged machine in the night to dismantle it in secret.

Poor Lord Kelvin, thought Kraken, shaking his head. The odd sight of the rocketing beasts had rather unnerved him—perhaps more so even than the ruination of his device. And the muck clogging the tube just before the explosion... Kraken giggled. But his success wasn't entirely a cause for celebration. There were questions of a philosophic nature to be asked, for sure—questions concerning his lordship's manufactured failure and the sleepless nights of vain speculation that failure would engender, questions of the expendability of dumb animals for the sake of saving mankind. Kraken wasn't sure he liked either notion, but he liked the idea of a mutant future even less.

These scientists, thought Kraken, there was no telling what sorts of tricks they'd get up to, scampering like so many grinning devils astride an engine, laboring to turn the old earth inside out like a pair of trousers, one of them yanking at a pant leg with a calipers while another filled the pockets with numbers and gunpowder. And here on the horizon, slipping as if by magic into the sky, rose the comet, the stars paling roundabout like lanterns enfeebled by sudden daylight.

Kraken tipped his hat at the sky and set out. He trudged past Westminster Pier and the Houses of Parliament and climbed into a waiting dogcart, pausing just a moment to look once again over his shoulder at the ascending comet. He took up the reins and shrugged, then reached out to pat the flank of his horse. Success, he thought to himself as he set out at a leisurely canter toward Chingford, is a relative business at best.

PART II

THE DOWNED SHIPS: JACK OWLESBY'S ACCOUNT

THE HANSOM CAB LUNATIC

I was coming along down Holborn Hill in December, beneath a lowering sky and carrying a tin of biscuits and a pound of Brazilian coffee, when a warehouse exploded behind Perkins inn. Smoke and lumber and a twisted sheet of iron, torn nearly in half from the blast, blew out of the mouth of the alley between Kingsway and Newton Street and scattered the half-dozen pedestrians like autumn leaves.

I was clear of it, thank God, but even so the concussion threw me into the gutter, and I dropped the biscuits and coffee and found myself on the seat of my pants, watching a man stagger away from the explosion, out of the mouth of the alley to collapse bloody on the pavement.

I jumped up and ran for the man on the ground, thinking to help but really not thinking at all, when a second blast ripped through and slammed me against a bakery storefront. Glass shattered where my elbow went through the window, and then the rest of me followed, snapping the mullions and tumbling through in an avalanche of buns.

Directly there was another roar—not an explosion this time, but a roof caving in, and then a billow of black smoke pouring out of the alley and a fire that reminded you of the Gordon Riots. I could walk, if you call it that, and between the two of us, the baker and I, we pulled the bloody man across to where my coffee lay spilled out in the gutter. We needn't have bothered; he was dead, and we could both see it straight off, but you don't leave even a dead man to burn, not if you can help it.

I couldn't see worth anything all at once, because of the reek. It was a paper company gone up—a common enough tragedy, except that there was an element or two that made it markedly less common: Mr. Theophilus Godall was there, for one. Maybe you don't know what that means yet; maybe you do. And the paper company wasn't just any paper company; it was next door but one to an empty sort of machine works overseen by the Royal Academy, specifically as a sort of closed-to-the-public museum used to house the contrivances built by the great Lord Kelvin and the other inventive geniuses of the Academy.

My name is Jack Owlesby, and I'm a friend of Professor Langdon St. Ives, who is perhaps the greatest, mostly unsung, scientist and explorer in the Western Hemisphere. Mr. Oscar Wilde said something recently along the following lines: "Show me a hero," he said, "and I will write you a tragedy." He might have taken St. Ives as a case in point. I'm rather more inclined to enlarge upon the heroism, which is easier, and of which you have a remarkable surplus when you tackle a subject like Langdon St. Ives. You yourself might have read about some few of his exploits;

and if you have, then I'll go as far as to tell you that this business of the exploding paper company won't turn out in the end to be altogether foreign to you.

As for Theophilus Godall, he owns the Bohemian Cigar Divan in Rupert Street, Soho; but there's more to the man than that.

L uckily there was a sharp wind blowing down Kingsway toward the Thames, which scoured the smoke skyward almost as soon as it flooded out of the alley, so that the street was clear enough in between billows. The blast brought a crowd, and they didn't stand and gawk, as crowds have got a reputation for. Two men even tried to get up the alley toward the fire, thinking that there might have been people trapped there or insensible, but the baker stopped them—and a good thing, too, as you'll see—pointing out quick that this being a Sunday the paper company was closed, as was everything else in that direction except Perkins Inn, which was safe enough for the moment. He had been out for a look, the baker had, not a minute before the explosion, and could tell us that aside from the dead man there hadn't been a soul dawdling in the alley except a tall gentleman of upright carriage in a greatcoat and top hat.

All of us looked as one down that grim black alley, all of us thinking the same thing—that the man in the coat, if he had in fact been dawdling there, was dead as a nailhead. The two men who had a minute earlier been making a rush in that direction were happy enough that they had held up, for the flames licked across at the brick façade opposite the paper company, and a wide section of wall crumbled outward in a roar of collapsing rubble.

The baker, as if coming to, clapped a hand onto the top of his bald head and sprinted for his own shop—thinking to get some few of his things clear before it went up too. The heat drove him back, though, and I can picture him clearly in my mind today, wringing his hands and scuffing his feet in the spilled coffee next to the dead man, and waiting for his shop to burn.

It didn't, though; thank heaven. It began to rain, is what it did, with such a crashing of thunder that, with the first bolt, we thought another roof had caved in. The drops fell thick and steady, as if someone were pouring it out of a bucket, and the baker fell to his knees right there in the street and clasped his hands together with the rainwater streaming down his face. I hope he said a word for the dead man behind him—although if he did, it was a brief one, for he stood up just as quick as he had knelt, and pointed across at a man in a greatcoat and hat, walking away in the direction of the river.

He carried a stick, and his profile betrayed an aquiline nose and a noble sort of demeanor—you could see it in his walk—that made him out to be something more than a gentleman: royalty, you'd think, except that his hat and coat had seen some wear, and his trousers were splashed with mud from the street.

The baker shouted. Of course it was the man he'd seen loitering in the alley directly before the blast. And two constables had the man pinned and labeled before he had a chance to run for it. He wouldn't have run for it anyway, of course, for it was Godall, as you've no doubt deduced by now.

I was possessed by the notion that I ought to go to his defense, tell the constables that they'd collared the wrong man. I didn't, though, having learned a lesson from that earlier unthinking dash of mine into what the newspapers, in their silly way, sometimes call "the devouring elephant," meaning the fire, and still limping from it, too. They would arrest me along with Godall, is what they would do, as an accomplice. My word is nothing to the constabulary. And I was certain that they wouldn't keep him two minutes anyway, once they knew who he was.

The rain fell harder, if that were possible, and the flames died away almost as fast as they'd risen, and the fire brigade, when it clanged up, had nothing at all to do but wait. The smoke boiled away, too, on the instant. Just like that. You would have thought there'd be a fresh billow, what with the sudden rain and all, but there wasn't; it was simply gone, leaving some whitish smoke tumbling up out of the embers of the dwindling fire.

It struck me as funny at the time, the fire and blast so quick and fierce, and then the smoke just dying like that. It's a consequence of hanging about with men like St. Ives and Godall, I guess, that you jump to conclusions about things; you want everything to be a mystery. No, that's not quite it: you *suspect* everything of being a mystery; what you *want* is a different story, which is to say, no story at all. There was a story in this, though. It took about thirty seconds of thought to conclude that it had been an incendiary bomb and a lot of chemical smoke, which had fairly quickly used itself up. The explosion had to have been manufactured.

My biscuits, it turned out—the tin I'd dropped in the road— had been trampled, and I left for Jermyn Street empty-handed. It's a good walk in the rain—by that I mean a long one—but it gave me time to think about two things: whether the tragedy that afternoon had anything to do with Lord Kelvin's machine (the presence of Godall rather argued that it had) and what I would tell Dorothy about it all. Dorothy, if you don't already know, is my wife, and at the moment she was a wife who wouldn't be keen on my getting caught up in another of St. Ives's adventures when the last one hadn't quite got cold yet. I had the unsettling notion that "caught up" was just the right verb, even if a little on the passive side; this had all the earmarks of that sort of thing.

St. Ives wasn't in Harrogate, at his laboratory. He was in London paying a visit to my father-in-law—Mr. William Keeble of Jermyn Street, the toy maker and inventor—consulting him on the building of an apparatus that doesn't concern us here, and is too wild and unlikely for me to mention without throwing a cloud of suspicion and doubt over the whole story. But it was fortuitous, St. Ives's being in London, because if he hadn't been I would have had to send a message up to Harrogate, and he would have come quick enough, maybe to find nothing at all and have wasted a trip.

As it was, I ran him down that night in an oyster bar near Leicester Square. The rain had given off, but the clouds hadn't, and it felt like snow. St. Ives sat reading a *Standard* that wasn't long off the presses. News of the explosion, however, didn't appear on the front page, which was fairly bursting with an extravagant story of another sort altogether. And here my own story digresses for a bit.

I wish I could quote it to you, this second story, but I haven't got it anymore; so I'll tell it to you straight out, although I warn you that I can't do it justice, and that you wouldn't half believe me if I could. Any good library, though, can afford you a copy of a London newspaper from the day in question, if you're the sort of Thomas in the popular phrase.

And note that I haven't tried to sandbag you with the notion that I'd *seen* this second tragedy as well as the explosion up in Holborn: what I'm telling you now is neither art nor journalism, but a sort of lager and lime mix-up of both, and maybe nearer the truth for that.

* * *

It was what the *Standard* referred to as an "imbroglio," although that, I'm afraid, is a small word, and this was no small matter. A lorry had very nearly overturned on Whitefriars Street. It had been running along south, heavily laden, toward the Embankment, its load covered in canvas, several layers, and lashed down against the wind and possible rain. Some few witnesses claimed that there was a man beneath the canvas, too, peering out at the day, although no one saw him so clearly as to identify him beyond their generally agreeing that he ran to tall and thin, and was hatless and nearly bald.

The lorry, angling round across Tudor Street and onto Carmelite, caught a bit of stone curb with its wheel. There was a shifting of cargo and a horrible shout from the half-hidden man on board, and the wagon, as if it were a great fish on the end of a played-out line, shuddered almost to a stop, the horses stumbling and their shoes throwing sparks on the pavement. A terrible mechanical howling set in, as if an engine had just that minute been started up.

The driver—an enormous man with a beard—cursed and slammed at the reins and whipped the poor beasts nearest him as if to take the hide off their flanks. They tried to drive on, too— desperately, to hear the witnesses tell of it—but the lorry, or rather the cargo, seemed to compel the horses back, and for the space of a long minute it looked as if time had stopped dead, except for the suddenly falling rain and the cursing and the flailing of the driver. Then there was the snap of a stay chain coming loose and the lorry lurched forward, the chain swinging round into the spokes, and there was such a groaning and screeching and banging that it seemed sure the wagon would go to pieces on the road and the horses plummet down Carmelite and into the river.

It wasn't the lorry, though, that was tearing itself apart. The air suddenly was full of flying debris, shooting out of the buildings along the street: nails and screws pried themselves out of door casings and clapboards; an iron pot flew from an open window as if it had been thrown; door knockers clanked and clattered and hammered in the hands of a dozen anxious ghosts and then tore away from their door-fronts with a screech of overstrained steel. Even the two iron hitching posts in front of the Temple Inn lurched out of the ground in a shower of dirt and stone fragments, and all of it shot away in the direction of that impossible lorry, a sort of horizontal hailstorm of hardware clanging and banging against the mysterious cargo and clamping tight to it as if glued there.

A man on the street, the paper said, was struck down by one of the posts, and wasn't expected to recover his senses, and two or three others had to be attended to by the surgeon, who removed "shrapnel and all manner of iron debris." Shop windows were shattered by stuff inside flying out through them, and the wagon itself, as if possessed, rocked up and down on its hounds like a spring pole.

During the mêlée there sounded an awful screaming and scrabbling from under the canvas, where the unfortunate passenger (fortunate, actually, that he was padded by several folds of heavy canvas) fought to clamber farther around behind the cargo. His cries attested to his partial failure to accomplish this feat, and if the strange business had gone on a moment longer he would have been beaten dead, and half a dozen houses along Tudor and Carmelite dismantled nail by nail and left in a heap.

The howling noise stopped, though, just like that. The horses jerked forward and away, hauling the lorry with its broken stay chain and spokes, and disappearing around onto the Embankment as the rush of iron debris fell straight to the roadway in a shower, clanking along in the wake of the wagon until it all tired out and lay still.

The street lay deathly silent after that, although the whole business took only about a minute and a half. Rain began to pour down (I've already described it; it was the same rain that saved the baker's shop up in Holborn), and the lorry got away clean, no one suspecting that the whole odd mess involved any definable crime until it was discovered later in the afternoon that a building owned by the Royal Academy—a machine works—had been broken into and a complicated piece of machinery stolen and the paper company next door ignited... It was thought at first (by anyone who wasn't certifiable) that this business of the flying iron might be connected to the theft of the machine.

The peculiar thing, then, was that a spokesman from the Royal Academy—the secretary, Mr. Parsons—denied it flat out and quick enough so that his denials were printed in the *Standard* by nightfall. There wasn't any connection, he said. Couldn't be. And he was extremely doubtful about any nonsense concerning flying door knockers. Science, Mr. Parsons seemed to say, didn't hold with flying door knockers.

Tell that to the man laid out by the iron post, I remember thinking, but it was St. Ives and Godall who between them made the whole thing plain. I forgot to tell you, in fact, that Godall was at the oyster bar, too—he and Hasbro, St. Ives's gentleman's gentleman.

But this is where art leans in and covers the page with her hand—she being leery of making things plain when the story would be better left obscure while the reader draws a breath. "All in good time" has ever been the way of art.

* * *

And anyway it wasn't until the first of the ships went down in the Dover Strait that any of us was certain—absolutely certain; or at least Godall was, from the deductive end of things, and St. Ives from the scientific. I wasn't certain of anything yet.

I was sitting on one of Godall's sofas, I remember, waiting for the arrival of St. Ives and thinking that I ought to take up a pipe and thinking too that I had enough vices already—indolence being one of them—when a man came in with a parcel. Godall reacted as if the Queen had walked in, and introduced the man to me as Isaac Laquedem, but aside from the odd name and his great age and frailty, there seemed to be nothing notable about him. He was a peddler, actually, and I forgot about him almost at once, their business having nothing to do with me—or with this story except in a peripheral way.

My father-in-law, William Keeble, had been teaching me the trade of toy-making, and I sat there meddling with an India-rubber elephant with enormous ears that I had finished assembling that very morning. Its trunk would rotate when you pushed its belly, and the ears would flap, and out of its mouth would come the magnified noise of ratcheting gears, which sounded, if you had an imagination, like trumpeting—or at least like the trumpeting of a rubber elephant with mechanical nonsense inside. It was funny to look at, though.

I remember wondering what it would have been like if Keeble himself had built it, and thinking that I at least ought to have given it a hat, maybe with a bird in it, and I listened idly to Godall and the old fellow talk about numismatics and about a clockwork match that the man was peddling. Then he left, very cheerfully, entirely forgetting his parcel of matches and going away up Rupert Street toward Brewer.

A minute passed, neither of us noticing the parcel. Then Godall spotted it and shouted damnation, or something, and I was up and out the door with it under my arm and with my elephant in my other hand. I ran up the street, dodging past people until I reached the corner, where I found the old man in a tearoom trying to sell little cheesecloth bags of green tea that could be dropped into a cup of boiling water and then retrieved again—not for the purpose of being reused, mind you, but so that the leaves wouldn't muck up the brew. The proprietor *read* tea leaves, though, as well as palms and scone crumbs, and wasn't at all interested in the invention, although I thought it was fairly clever and said so when I returned his automatic matches. He said that he admired my elephant, too, and I believe he did. We chatted over a cup of tea for ten minutes and then I strolled back down, thinking correctly that St. Ives would have shown up by then.

There at the side of the street, half a block up from the cigar divan, was a hansom cab, rather broken-down and with a curtain of shabby velvet drawn across the window. As I was passing it, the curtain pushed aside and a face popped out. I thought at first it was a woman, but it wasn't; it was a man with curled hair to his shoulders. His complexion was awful, and he had a sort of greasy look about him and a high effeminate collar cut out of a flowery chintz. It was his eyes, though, that did the trick. They were filled with a mad unfocused passion, as if everything around him—the cab, the buildings along Rupert Street, me—signified something to him. His glance shot back and forth in a cockeyed vigilance, and he said, almost whispering, "What is that?"

He was looking up the street at the time, so I looked up the street too, but saw nothing remarkable. "Beg your pardon," I said.

"That there."

He peered down the street now, so I did too.

"There."

Now it was up into the air, toward a bank of casements on the second floor. There was a man staring out of one, smoking a cigar.

"Him?" I asked.

He gave me such a look that I thought I'd landed upon it at last, but then I saw that I was wrong.

"That. In your hand."

The elephant. He blinked rapidly, as if he had something in his eye. "I like that," he said, and he squinted at me as if he knew me. There was something in his face, too, that I almost recognized. But he was clearly mad, and the madness, somehow, had given him a foreign cast, as if he were a citizen from nowhere on earth and had scrambled his features into an almost impenetrable disguise.

I felt sorry for him, to tell you the truth, and when he reached for the rubber elephant, I gave it to him, thinking, I'll admit, that he'd give it back after having a look. Instead he disappeared back into the cab, taking the elephant with him. The curtain closed, and I heard from him no more. I knocked once on the door. "Go away," he said.

So I did. He wanted the creature more than I wanted it. What did I want to build toys for, anyway, if not for the likes of him? And besides, it pretty clearly needed a hat. That's the sort of thing I told myself. It was half cowardice, though, my just walking away. I didn't want to make a scene by going into the cab after him and be found brawling with a madman over a rubber elephant. I argued it out in my head as I stepped into Godall's shop, ready to relate the incident to my credit, and there, standing just inside the threshold, impossibly, was the lunatic himself.

I must have looked staggered, for Hasbro leaped up in alarm

at the sight of my face, and the person in the doorway turned on her heel with a startled look. She wasn't the fellow in the truck; she was a woman with an appallingly similar countenance and hair, equally greasy, and with a blouse of the same material. This one wore a shawl, though, and was older by a good many years, although her face belied her age. It was almost unlined due to some sort of unnatural puffiness—as if she were a goblin that had come up to Soho wearing a cleverly altered melon for a head. This was the mother, clearly, of the creature in the cab.

She smiled theatrically at me. Then, as if she had just that instant recognized me, her smile froze into a look of snooty reproach, and she ignored me utterly from then on. I had the distinct feeling that I'd been cut, although you'd suppose that being cut by a madwoman doesn't count for much—any more than having one's rubber elephant stolen by a madman counts for anything.

"A man like that ought to be brought to justice," she said to St. Ives, who gestured toward the sofa and raised his eyebrows at me.

"This is Mr. Owlesby," he said to the woman. "You can speak freely in front of him."

She paid me no attention at all, as if to say that she would speak freely, or would not, before whomever she chose, and no one would stop her. I sat down.

"Brought to justice," she said.

"Justice," said St. Ives, "was brought to him, or he to it, sometime back. He died in Scandinavia. He fell into a lake where he without a doubt was frozen to death even before he drowned. I… I saw him tumble into the lake myself. He didn't crawl out."

"He did crawl out."

"Impossible," said St. Ives—and it *was* impossible, too. Except that when it came to the machinations of Dr. Narbondo you were stretching a point using the word *impossible,* and St. Ives knew it. Doubt flickered in his eyes, along with other emotions, too complex to fathom. I could see that he was animated, though. Since his dealings with the comet and the death of Ignacio Narbondo, St. Ives had been enervated, drifting from one scientific project to another, finishing almost nothing, lying on the divan in his study through the long hours of the afternoon, drifting in and out of sleep. For the space of a few days he had undertaken to restore Alice's vegetable garden, but the effort had cost him too much, and he had abandoned it to the moles and the weeds. I could turn this last into a metaphor of the great man's life over the last couple of years, but I won't. I promised to leave tragedy alone.

"Look here," the woman said, handing across what appeared to be a letter. It had been folded up somewhere for years, in someone's pocket from the look of it, and the cheap paper was yellowed and torn. It was addressed to someone named Kenyon, but the name was new to me and the contents of the letter were nothing of interest. The handwriting was the point as was the signature: Dr. Ignacio Narbondo. St. Ives handed it across to Godall, who was measuring out tobacco on a balance scale in the most disinterested way imaginable.

She handed over a second letter, this one fresh from last week's post. It was in an envelope that appeared to have been dropped in the street and trod upon by horses, and part of the letter inside, including the salutation, was an unreadable ruin. The first two paragraphs were written in a plain hand, clearly by a man who cared little for stray blots and smudges. And then, strangely, the final several sentences were inscribed by the man who had written the first missive. It didn't take an expert to see that. There was a flourish in the *T*'s, and the uppercase *A*, of which there were two, was several times the size of any other letter, and was printed rather than enscripted, and then crossed pointlessly at the top, giving it an Oriental air. In a word, the handwriting at the end of this second letter was utterly distinct, and utterly identical to that of the first. The signature, however, was different. "H. Frost," it read, with a scattering of initials afterward that I don't recall.

The text of this second letter was interesting. It mentioned certain papers that this H. Frost was anxious to find, and would pay for. He was a professor, apparently, at Edinburgh University, a chemist, and had heard rumors that papers belonging to our madwoman's father were lost in the vicinity of the North Downs some forty years ago. He seemed to think that the papers were important to medical science, and that her father deserved a certain notoriety that he'd never gotten in his tragic life. It went on so, in flattering and promising tones, and then was signed, as I said, "H. Frost."

St. Ives handed this second letter to Godall and pursed his lips. I had the uncanny feeling that he hesitated because of his suspicions about the woman, about her reasons for having come round with the letters at all. "The doctor is dead, madam," was what he said finally.

She shook her head. "Those letters were written with the same hand; anyone can see that."

"In fact," said St. Ives, "the more elaborate the handwriting, the easier it is to forge. The reproduction of eccentricities in handwriting is cheap and easy; it's the subtleties that are difficult. Why someone would want to forge the doctor's hand, I don't know. It's an interesting puzzle, but one that doesn't concern me. My suggestion is to ignore it utterly. Don't respond. Do nothing at all."

"He ought to be brought to justice is what I'm saying."

"He's dead," said St. Ives finally. And then, after a moment of silence, he said, "And if this mystery were worth anything to me at all, then I'd have to know a great deal more about the particulars, wouldn't I? What papers, for example? Who was your father? Do you have any reason to think that his lost papers are valuable to science or were lost in the North Downs forty years ago?"

Now it was her turn to hesitate. There was a good deal that she wasn't saying. Bringing people to justice wasn't her only concern; that much was apparent. She fiddled with her shawl for a moment, pretending to adjust it around her shoulders but actually casting about her mind for a way to reveal what it was she was after without really revealing anything at all. "My father's name was John Kenyon. He was… misguided when he was young," she said. "And then he was misused when he was older. He associated with the grandfather of the man you think is dead, and he developed a certain serum, a longevity serum, out of the glands of a fish, I misremember which one. When the elder Narbondo was threatened with transportation for experiments in vivisection, my grandfather went into hiding. He went over to Rome…"

"Moved to the Continent?" asked St. Ives.

"No, he became a papist. He repented of all his dealings in alchemy and vivisection, and would have had me go into a nunnery to save me from the world, except that I wouldn't have it. His manuscripts disappeared. He claimed to have destroyed them, but I'm certain he didn't, because once, when I was about fifteen, my mother found what must have been them, in a trunk. They were bound into a notebook, which she took and tried to destroy, but he stopped her. They fought over the thing, she calling him a hypocrite and he out of his mind with not knowing *what* he intended to do.

"But my father was a weak man, a worm. He saved the notebook right enough and beat my mother and went away to London and was gone a week. He came home drunk, I remember, and penitent, and I married and moved away within the year and didn't see him again until he was an old man and dying. My mother was dead by then for fifteen years, and he thought it had been himself that killed her— and it no doubt was. He started in to babble about the notebook, again, there on his deathbed. It had been eating at him all those years. What he said, as he lay dying, was that it had been stolen from him by the Royal Academy. A man named Piper, who had a chair at Oxford, wanted the formulae for himself, and had got the notebook away from him with strong drink and the promise of money. But there had never been any money. I ought to find the notebook and destroy it, my father said, so that he might rest in peace.

"Well, the last thing I cared about, I'll say it right out, was him resting in peace. The less peace he got, the better, and amen. So I didn't do anything. I had a son, by then, and a drunk for a husband who was as pitiful as my father was and who I hadn't seen in a fortnight and hoped never to see again. But I was never a lucky one. That part don't matter, though. What matters is that there *are* these papers that he mentions, this notebook. And I know that it's him—the one you claim is dead up in Scandinavia—that wants the papers now. No one else knows about them, you see, except him and a couple of old hypocrites from the Royal Academy, and they wouldn't need to ask *me* about them, would they, having stolen the damned things themselves. He's got his methods, the doctor has, and this letter doesn't come as any surprise to me, no surprise at all. If you know him half as well as you claim to, gentlemen, then it won't come as any surprise to you either, no matter how many times you think you saw him die."

And so ended her speech. It just rushed out of her, as if none of it were calculated, and yet I was fairly certain that every word had been considered and that half the story, as they say, hadn't been told. She had edited and euphemized the thing until there was nothing left but the surface, with the emotional nonsense put in to cover the detail that was left out.

She had got to St. Ives, too. And Godall, it seemed to me, was weighing out the same bag of tobacco for the tenth time. Both of them were studying the issue hard. If she had come in through the door intending to address their weightiest fear, she could hardly have been more on the money than she was. Something monumental was brewing, and had been since the day of the explosion and the business down by the Embankment. No run-of-the-mill criminal was behind it; that weeks had gone by in the meantime was evidence only that it was brewing slowly, that it wouldn't be rushed, and was ominous as a result.

"May we keep the letters?" asked St. Ives.

"No," she replied, snatching both of them off the counter where Godall had laid them. She turned smiling and stepped out onto the sidewalk, climbing into the waiting cab and driving away, just like that, without another word. She had got us, and that was the truth. St. Ives asking for the letters had told her as much.

Her sudden departure left us just a little stunned, and it was Godall who brought us back around by saying to St. Ives, "I fancy that there is no Professor Frost at Edinburgh in any capacity at all."

"Not a chemist, certainly. Not in any of the sciences. That much is a ruse."

"And it's his handwriting, too, there at the end."

"Of course it is." St. Ives shuddered. Here was an old wound opening up—Alice, Narbondo's death in Scandinavia, St. Ives once again grappling with weighty moral questions that had proven impossible to settle. All he could make out of it all was guilt—his own. And finally he had contrived, by setting himself adrift, simply to wipe it out of his mind. Now this—Narbondo returning like the ghost at the feast...

"It's just the tiniest bit shaky, though," Godall said, "as if he were palsied or weak but was making a great effort to disguise it, so as to make the handwriting of this new letter as like the old as possible. I'd warrant that he wasn't well enough to write the whole thing, but could only manage a couple of sentences; the rest was written for him."

"A particularly clever forger, perhaps..." began St. Ives. But Godall pointed out the puzzle:

"Why forge another man's handwriting but not use his name? That's the key, isn't it? There's no point in such a forgery unless these are deeper waters than they appear to be."

"Perhaps someone wanted the letter to get round to us, to make us believe Narbondo is alive..."

"Then it's a puzzling song and dance," said Godall, "and far more a dangerous one. We're marked men if she's right. It's Narbondo's way of calling us out. I rather believe, though, that this is his way of serving her a warning, of filling her with fear; he's come back, he means to say, and he wants that notebook."

"I believe," said St. Ives, "that if I were her I'd tell him, if she knows where it is."

"That's what frightens me about the woman," said Godall, sweeping tobacco off the counter. "She seems to see this as an opportunity of some sort, doesn't she? She means to tackle the monster herself. My suggestion is that we find out the whereabouts of this man Piper. He must be getting on in age, probably retired from Oxford long ago."

Just then a lad came in through the door with the *Standard*, and news that the first of the ships had gone down off Dover. It was another piece to the puzzle, anyone could see that, or rather could sense it, even though there was no way to know how it fit.

The ship had been empty, its captain, crew, and few paying passengers having put out into wooden boats for the most curious reason. The captain had found a message in the ship's log—scrawled into it, he thought, by someone on board, either a passenger or someone who had come over the side. It hadn't been there when they'd left the dock at Gravesend; the captain was certain of it. They had got a false start, having to put in at Sterne Bay, and they lost a night there waiting for the cargo that didn't arrive.

Someone, of course, had sneaked on board and meddled with the log; there had never been any cargo.

What the message said was that every man on board must get out into the boats when the ship was off Ramsgate on the way to Calais. They must watch for a sailing craft with crimson sails. This boat would give them a sign, and then every last one of them would take to the lifeboats and row for all he was worth until they'd put a quarter mile between themselves and the ship. Either that or they would die—all of them.

It was a simple mystery, really, baffling, but with nothing grotesque about it. Until you thought about it—about what would have happened if the captain hadn't opened the logbook and those men hadn't got into the boat. The message was in earnest. The ship sank, pretty literally like a stone, and although the crew was safe, their safety was a matter of dumb luck. Whoever had engineered the disaster thought himself to be Destiny, and had played fast and high with the lives of the people on board. That had been the real message, and you can bank on it.

The captain lost his post as well as his ship. Why hadn't he turned about and gone back to Dover? Because the note in the log didn't hint that the ship would be destroyed, did it? It was more than likely a hoax, a prank—one that would kill a couple of hours while they tossed in the lifeboat and then rowed back over to her and took possession again. He had never even expected to see the doubtful sailcraft. And they were already a day late because of the stopover at Sterne Bay. It was all just too damned unlikely to take seriously, except the part about getting into the boats. The captain wouldn't risk any lives, he said.

But there it was: the ship had gone down. It hadn't been the least bit unlikely in the end. There were only two things about it that *were* unlikely, it seemed to us: one was that the crew, every man jack of them, had remained in Dover, and shipped out again at once. The word of the captain was all that the authorities had; and he, apparently, was a Yank, recently come over from San Francisco. The second unlikelihood was that this business with the ship was unrelated to the two London incidents.

THE PRACTICING DETECTIVE
AT STERNE BAY

We had no choice but to set out for the coast by way of Sterne Bay. It wasn't just the business of the downed ship; it was that St. Ives discovered that Dr. Piper, of the Academy, had retired years past to a cottage down the Thames, at Sterne Bay. Godall stayed behind. His business didn't allow for that sort of jaunt, and there was no reason to suppose that London would be devoid of mysteries just because this most recent one had developed a few miles to the east.

St. Ives had put in at the Naval Office, too, in order to see if he couldn't discover something about this Captain Bowker, but the captain was what they call a shadowy figure, an American whose credentials weren't at all clear, but who had captained small merchant ships down to Calais for a year or so. There was no evidence that he was the sort to be bought off—no recorded trouble. That was the problem; nothing was known about the man, and so you couldn't help jumping to the conclusion that he was just the sort to be bought off. It seemed to stand to reason.

We rattled out of Victoria Station in the early morning and

arrived in time to breakfast at the Crown and Apple in Sterne Bay before setting about our business. Nothing seemed to be particularly pressing. We took over an hour at it, shoving down rashers and eggs, and St. Ives all the while in a rare good humor, chatting with the landlady about this and that—all of it entirely innocent—and then stumbling onto the subject of the ship going down and of Captain Bowker. Of course it was in all the papers, being the mystery that it was, and there was nothing at all to suggest that we had anything but a gossip's interest in it.

Oh, she knew Captain Bowker right enough. He was a Yank, wasn't he, and the jolliest and maybe biggest man you'd meet in the bay. He hadn't an enemy, which is what made the business such a disaster, poor man, losing his ship like that, and now out of a situation. Well, not entirely; he had taken a position at the icehouse, tending the machinery—a good enough job in a fishing town like Sterne Bay. He was generally at it from dawn till bedtime, and sometimes took dinner at the Crown and Apple, since he didn't have a family. He slept at the icehouse too, now that his ship was gone and he hadn't got a new one. He was giving up the sea, he said, after the disaster, and was happy only that he hadn't lost any men. The ship be damned, he liked to say—it was his men that he cared about; that was ever the way of Captain Bowker.

St. Ives said that it was a good way, too, and that it sounded to him as if the world ought to have a dozen more Captain Bowkers in it, but I could see that he was being subtle. His saying that had the effect of making her think we were the right sort, not busybody tourists down from London. That was St. Ives's method, and there was nothing of the hypocrite in it. He meant every bit of it, but if being friendly served some end too, before we were done, then so much the better.

Now it happened that Hasbro had an aunt living in the town, his jolly old Aunt Edie. She had been a sort of lady-in-waiting to St. Ives's mother—almost a nanny to him—and now, as unlikely as it sounds, she had taken to the sea, to fish, on a trawler owned by her dead husband's brother, Uncle Botley. So after breakfast St. Ives and Hasbro went off to pay her a visit, leaving me to myself for an hour. I wanted to sightsee, although to tell you the truth, I felt a little guilty about it because Dorothy wasn't along. I've gotten used to her being there, I guess, over the years, and I'm glad of it. It's one of the few things that I've got right.

It was a damp and foggy morning, getting along toward late— the sort of morning when every sound is muffled, and even though there are people out, there's a sort of curtain between you and them and you walk along the damp cobbles in a gray study, lost in thought. I strolled down the waterfront, thinking that Sterne Bay was just the sort of place to spend a few leisurely days, maybe bring along a fishing rod. Dorothy would love it. I would propose it to her as soon as we got back. The thought of proposing it to her, of course, was calculated to rid me of some of the guilt that I was feeling, out on holiday, really while Dorothy was stuck up in London, trapped in the old routine.

Then I thought of poor St. Ives, and of Alice, whom he had loved for two short years before that awful night in the Seven Dials. Thank God I wasn't there. It's a selfish thing to say, perhaps, but I can't help that. The man had lived alone before Alice, and has lived alone since. And although he'll fool most people, he doesn't fool me—he wasn't born to the solitary life. He's been worn thin by it. Every emotional shilling was tied up in Alice. He had put the lot of it in the savings bank until he had the chance to invest it in her, and it had paid off with interest. All that was gone now, and the very idea of a romantic holiday on the water was impossible for him to bear. He's been disallowed from entertaining notions that other people find utterly pleasant and common...

And just then, as I was strolling along full of idle and sorrowful thoughts, I looked up and there was a three-story inn, like something off a picture postcard.

It was painted white with green gingerbread trim and was hung with ivy vines. From what I could see, a broad veranda ran around three sides of it. On the veranda sat pieces of furniture, and on the willow furniture sat a scattering of people who looked just about as contented as they had any right to look—a couple of them qualifying as "old salts," and very picturesque. There was a wooden sign over the stairs that read THE HOISTED PINT, which struck me as calculated, but very friendly and with the right general attitude.

I stepped up onto the veranda, nodding a hello in both directions, and into the foyer, thinking to inquire about rates and availability. Spring was on the horizon, and there would be a chance of good weather—although the town was admirably suited to dismal weather too—and there was no reason that I shouldn't simply cement the business of a holiday straightaway, so as to make Dorothy happy.

She would love the place; any doubts I might have had from the street were vanished. There were wooden floors inlaid with the most amazing marquetry depicting a whale and whaling ship—the sort of work you don't see anymore—and there were potted plants and a great stone fireplace with a log fire burning and not a piece of coal to be seen. A small woman worked behind the long oak counter, meddling with papers, and we talked for a moment about rooms and rates. Although I didn't like her very much, or entirely trust her, I set out finally for the door very well satisfied with the inn and with myself both.

That's when I thought I saw my rubber elephant lying atop a table, half hidden by a potted palm. I was out the door and onto the veranda before I knew what it was that I'd seen—just the bottom of him, his round feet and red-painted jumbo trousers. It was the impossibility of it that made it slow to register, and even by the time it did, by the time I was sure of it, I had taken another step or two, half down the stairs, before turning on my heel and walking back in.

The woman looked up from where she dusted at furniture now with a clutch of feathers. She widened her eyes, wondering, perhaps, if I hadn't forgotten something, and I smiled back, feeling like a fool, and asking weakly whether I didn't need some sort of receipt, a confirmation—implying by it, I suppose, that her bookwork there behind the counter wasn't sufficient. She frowned and said that she supposed she could work something up, although... And I said quite right, of course but that as a surprise to my wife I thought that a little something to put into an envelope on her breakfast plate... That made her happy again. She liked to see that in a man, and said that she was anxious to meet the young lady. When I glanced across the room there wasn't any elephant, of course, or anything like it.

I don't doubt that you're going to ask me why I didn't just *inquire* about the woman and her son, who carried a rubber elephant with enormous ears. There would have been a hundred friendly ways to phrase it. Well, I didn't. I still felt like half a fool for having blundered back in like that and going through the song and dance about the breakfast plate, and I was almost certain by then that I hadn't seen anything at all, that I had invented it out of the curve of a leaf and the edge of a pot. It was a little farfetched, wasn't it? Just as it had seemed improbable to the captain of the downed ship that the nonsense in his log ought to be taken seriously.

I had imagined it, and I told myself so as I set out toward the pier again, where, just like that, I nearly ran over old Parsons, the secretary of the Royal Academy of Sciences, coming along with a bamboo pole and creel in his hand, got up in a woolen sort of fishing uniform and looking as if even though he mightn't catch a single fish, at least he had got the outfit right, and that qualified him, as the scriptures put it, to walk with the proud.

I was surprised to see him. He was thoroughly disappointed to see me. It was the company I kept. He assumed straight off that St. Ives was lurking somewhere about, and that meant, of course, that the business of the Royal Academy was being meddled in again. And he was right. *His* being there said as much. It was an altogether unlikely coincidence. If I had looked at it from the angle of a practicing detective, then I'd have had suspicions about his angling outfit, and I'd have concluded that he was trying too hard to play a part. He was up to something, to be sure.

"What are *you* doing here?" he asked.

I gave him a jolly look, and said, "Down on holiday, actually. And you, going fishing?"

Foolish question, I guess, given what he looked like, but that didn't call for him to get cheeky. "I'm *prospecting*," he said, and held up his bamboo pole. "This is an alchemical divining rod, used to locate fishes with coins in their bellies."

But just then, when I was going to say something clever, up came a gentleman in side whiskers and interrupted in order to wring Parsons's hand. "Dreadfully sorry, old man," he said to Parsons. "But he was tired, and he'd lived a long life. Very profitable. I'm happy you could come down for the funeral."

Parsons took him by the arm and led him away down the pier pretty briskly, as if to get him away from me before he said anything more. He had already said enough, though, hadn't he? This man Piper was dead, and Parsons had come down to see him buried.

It was a full morning, taken all the way around. There was a half hour yet before I was to meet St. Ives and Hasbro back at the Apple. I was feeling very much *like* a detective by then, although I couldn't put my finger on exactly what it was I had detected, besides this last bit. I decided that wasn't enough, and went across toward the ramshackle icehouse, a wooden sort of warehouse in a weedy lot not far off the ocean.

I went in at a side door without knocking. The place was cold, not surprisingly, and I could hear the hiss of steam from the compressors. The air was tinged with the smell of ammonia and wet straw. The jolly captain wasn't hard to find; he confronted me as soon as I came in through the door. He seemed to be the only one around, and he was big, and he talked with an accent, stretching out his vowels as if they were made of putty. I won't try to copy it, since I'm no good at tricking up accents, but he was full of words like *tarnation* and *fleabit* and *hound dog* and *ain't* and talked altogether in a sort of apostrophic "Out West" way that struck me as out of character in a sea captain. I expected something salty and maritime. I made a mental note of it.

That was after I had shaken his hand and introduced myself. "I'm Abner Benbow," I said, thinking this up on the spot and almost saying "Admiral Benbow," but stopping myself just in time. "I'm in the ice trade, up in Harrogate. They call me 'Cool Abner Benbow,'" I said, "but they don't call me a cold fish." I inclined my head just a little, thinking that maybe this last touch was taking it too far. But he liked it, saying he had a "monicker" too.

"Call me Bob," he said, "Country Bob Bowker. Call me anythin' you please, but don't call me too late for dinner."

And with that admonition he slammed me on the back with his open hand and nearly knocked me through the wall. He was convulsed with laughter, wheezing and looking apoplectic, as if he had just that moment made up the gag and was listening to himself recite it for the first time. I laughed too, very heartily, I thought, wiping pretended tears from my eyes.

"You're a Yank," I said. And that was clever, of course, because it rather implied that I didn't already know who he was, despite his recent fame.

"That's a fact. Wyoming man, born and bred. Took to the sea late and come over here two years ago just to see how the rest of the world got on. I was always a curious man. And I was all alone over there, runnin' ferries out of Frisco over to Sarsleeto, and figured I wouldn't be no more alone over here."

No more than any common criminal, I thought, assuming straight off, and maybe unfairly, that there was more to Captain Bowker's leaving America than he let on. I nodded, though, as if I thought all his nonsense very sage indeed.

"Been here long?" I asked, nonchalant.

He gave me a look. "Didn't I just say two year?"

"I mean here, at the icehouse."

"Ah!" he said, suddenly jolly again. "No. *Just* got on. If you'd of come day before yesterday you wouldn't have found me. Old man who ran the place up and died, though. Pitched over like he was poisoned, right there where you're a-standing now, up and pitched over, and there I was an hour later, looking in at the door with my hat in my hands. I knew a little about it, being mechanical and having lived by the sea, so I was a natural. They took me right on. What's all that to you?"

"Nothing. Nothing at all," I said, realizing right off that I shouldn't have said it twice; there was no room here to sound jumpy. But he had caught me by surprise with the question, and all I could think to say next, rather stupidly, was, "*Up* and died?" thinking that the phrase was a curious one, as if he had done it on purpose, maybe got up out of a chair to do it.

You can see that I had got muddled up. This wasn't going well. Somehow I had excited his suspicions by saying the most arbitrary and commonplace things. Captain Bowker was another lunatic, I remember thinking—the sort who, if you passed him on the street and said good-morning, would squint at you and ask what you *meant* by saying such a thing.

"Dropped right over dead on his face," said Captain Bowker, looking at me just as seriously as a stone head.

Then he grinned and broke into laughter, slapping me on the back again. "Cigar?" he asked.

I waved it away. "Don't smoke. You have one. I like the smell of tobacco, actually. Very comfortable."

He nodded and said, "Drives off the 'monia fumes," and then he gnawed off the end of a fat cigar, spitting out the debris with about twice the required force.

"So," I said. "Mind if I look around?"

"Yep," he said.

I started forward, but he stepped in front of me. "Yep," he said again, talking past his cigar. "I *do* mind if you look around." Then he burst into laughter again so that there was no way on earth that I could tell what he minded and what he didn't mind.

He plucked the unlit cigar out of his mouth and said, "Maybe tomorrow, Jim. Little too much going on today. Too busy for it. I'm new and all, and can't be showing in every Dick and Harry." He managed, somehow, to get me turned around and propelled toward the door. "*You* understand. You're a *businessman.* Tomorrow afternoon, maybe, or the next day. That's soon enough, ain't it? You ain't going nowhere. Come on back around, and you can have the run of the place. Bring a spyglass and a measure stick."

And with that I was out in the fog again, wondering exactly how things had gone so bad. In the space of ten minutes I'd been Abner and Jim and Dick and Harry, but none of us had seen a thing. At least I hadn't given myself away, though. Captain Bowker couldn't have guessed who I really was. I could relate the incident to St. Ives and Hasbro without any shame. There was enough in the captain's manner to underscore any suspicions that we might already have had of the man, and there was the business of his not wanting me to see the workings of the icehouse, innocent as such workings ought to be.

I lounged along toward the Apple—it wasn't the weather for hurrying—and had got down past the market, maybe a hundred yards beyond The Hoisted Pint, when I heard the crack of what sounded like a firecracker from somewhere above and behind me. Immediately an old beggar with his shoes wound in rags, standing just in front of me, stiffened up straight, as if he'd been poked in the small of the back, and a wash of red blood spread out across his shirtfront where you could see it through his open coat.

Before I could twitch, he sat down in the weeds and then slumped over backward and stared at the sky, his mouth working as if he were trying to pray, but had forgot the words. He had been shot, of course—in the heart—by someone with a dead-on aim.

A woman screamed. There was the sound of a whistle. And without half knowing what I was about, I had the man's wrist in my hand and was feeling for a pulse. It was worthless. Where the *hell* do you find a man's pulse? I can't even find my own half the time. I slammed my hand over the hole in his chest and leaned into it, trying to shut off the rush of blood and feeling absolutely futile and stupid until a doctor strode up carrying his black bag. He crouched beside me, squinted at the corpse, and shook his head softly to tell me that I was wasting my time.

Reeling just a little from the smell of already-drying blood, I stood up and stumbled over to sit on a bench, where I hunched forward and pretended for a bit to be searching for a lucky clover until my head cleared. I sat up straight, and there was a constable looming over me with the look in his eye of a man with a few pressing questions to ask. If I was a rotten actor in front of Captain Bowker, I had improved a bit in the score of minutes since, and it was a simple thing to convince the constable that I knew nothing of the dead man.

I avoided one issue, though: I seemed to be *collecting* dead men all of a sudden. First there was the tragedy up in Holborn, now a man drops dead at my feet, shot through the heart. Most of us go through our lives avoiding that sort of thing. Now I was getting more than my share of it. It was evidence of something, but not the sort of evidence that would do the constable any good, not yet anyway.

It wasn't quite noon when I got back to the Crown and Apple and cleaned myself up, and when St. Ives and Hasbro found me I was putting away my second pint and not feeling any better at all. This last adventure had taken the sand out of me, and I couldn't think in a straight enough line to put the pieces of the morning together in such a way that they would signify.

"You're looking rotten," said St. Ives with his customary honesty. He ordered a pint of bitter, and so did Hasbro, although St. Ives had lately been under a new regime and had taken to drinking nothing but cider during the day. They were following my lead in order to make it seem perfectly natural that I was swilling beer before lunch. St. Ives winked at Hasbro. "It's the clean sea air. You're missing the London fogs. Your lungs can't stand the change. Send for Dorothy." He said this last to Hasbro, who pretended to get up, but then sat back down when the two fresh pints hove into view.

They were joking, of course—being jolly after their morning visit. And I was happy for it, not for myself, but for St. Ives. I hated to tell them the truth, but I told them anyway. "There's been a man shot," I said.

St. Ives scowled. "The news is up and down the bay by now. We heard a lad shouting it outside the window of Aunt Edie's cottage. Sterne Bay doesn't get many shootings."

"I saw the whole thing. Witnessed it."

St. Ives looked up from his pint glass and raised his eyebrows.

"He wasn't a half step in front of me. A tramp from the look of him, just about to touch me for a shilling, I suppose, and then, crack! just like that, and he's on his back like a bug, dead. Shattered his heart."

"He was a *half step* in front of you? That's hyperbole, of course. What you meant to say is that he was nearby."

"As close to me as I am to you," I said, thinking what he was thinking.

St. Ives was silent for a moment, studying things. It had taken me a while to see it too, what with all the complications of the morning. Clearly the bullet hadn't been meant for the beggar.

There's no profit in shooting a beggar, unless you're a madman. And I had been running into too many madmen lately. The odds against there being another one lurking about were too high. Picture it: there's the beggar turning toward me. From back toward The Hoisted Pint, I must have half hidden him. The bullet that struck him had missed me by a fraction.

So who had taken a shot at me from The Hoisted Pint, from a second-story window, maybe? Or from the roof of the icehouse; that would have served equally well. I thought about the disappeared elephant and about the captain and his "Out West" mannerisms. But why on earth…?

I ordered a third pint, swearing to myself to drink it slowly and then go up to take a nap. I'd done my work for the day; I could leave the rest to Hasbro and St. Ives.

"I saw Parsons on the pier," I said. "And I talked to Captain Bowker. And I think your woman with the letters is skulking around, probably staying at The Hoisted Pint, down toward the pier." That started it. I told them the whole story, just as it happened—the toy on the table, Parsons in his fishing regalia, the captain jollying me around—and they sat silent throughout, thinking, perhaps, that I'd made a very pretty morning of it while they were off drinking tea and listening to rumors through the window.

"He thought you were an agent," said St. Ives, referring to Captain Bowker. "Insurance detective. What's he hiding, though, that he wouldn't let you look around the icehouse? This log of his, maybe? Not likely. And why would he try to shoot you? That's not an act calculated to cement the idea of his being innocent. And Parsons here too…" St. Ives fell into a study, then thumped his fist on the table, standing up and motioning to Hasbro, who stood up too, and the both of them went out leaving their glasses two-thirds full on the table. Mine was empty again, and I was tempted to pour theirs into mine in order to secure a more profound nap and to avoid waste. But there was the landlady, grinning toward me and the clock just then striking noon.

She whisked the glasses away with what struck me as a sense of purpose, looking across her spectacles at me. I lurched up the stairs and collapsed into bed, making up for our early rising with a nap that stretched into the late afternoon.

I was up and pulling on my shoes when there was a knock on the door. It's St. Ives, I thought, while I was stepping across to throw it open. It might as easily have been the man with the gun— something that occurred to me when the door was halfway open. And for a moment I was tempted to slam it shut, cursing myself for a fool and thinking at the same time that half opening the door and then slamming it in the visitor's face would paint a fairly silly picture of me, unless, of course, it *was* the man with the gun...

It wasn't. It was a man I had never seen before. He was tall, gaunt, and stooped, almost cadaverous. He wore a hat, but it was apparent that he was bald on top and didn't much bother to cut the tufts of hair above his ears. He would have made a pretty scarecrow. There were deep furrows around his lips, the result of a lifetime of pursing them, I suppose, which is just what he was doing now, glaring down his hooked nose at me as if he didn't quite approve of the look on my face.

Afternoon naps always put me in a wretched mood, and the sight of him doubled it. "You've apparently got the wrong room," I said, and started to shut the door. He put his foot in the way.

"I'm an insurance agent," he said, glancing back down the hallway. "Lloyd's. There's a question or two…"

"Of course," I said. So that was it. Captain Bowker *was* under investigation. I swung the door open and in he came, looking around the room with a slightly appalled face, as if the place was littered with dead pigs, say, and they were starting to stink. I didn't like him at all, insurance agent or not.

He started in on me, grilling me, as they say. "You were seen talking to Captain Bowker today."

I nodded.

"About what?"

"Ice," I said. "My name is Adam Benbow, from up in Harrogate. I'm a fish importer down on holiday."

He nodded. He was easier to fool than the captain had been. I was bothered, though, by the vague suspicion that I had gotten my name wrong. I had, of course. This morning it had been Abner. I could hardly correct it, though, not now. And how would he know anyway? What difference did my name make to him?

"We're investigating the incident of the downed ship. Did you talk to him about that?"

"Which ship?"

"The *Landed Catch*, sunk off Dover days ago. What do you know about that ship?"

"Not a thing. I read about it in the papers, of course. Who hasn't?"

"Are you acquainted with a man named Langdon St. Ives?" he asked abruptly. He half spun around when he said this, as if to take me by surprise.

It worked, too. I sputtered there for a moment, blinking at him. And when I said, "Langdon who?" the attempt was entirely worthless. I was as transparent as window glass.

He acted as if I had admitted everything. "We believe that Mr. St. Ives is also investigating the business of the *Landed Catch*, and we're wondering why."

"I'm sure I don't know. Who was it again? Saint what?" It was worthless pretending, and I knew it. I had to dummy up, though. I wasn't about to answer the man's questions. St. Ives could do that for himself. On the other hand, I suppose it was pointless to insist that I didn't know St. Ives. The man was onto my game, what with the false names and the Harrogate business.

"What did you *see*, exactly, at the icehouse?"

"*See?* Nothing. The man wouldn't allow me in. He seemed anxious, to tell you the truth. Like he didn't want me snooping around. He has something to hide there; you can take that much from me."

"Something to hide, you think?"

"Bank on it."

The man nodded, suddenly jolly, grinning at me. "I think you're right," he said. "He's hiding something horrible, is what I think. These are dangerous waters. Very rocky and shallow. He's a subtle man, Captain Bowker is. My advice is to steer clear of him. Leave him to us. He'll be in Newgate Prison waiting to swing, if only for this morning's shooting."

I must have jerked my eyes open when he said this last, for he grinned at the look on my face and nodded, pursing his lips so that his mouth almost disappeared. "You were a lucky man," he said. "But you're safe now. We're onto him, watching him from every angle. You don't have to hide in your room like this."

"I wasn't hiding, actually. I…"

"Of course, you weren't," he said, turning toward the door.

"Quite a welcome you've had. Don't blame you. Look me up. Binker Street."

He was out the door then, striding away down the hall. I shut the door and sat on the edge of the bed, studying things out. I understood nothing—less than before. I was vaguely happy, though, that someone was watching the captain. Of course it must have been him who had fired the shot—him and his cowboy upbringing and all. Much more likely than my hansom cab lunatic. I could see that now.

There was another knocking on the door. It's the agent, I thought, back again. But it wasn't. It was the landlady with a basket of fruit. What a pleasant surprise, I remember thinking, taking the basket from her. "Grape?" I asked, but she shook her head.

"There's a note in it," she said, nodding at the basket.

From Dorothy, I thought, suddenly glad that I'd made the reservation at The Hoisted Pint. Absence was making hearts grow fonder. And quickly, too. I'd only left that morning. There was the corner of an envelope, sticking up through the purple grapes and wedged in between a couple of tired-looking apples. The whole lot of fruit lay atop a bed of coconut fiber in a too-heavy and too-deep basket.

It was the muffled ticking that did the trick, though—the ticking of an infernal machine, hidden in the basket of fruit.

My breath caught, and I nearly dropped the basket and leaped out the door. But I couldn't do that. It would bring down the hotel, probably with me still in it. I hopped across to the window, looking down on what must have been a half-dozen people, including St. Ives and Hasbro, who were right then heading up the steps. I couldn't just pitch it out onto everybody's heads.

So I sprinted for the door, yanking it open and leaping out into the hallway. My heart slammed away, flailing like an engine, and without bothering to knock I threw open the door to the room kitty-corner to my own, and surprised an old man who sat in a chair next to a fortuitously open casement, reading a book.

It was Parsons, not wearing his fishing garb anymore.

⟅⟞ ALOFT IN A BALLOON ⟝⟆

Parsons leaped up, wild with surprise to see me rushing at him like that, carrying my basket. "It's a bomb!" I shouted. "Step aside!" and I helped him do it, too, with my elbow. He sprawled toward the bed, and I swung the basket straight through the open casement and into the bay in a long, low arc. If there had been boats roundabout, I believe I would have let it go anyway. It wasn't an act of heroics by that time; it was an act of desperation, of getting the ticking basket out of my hand and as far away from me as possible.

It exploded. Wham! Just like that, a foot above the water, which geysered up around the sailing fragments of basket and fruit. Everything rained down, and then there was the splashing back and forth of little colliding waves. Parsons stood behind me, taking in the whole business, half scowling, half surprised. I took a couple of calming breaths, but they did precious little good. My hand—the one that had held the basket—was shaking treacherously, and I sat down hard in Parsons's chair.

"Sorry," I said to him. "Didn't mean to barge in."

But he waved it away as if he saw the necessity of it. It was obvious that the device had been destined to go out through the window and into the sea. There had been no two ways about it. I could hardly have tucked it under my coat and forgotten about it. He stared for a moment out the window and then said, "Down on holiday," in a flat voice, repeating what I'd said to him on the pier that morning and demonstrating that, like everyone else, he had seen through me all along. I cleared my throat, thinking in a muddle, and just then, as if to save me, St. Ives and Hasbro rushed in, out of breath because of having sprinted up the stairs when they'd heard the explosion.

The sight of Parsons standing there struck St. Ives dumb, I believe. The professor knew that Parsons was lurking roundabout, because I'd told him, but here, at the Apple? And what had Parsons to do with the explosion, and what had I to do with Parsons?

There was no use this time in Parsons's simply muttering, "Good day," and seeing us all out the door. It was time for talking turkey, as Captain Bowker would have put it. Once again, I was the man with the information. I told them straight off about the insurance agent.

"And he knew my name?" said St. Ives, cocking his head.

"That's right. He seemed to know…" I stopped and glanced at Parsons, who was listening closely.

St. Ives continued for me. "He made sure who you were, and he found out that you had suspicions about what was going on at the icehouse, and then he left. And a moment later the basket arrived."

I nodded and started to tell the story my way, to put the right edge on it, but St. Ives turned to Parsons and, without giving me half a chance, said, "See here. We're not playing games anymore. I'm going to tell you, flat out and without any beating about the bush, that we know about Lord Kelvin's machine being stolen. A baby could piece that business together, what with the debacle down on the Embankment, the flying iron and all. What could that have been but an electromagnet of astonishing strength? There's no use your being coy about it any longer. I've got a sneaking hunch what they've done with it, too. Let's put everything straight. I'll tell you what I know, and you tell me what you know, and together maybe we'll see to the bottom of this murky well."

Parsons held his hands out in a theatrical gesture of helplessness. "I'm down here to catch a fish," he said. "It's you who are throwing bombs through the window. You seem to attract those sorts of things—bombs and bullets."

St. Ives gave Parsons a weary glance. Then he said to me, "This agent, Jack, what did he look like?"

"Tall and thin, and with a hook nose. He was bald under his hat, and his hair stuck out over his ears like a chimney sweep's brush."

Parsons looked as though he'd been electrocuted. He started to say something, hesitated, started up again, and then, pretending that it didn't much matter to him anyway, said, "Stooped, was he?"

I nodded.

"Tiny mouth, like a bird?"

"That's right."

Parsons sagged. It was a gesture of resignation. We waited him out. "That wasn't any insurance agent."

The news didn't surprise anyone. Of course it hadn't been an insurance agent. St. Ives had seen that at once. The man's mind is honed like a knife. Insurance agents don't send bombs around disguised as fruit baskets. We waited for Parsons to tell us who the man was, finally, to quit his tiresome charade, but he stood there chewing it over in his mind, calculating how much he could say.

Parsons is a good man. I'll say that in the interests of fair play. He and St. Ives have had their differences, but they've both of them been after the same ends, just from different directions. Parsons couldn't abide the notion of people being shot at, even people who tired him as much as I did. So in the end, he told us:

"It was a man named Higgins."

"Leopold Higgins!" cried St. Ives. "The ichthyologist. Of course." St. Ives somehow always seemed to know at least half of everything—which is a lot, when you add it up.

Parsons nodded wearily. "Oxford man. Renegade academician. They're a dangerous breed when they go feral, academics are. Higgins was a chemist, too. Came back from the Orient with insane notions about carp. Insisted that they could be frozen and thawed out, months later, years. You could keep them in a deep freeze, he said. Some sort of glandular excretion, as I understand it, that drained water out of the cells, kept them from bursting when they froze. He was either an expert in cryogenics or a lunatic. It's your choice. He was clearly off his head, though. I think it was opium that did it. He claimed to dream these things.

"Anyway, it was a glandular business with carp. That was his theory. All of it, mind you, was wrapped up in the notion that it was these secretions that were the secret of the astonishing longevity of a carp. He hadn't been back from China a year when he disappeared. I saw him, in fact, just two days earlier, in London, at the club. He burst in full of wild enthusiasm, asking after old—after people I'd never heard of, saying that he was on the verge of something monumental. And then he was gone—out the door and never seen again."

"Until now," said St. Ives.

"Apparently so."

St. Ives turned to Hasbro and myself and said, "Our worst fears have come to pass," and then he bowed to Parsons, thanked him very much, and strode out with us following, down the hallway and straightaway to the train station.

We spent the night on the Ostende ferry. I couldn't sleep, thinking about the *Landed Catch* sinking like a brick just to the south of the very waters we were plowing, and I was ready at the nod of a head to climb into a lifeboat and row away. The next day found us on a train to Amsterdam, and from there on into Germany and Denmark, across the Skaggerak and into Norway. It was an appalling trip, rushing it like that, catching little bits of hurried sleep, and the only thing to recommend it was that there was at least no one trying to kill me anymore, not as long as I was holed up in that train.

St. Ives was in a funk. A year ago he had made this same weary journey, and had left Narbondo for dead in a freezing tarn near Mount Hjarstaad, which rises out of the Norwegian Sea. Now what was there but evidence that the doctor was alive and up to mischief? It didn't stand to reason, not until Parsons's chatter about cryogenics. Two things were bothering St. Ives, wearing him thinner by the day. One was that somehow he had failed once again. Thwarting Narbondo and diverting the earth from the course of that ghastly comet had stood as his single greatest triumph; now it wasn't a triumph anymore. Now it was largely a failure, in his mind, anyway. Just like that. White had become black. He had lived for months full of contradictions of conscience. Had he brought about the doctor's death, or had he tried to prevent it? And never mind that—*had* he tried to prevent it, or had he attempted to fool himself into thinking he had? He couldn't abide the notion of working to fool himself. That was the avenue to madness. So here, in an instant, all was effaced. The doctor was apparently alive after all and embarked on some sort of murderous rampage. St. Ives hadn't been thorough enough. What Narbondo wanted was a good long hanging.

And on top of that was the confounding realization that there wasn't an easier way to learn what we had to learn. St. Ives knew no one in the wilds of Norway. He couldn't just post a letter asking whether a frozen hunchback had been pulled from a lake and revived. He had to find out for himself. I think he wondered, though, whether he hadn't ought simply to have sent Hasbro about the business, or me, and stayed behind in Sterne Bay.

We were in Trondheim, still hurtling northward, when the news arrived about the sinking of the other two ships, just below where the first had disappeared. Iron-hulled vessels, they'd gone down lickety-split, exactly the same way. The crew had abandoned the first one, but not the second. Ten men were lost in all. It had been Godall who sent the cable to Norway. He had prevailed upon the prime minister to take action. St. Ives was furious with himself for having done nothing to prevent the debacle.

What could he have done, though? That's what I asked him. It was useless to think that he could have stopped it. Part of his fury was directed at the government. They had been warned, even before Godall had tackled them. Someone—Higgins, probably— had sent them a monumental ransom note. They had laughed it away, thinking it a hoax, even though it had been scrawled in the same hand as had Captain Bowker's note, and warned them that more ships would be sunk. The Royal Academy should have urged them to take it seriously, but they had mud on their faces by now, and had hesitated. All of them had been fools.

Shipping now was suspended in the area, from the mouth of the Thames to Folkestone, at an inconceivable expense to the Crown and to private enterprise. Half of London trade had slammed to a halt, according to Godall. It was a city under siege, and no one seemed to know who the enemy was or where he lay... St. Ives was deadly silent, frustrated with our slow travel northward, with the interminable rocky landscape, the fjords, the pine forests.

What could he do but carry on? That's what I asked him. He could turn around, that's what. He made up his mind just like that. We were north of Trondheim and just a few hours from our destination. St. Ives would take Hasbro with him. I would go on alone, and see what I could see. He and Hasbro would rush back to Dover where St. Ives would assemble scientific apparatus. He had been a fool, he said, a moron, a nitwit. It was he and he alone who was responsible for the death of those ten men. He could have stopped it if he hadn't been too muddleheaded to see. That was ever St. Ives's way, blaming himself for all the deviltry in the world, because he hadn't been able to stop it. The sheer impossibility of his stopping all of it never occurred to him.

Hasbro gave me a look as they hefted their luggage out onto the platform. St. Ives was deflated, shrunken almost, and there shone in his eyes a distant gleam, as if he were focused on a single wavering point on the horizon—the leering face of Ignacio Narbondo—and he would keep his eyes fixed on that face until he stared the man into oblivion.

Hasbro took me aside for a moment to tell me that he would take care of the professor, that I wasn't to worry, that we would all win through in the end. All I had to do was learn the truth about

Narbondo. St. Ives must be desperately certain of the facts now; he had become as methodical as a clockwork man. But like that same man, he seemed to both of us to be running slowly down. And for one brief moment there on the platform, I half hoped that St. Ives would never find Narbondo, because, horrible as it sounds, it was Narbondo alone that gave purpose to the great man's life.

Narbondo had had a long and curious criminal history: vivisection, counterfeiting, murder—a dozen close escapes capped by his fleeing from Newgate Prison very nearly on the eve of his intended execution. There was nothing vile that he hadn't put his hand to. He dabbled in alchemy and amphibian physiology, and there was some evidence that, working with the long-forgotten formulae of Paracelsus, he had developed specifics that would revive the dead. His grandfather, the elder Narbondo, had elaborated the early successes of those revivification experiments in journals that had been lost long ago. And those, of course, were the papers alluded to by the woman in Godall's shop.

It was a mystery, this business of the lost journals—a far deeper mystery than it would seem on the surface, and one that seemed to have threads connecting it to the dawn of history and to the farthest corners of the earth. And it was a mystery that we wouldn't solve. We would tackle only the current manifestation of it, this business of Higgins the academician and Captain Bowker and the revived Narbondo and the ships sinking in the Dover Strait. There was enough in that to confound even a man like St. Ives.

It was St. Ives's plan to resort again to the dirigible. I would proceed to Mount Hjarstaad by train and make what discoveries I could, while waiting for the arrival of the dirigible, which would put out of Dover upon St. Ives's return to that city. Ferries were still docking there, but only if they had come in from the north:

Flanders and Normandy ferries had stopped running altogether. So St. Ives would send the dirigible for me, in an effort to fetch me back to England in time to be of service.

We should have hired the dirigible in the first place, lamented St. Ives, standing on the platform in the cold arctic wind. We should have this, we should have that. I muttered and nodded, never having seen him in such despair. There was no arguing with him there in that rocky landscape, which did its part to freeze one's hope. I would have to go on with as stout a heart as I could fabricate.

And so away they went south, and I north, and I didn't learn another thing about their adventures until I met up with them again, days later, back in Sterne Bay, the dirigible rescue having come off without a hitch and skived at least a couple of days off my wanderings about Norway, but having sailed me into Dover too late to join my comrades in their dangerous scientific quest. I'm getting ahead of myself, though. It's what I found out in Hjarmold, near the mountain, that signifies.

Narbondo *had* been fished out of his watery grave, all right— by a tall thin man with a bald head. It had to have been Leopold Higgins, although he had registered at the hostel under the name Wiggins, which was evidence either of a man gone barmy or of a man remarkably sure of himself. I got all this from the stableboy, whose room lay at the back of the stables, and who had seen a good deal of what transpired there. No real effort had been made for secrecy. Higgins and an accomplice—Captain Bowker, from the description of him—had ridden in late one afternoon with Narbondo lying in the back of the wagon, stiff as a day-old fish. They claimed that he had just that morning fallen into the lake, that they had been on a climbing expedition. There was nothing in their story to excite suspicions. Higgins had professed to be a doctor and had stopped them from sending up to Bodø for the local medicine man.

Curiously, he hadn't taken Narbondo inside the hostel to thaw him out; he had set up camp in the stables instead, insisting that Narbondo's recovery must be a slow business indeed, and for the first two nights Narbondo slept on his table without so much as a blanket for covering. Higgins fed him nothing but what he said was cod-liver oil, but which he referred to as "elixir." And once, when Narbondo began to moan and shudder, Higgins said that he was "coming round too soon," and he hauled Narbondo out into the freezing night and let him stiffen up some.

The stableboy who told me all of this was a bright lad, who had smelled something rotten, as it were, and it wasn't the fish oil, either. He had a sharp enough eye to recognize frauds like Higgins and Bowker, and he watched them, he said, through a knothole when they thought he was asleep. It was on the fourth night that Narbondo awakened fully, if only for a few seconds. Higgins had set up some sort of apparatus—hoses, bladders, bowls of yellow liquid. Throughout the night he had sprayed the doctor with mists while Captain Bowker snored in the hay. An hour before dawn, Narbondo's eyes blinked open in the lamplight, and after a moment of looking around himself, puzzled at what he saw, he smiled a sort of half-grin and said the single word, "Good," and then lapsed again into unconsciousness.

I knew by then what it was I had come for, and I had learned it in about half an hour. St. Ives had been right to turn around; it didn't take three men to talk to a stableboy. After that I was forced to lounge about the village, eating vile food, wondering what it was that my companions were up to and when my dirigible would arrive, and worrying finally about one last bit of detail: the frozen man, according to my stableboy, had had milky-white hair and pale skin, like a man carved out of snow or dusted with frost; and yet Narbondo had had lanky black hair, just going to gray, when he had catapulted into that tarn.

The phrase "dusted with frost" wasn't my own; it was the artful creation of my stableboy, who had lived for ten years in York and might have been a writer, I think, if he had put his mind to it. Here he was mucking out stables. It made me wonder about the nature of justice, but only for a moment. Almost at once it brought to mind the letter we had read in Godall's shop, the one signed H. Frost, of Edinburgh University.

Meanwhile, Langdon St. Ives and Hasbro arrived back in Dover without incident—no bombs, no gunfire, no threats to the ship. I believe that our sudden disappearance from Sterne Bay had confounded our enemies. Perhaps they thought that the fruit-basket bomb had frightened us away, although Narbondo— or Frost—knowing St. Ives as well as he did, shouldn't have made that mistake. Anyway, in Dover, St. Ives arranged for the dirigible to fetch me out of Norway, and then set about hiring a balloon for himself and Hasbro. They didn't wait for me—they couldn't—and I'm narrating their exploits as accurately as I can, having got the story secondhand, but straight from the horse's mouth, of course.

St. Ives set about constructing a bismuth spiral, which, for the reader unfamiliar with the mysteries of magnetism, is a simple snail-shell spiral of bismuth connected to a meter that reads changes of resistance in the spiral to determine intensities of magnetic fields. It's a child's toy, comparatively speaking, but foolproof. The very simplicity of St. Ives's notion infuriated him even further. It was something that ought to have been accomplished a week earlier, in time to save those ten men.

He affixed the spiral to a pole that they could slip down through a small hiatus in the basket of the balloon, so as to suspend the spiral just above the waves, making the whole business of taking a reading absolutely dangerous—almost deadly, as it turned out—because it required their navigating the balloon perilously close to the sea itself. Why didn't they use a length of rope, instead—play out the line while staying safely aloft? That was my question too; and the answer, in short, is that the science of electricity and magnetism wouldn't allow for it: the length of wire connecting the bismuth to the meter must be as short as possible for the reading to be accurate—that was how St. Ives understood it, although his understanding was nearly the death of him.

He meant to discover where Lord Kelvin's machine—the enormously powerful electromagnet stolen from the machine works in Holborn—lay beneath the sea, somewhere in the Dover Strait. He assumed that it rested on a submerged platform or on a shallow sandy shoal. Maybe it was anchored, but then again maybe it was slowly drifting at the whim of deepwater currents. He suspected the existence of a float or buoy of some sort, both to locate it and, perhaps, to effect its switching on and off.

The two of them were aloft within a day. It was doubtful that the ban on local shipping would last out the week; the economy wouldn't stand it. The government would pay the ransom or get used to the notion of losing ships. The Royal Academy still denied everything, right down to the ground, while at the same time working furiously to solve the mystery themselves.

St. Ives and Hasbro scoured the surface of the sea, from

Ramsgate to Dungeness. Hasbro, an accomplished balloonist—the blue-ribbon winner, in fact, of the Trans-European balloon races of 1883—grappled with the problem of buoyancy, of keeping the basket above the licking waves in order not to drown St. Ives's apparatus. The wind blew down out of the North Sea in gusts, buffeting them southward toward the coast of France, and it took all of Hasbro's skill to steady their course at all. St. Ives had fashioned a sort of ballasted sea anchor that they dragged along and so avoided being blown across the coast of Normandy before discovering anything.

Even so, it finally began to seem as if their efforts were in vain—the Strait being almost inconceivably vast from the perspective of two men in a balloon. It was sometime late in the afternoon, when they were just on the edge of giving up, that they saw a sloop flying the ensign of the Royal Academy. St. Ives could see Parsons on the deck, and he waved to the man, who, after seeming to ascertain who it was that hailed him, replied with a perfunctory little nod and went immediately below decks. There was the chance, of course, that the Academy had already discovered the spot where the device had been sunk. And there was the chance that they were still searching. What would St. Ives do? What *could* he do?

They swept across her bow and passed her, St. Ives lowering the bismuth spiral one last time to take another reading. It registered some little bit of deviation, the needle swinging around fairly sharply as they drove along south and west, away from Parsons's sloop.

They were two hundred yards off his port bow when the balloon lurched, throwing both the professor and Hasbro into the basket wall in a tangle of arms and legs. The basket tilted ominously, nearly pouring them into the sea. Hasbro hacked furiously at the rope holding the sea anchor, thinking that it had caught itself in something, while St. Ives held on to his pole and meter, which burst suddenly in his hands. That is to say the meter did—exploded—its needle whirling around and around like a compass gone mad, until it twisted itself into ruin.

St. Ives let go of the apparatus, which shot straight down into the water as the balloon strained at her lines, trying to tug the basket skyward, but having no luck. The basket, torn in the opposite direction by an unseen force, spun and dipped crazily, fighting as if it had been grappled by a phantom ship.

The crew of the sloop, including Parsons, lined the deck, watching the wild balloon and the two men clinging helplessly to her. It must have appeared as if she were being torn asunder by warring spirits—which she was, in a sense, for it was the powerful forces of hot air and magnetism that tugged her asunder. The ruined meter told the tale. St. Ives had found the sunken device right enough; the iron-reinforced base of the balloon basket was caught in its electromagnetic grip.

With a tearing of canvas and snapping of line, the basket lurched downward, almost into the ocean. A ground swell washed across them, and in an instant they were foundering. St. Ives and Hasbro had to swim for it, both of them striking out through the cold water toward the distant sloop, the nails in their bootheels prising themselves out. St. Ives fished out his clasp knife and offered it up to the machine in order that his trousers pocket might be saved. Finally, when they were well away from the snapping line and rollicking bag, they stopped swimming to watch.

For a moment their basket still tossed on the surface of the water. Then it was tugged down into the depths, where it hung suspended just below the surface. The still-moored balloon flattened itself against the sea, humping across the rolling swell, the gasses inside snapping the seams apart with Gatling-gun bursts of popping, the hot air inside whooshing into the atmosphere as if a giant were treading the thing flat.

Within minutes the deflated canvas followed the basket down like a fleeing squid and was gone, and St. Ives and Hasbro trod water, dubious about their obvious success. If it weren't for the sloop sending a boat out after them, they would have drowned, and no doubt about it. Parsons, seeing that clearly, welcomed them aboard with a hearty lot of guffawing through his beard.

"Quite a display," he said to St. Ives as the professor slogged toward a forward cabin. "That was as profitable an example of scientific method as I can remember. I trust you took careful notes. There was a look on your face, man—I could see it even at such a distance as that—a look of pure scientific enlightenment. If I were an artist I'd sketch it out for you…" He went on this way, Parsons did, laughing through his beard and twigging St. Ives all the way back to Dover, after leaving the area encircled with red-painted buoys.

A t the very moment that they were aloft over the Strait, I was aloft in the dirigible, watching the gray seas slip past far below, and captain of nothing for the moment but my own fate. I was bound for Sterne Bay. The business of the icehouse had become clear to me while I lounged in Norway. Days had passed, though, since my confrontation with Captain Bowker, and in that time just about anything could have happened. I might rush back to find them all gone, having no more need of ice. On the other hand, I might easily find a way to do my part.

At the Crown and Apple I discovered that St. Ives and Hasbro hadn't yet returned from their balloon adventure. Parsons was gone too. I was alone, and that saddened me. Parsons's company would have been better than nothing. I sat on the edge of the bed contemplating a pint or two and a nap, wanting to escape my duty by going to sleep—drink and sleep being a substitute, albeit a poor one, for company. Sitting there reminded me of that last fateful knock on the door, though—reminded me that while I slept, no end of frightful business might be transpiring. Who could say that the door mightn't swing open silently and an infernal machine, fuse sputtering, mightn't roll like a melon into the center of the floor…

A nap was out of the question. But what would I do instead? I would go to the icehouse. There was no percentage in my pretending to be Abner Benbow any longer. Might I disguise myself? A putty nose and a wig might accomplish something. I dismissed the idea. That was the sort of thing they would expect. My only trump card was that they would have no notion of my having returned to Sterne Bay.

Still, I wouldn't take any unnecessary risks. I was ready for them now. I went out through the second-story door at the back of the inn, and down rickety steps that led out past a weedy bit of garden and through a gate, right to the edge of the bay. A half score of rowboats were serried along a dock of rotting wooden planks that ran out into the water fifty good yards or so before becoming a mere thicket of broken pilings. There was no one about.

The tide was out, leaving a little stretch of shingle running along beside a low stone seawall. I clambered down and picked my way along the shingle, thinking to emerge into the village some distance from the Apple, so that if they *were* onto me, and someone was watching the inn, I'd confound them.

Some hundred yards down, I slipped back over the seawall and followed a narrow boardwalk between two vine-covered cottages, squeezing out from between them only a little ways down from where my beggar man was shot before he could borrow any money from me. I hiked along pretty briskly toward the icehouse, but the open door of The Hoisted Pint brought me up short.

I had never discovered whether my rubber elephant inhabited a room there, largely because I had been coy, playing the detective, and was overcome by the woman behind the counter, who, I was pretty sure, had taken me for a natural fool. The truth of it is that I'm too easily put off by an embarrassment. This time I wouldn't be. I angled toward the door, up the steps, and into the foyer. She stood as ever, meddling with receipts, and seemed not to recognize me at all. My hearty, "Hello again," merely caused her to squint.

She pushed her spectacles down her nose and looked at me over them. "Yes?" she said.

Somehow the notion of her having forgotten me, after all the rigamarole just a few days earlier, put an edge on my tone. I was through being pleasant. I can't stand cheeky superiority in people, especially in clerks and waiters, who have nothing to recommend them but the fact of their being employed. What was this woman but a high-toned clerk? Perhaps she owned the inn; perhaps she didn't. There was nothing in any of it that justified her putting on airs.

"See here," I said, leaning on the counter. "I'm looking for a woman and her son. I believe they're staying here or at any rate were staying here last week. They look remarkably alike, frighteningly so, if you take my meaning. The son, who might be as old as thirty, carries with him an India-rubber elephant that makes a noise."

"A *noise*?" she said, apparently having digested nothing of the rest of my little speech. The notion of an elephant making a noise, of my having gone anatomical on her, had shattered her ability to understand the clearest sort of English, had obliterated reason and logic.

"Never mind the noise," I said, losing my temper. "Disregard it." I caught myself, remembering St. Ives's dealings with the landlady at the Crown and Apple. Tread softly, I reminded myself, and I forced a smile. "That's right. It's the woman and her son that I wanted to ask you about. She's my mother's cousin, you see. I got a letter in the post, saying that she and her son—that would be, what? my cousin twice removed, little Billy, we used to call him, although that wasn't his name, not actually—anyway, that she's here on holiday, and I'm anxious to determine where she's staying."

The woman still looked down her nose at me, waiting for me to go on, as if what I had said so far hadn't made half enough sense, couldn't have begun to express what it was I wanted.

I winked at her and brassed right along. "I asked myself, 'Where in all of Sterne Bay is my mother's favorite cousin likely to stay? Why, in the prettiest inn that the town has to offer. That's the ticket.' And straightaway I came here, and I'm standing before you now to discover whether she is indeed lodged at this inn."

That ought to have made it clear to the woman, and apparently it did, for the next thing she said was, "What is the lady's name?" in a sort of schoolteacher's voice, a tone that never fails to freeze my blood—doubly so this time because I hadn't any earthly idea what the woman's name was.

"She has several," I said weakly, my brain stuttering. "In the Spanish tradition. She might be registered under Larson, with an *o*."

I waited, drumming my fingers on the oak counter as she perused the register. Why had I picked Larson? I can't tell you. It was the first name that came to mind, like Abner Benbow.

"I'm sorry," she said, looking up at me.

"Perhaps…" I said, gesturing toward the book. She hesitated, but apparently couldn't think of any good reason to keep it away from me; there was nothing in what I asked to make her suspicious, and she wouldn't, I suppose, want to insult the favored cousin several times removed of one of her registered guests. So she pushed her glasses back up her nose, sniffed at me, and turned the book around on the counter.

Fat lot of good it would do me. *I* didn't know what the woman's name was. What sort of charade was I playing? The rubber elephant had been my only clue, and that hadn't fetched any information out of her. If I brought it back into the conversation now, she'd call the constable and I'd find myself strapped to a bed in Colney Hatch. I was entirely at sea, groping for anything at all to keep me afloat.

I gave the list a perfunctory glance, ready to thank her and leave. One of the names nearly flew out at me: Pule, Leona Pule.

Suddenly I knew the identity of the madman in the coach. I knew who the mother was. I seemed to know a thousand things, and from that knowledge sprang two thousand fresh mysteries. It had been Willis Pule that had stolen my elephant. I should have seen it, but it had been years since he had contrived a wormlike desire for my wife Dorothy, my fiancée then. You wouldn't call it love; not if you knew him. He went mad when he couldn't possess her, and very nearly murdered any number of people. He was an apprentice of Dr. Narbondo at the time, but they fell out, and Pule was last seen insane, comatose in the back of Narbondo's wagon, being driven away toward an uncertain fate.

I noted the room number. They hadn't left. They might be upstairs at the moment. The nonsense in the coach—his taking the elephant—was that a charade? Was that his way of toying with me? Was it Willis Pule that had shot my beggar man? I thanked the woman at the counter and stepped away up the shadowy stairs, half thinking to discover whether from room 312 a man might have a clear rifle shot down toward the green.

I'll admit it: right then I was foolishly proud of myself for being "on the case," and was half wondering about the connection between Pule's grandfather and the elder Narbondo, which mirrored, if I saw things aright, the relationship between Pule and the doctor. How did Higgins fit, though? Had he discovered references to the lost alchemical papers that had ruined Mrs. Pule's family? Had he thought to revive Narbondo in order to enlist his aid in finding them? And now they were all skulking about in Sterne Bay, perhaps, carrying out their deadly plans for the machine, waiting for the ransom, thawing Narbondo out slowly at the icehouse.

I felt awfully alone at the moment, and wished heartily that St. Ives and Hasbro weren't off doing whatever they were doing. The stairs creaked. The evening sunlight filtering through the landing windows was insufficient, and the deepening shadows above me seemed to be a waiting ambush as I stepped cautiously out onto the dim third-floor landing.

An empty hallway stretched away in either direction. Room 312 was either up or down; it didn't matter to me, for it was clear at once that the landing window would suffice if what you wanted to do was shoot a man. The iron hinges of the double casement were rusted. I got onto my hands and knees and peered at the floor in the failing light. It was swept clean, except for right along the floor moldings, where flakes of rust dusted the very corner. The window wasn't opened very often; but it had been recently. The varnished wood of the sill was etched with a scraped indentation where someone had forced open the jammed casement, the wood beneath the scratch still fresh and clean, barely even dusty.

I slipped the latch and pulled, but the old window, swollen by sea air and the wet spring weather, was jammed shut. I wiggled it open just far enough to wedge my fingers in behind it, and then it was easy enough to work the window open, scraping it again across the sill. I leaned out then, peering through the gloom toward the green where the beggar had died.

The sounds of the village settling into evening struck me as being very pleasant, and the rush of sea wind in my face awakened me from the morbid reverie of dread that I'd slipped into while climbing the darkened stairs. I could even see the lights of the Crown and Apple, and they reminded me of supper and a pint. But then I looked down three long stories to the paving stones of the courtyard below, and with a dreadful shudder I was reminded of danger in all its manifold guises, and I bent back into the safety of the hallway, imagining sudden hands pushing against the small of my back, and me tumbling out and falling headlong… Being handed a bomb in a basket has that effect on me.

I knew what I had to know. Confrontations would accomplish nothing, especially when I had no idea on earth what it was, exactly, I would discover upon knocking on the door of the Pules' room. Better to think about it over supper.

I forced the window shut, then stood up and turned around, thinking to steal back down the stairs and away. But I found myself staring into the face of the ghastly Mrs. Pule, the woman in Godall's shop.

MY ADVENTURE AT
THE HOISTED PINT

I gasped out a sort of hoarse yip while she grinned out of that melon face of hers—a hollow grin, empty of any real amusement. She pointed a revolver at me.

Down the hall we went. I would be visiting their room after all, and I'll admit that I didn't like the notion a bit. What would St. Ives do? Whirl around and disarm her? Talk her out of whatever grisly notion she had in mind? Prevail upon her better judgment? I didn't know how to do any of that. St. Ives wouldn't have gotten himself into this mess in the first place.

She knocked twice on the door of the room, then paused, then knocked once. It swung open, but nobody stood there; whoever had opened the door was hidden behind it, not wanting to be seen. Who would it be? Captain Bowker, perhaps, waiting to lambaste me with a truncheon. I couldn't have that. Ignoring the revolver, I ducked away to the left into the room and spun around to face whoever it was that would emerge when the door swung shut.

It was the lunatic son—Willis Pule. He peeked out coyly, just his head, and his mother had to snatch the door shut because he didn't want to let go of it. She reached across and pinched him on the ear, and his coy smile evaporated, replaced by a look of theatrical shock, which disappeared in turn when he got a really good glimpse at the fright that must have been plain on my face. Then, suddenly happy, he affected the wide-eyed and round-mouthed demeanor of the fat man in the comical drawing, the one who has just that moment noted the approach of someone bearing an enormous plate of cream tarts. Pule pulled his right hand from behind his back and waved my elephant at me.

There was a buzzing just then, and the woman strode across to where the outlet of a speaking tube protruded from the wall. She slid open its little hatch-cover, jammed her ear against it, listened, and then, speaking into the tube, she said, "Yes, we've got him." She listened again and said, "No, in the hallway." And after another moment of listening she snickered out, "Him? Not hardly," and closed the hatch-cover and shut off the tube.

She had obviously just spoken to the landlady. The place was a rat's nest. Everything was clear to me as I slumped uninvited into a stuffed chair. All my detective work was laughable; I'd been toyed with all along. Even the elephant under the potted plant—that had been the work of the landlady too. She had snatched it away, of course, when I'd gone out through the door. She was the only one who was close enough to have got to it and away again before I had come back in. And all the rigamarole about my mother's cousin with the improbable names... She must have taken me for a child after that, watching me stroll away up the stairs to my probable doom. "Him, not hardly..." I grimaced. I thought I knew what that meant, and I couldn't argue with it. Well, maybe it would serve me some good in the end; maybe I could turn it to advantage. I would play the witless milksop, and then I would strike. I tried to convince myself of that.

Willis Pule tiptoed across to a pine table with a wooden chair alongside it. His tiptoeing was exaggerated, this time like a comic actor being effusively quiet, taking great silent knee-high steps. What was a madman but an actor who didn't know he was acting, in a play that nobody else had the script for? He sat in the chair, nodding at me and working his mouth slowly, as if he were chewing the end of a cigar. What did it all mean, all his mincing and posing and winking? Nothing. Not a damned thing. All the alterations in the weather of his face were nonsense.

He laid the elephant on the table and removed its red jumbo pants with a sort of infantile glee. Then he patted his coat pocket, slipped out a straight razor, and very swiftly and neatly sawed the elephant's ears off. A look of intense pity and sadness shifted his eyes and mouth, and then was gone.

I forgot to breathe for a moment, watching him. It wasn't the ruining of the toy that got to me. I had built the thing, after all, and I've found that a man rarely regrets the loss of something he's built himself; he's always too aware of the flaws in it, of the fact that it wants a hat, but it's too late to give it one. It was the beastly cool way that he pared the thing up—that's what got to me: the way he watched me out of the corner of his eye, and looked up once to wink at me and nod at the neat bit of work he was accomplishing, almost as if to imply that it was merely practice, sawing up the elephant was. And, horribly, he was dressed just like his mother, too, still got up in the same florid chintz.

His mother walked past him, ignoring him utterly. I hoped that she might take the razor away from him. A razor in the hands of an obvious lunatic, after all… But she didn't care about the razor. She rather approved of it, I think.

"Willis likes to operate on things," she said matter-of-factly, the word *operate* effecting a sort of ghastly resonance in my inner ear. I nodded a little, trying to smile, as if pleased to listen to the chatter of a mother so obviously proud of her son. "He cut a bird apart once, and affixed its head to the body of a mouse."

"Ah," I said.

She cocked her head and favored me with a horrid grimace of sentimental wistfulness. "It lived for a week. He had to feed it out of a tiny bottle, poor thing. It was a night-and-day job, ministering to that helpless little creature. A night-and-day job. It nearly wore him out. And then when it died I thought his poor heart would break, like an egg. He enshrined it under the floorboards along with the others. Held a service and all."

I shook my head, wondering at the notion of a heart breaking like an egg. They were both barmy, and no doubt about it. And given Pule's years in apprenticeship with Narbondo, all this stuff about vivisection very likely wasn't just talk. I glanced over at the table. Pule had managed to stuff a piece of candle through the holes where the beast's ears had been. He lit it with a match at both ends, so that the twin flames shot out on either side of its head, melting the wax all over the tabletop and filling the room with the reek of burning rubber.

"Willis!" shrieked the mother, wrinkling up her nose at the stink. In a fit of determination she leaped up and raced toward the sleeping room. She was immediately out again, brandishing a broad wooden paddle, and her son, suddenly contrite, began to howl and beg and cry. Then, abruptly, he gave off his pleading and started to yell, "Fire! Fire!" half giggling, half sobbing, as he slammed away at the burning elephant with his cap, capering around and around the table and chair as his mother angled in to swat him with the paddle.

It was an appalling sight—one I hope never again to witness as long as I live. I was up in a shot, and leaping for the door, getting out while the getting was good. The getting wasn't any good, though; the door was locked tight, and both the mother and son turned on me together, he plucking up the razor and she waving the paddle.

I apologized profusely. "Terribly sorry," I said. "Terribly, terribly sorry." I couldn't think of anything else. But all the while I looked around the room, searching out a weapon, and there was nothing at all close to hand except a chair cushion. I believe that if I could have got at something with a little weight to it I would have pounded them both into jelly right then and there, and answered for the crime afterward. There wasn't a court in all of England that would have condemned me, not after taking a look at that mad pair and another look beneath the floorboards of their house in London.

They advanced a step, so I shouted, "I know the truth!" and skipped away against the far wall. It was a nonsensical thing to shout, since I didn't any more know the truth than I knew the names of my fictitious cousins, but it stopped them cold. Or at least it stopped her. He, on the other hand, had fallen entirely into the role of being a menace, and he stalked back and forth eyeing me like a pirate, and she eyeing him, until, seeing her chance, she walloped him on the posterior with the paddle, grinning savagely, and very nearly throwing him straight razor and all into the chair I'd been sitting in.

He crept back to his table tearfully, like a broken man, whimpering nonsense at her, apologizing. He slumped over the ravaged elephant, hacking off its feet with the razor and then slicing its legs to ribbons, the corners of his mouth turned down in a parody of grief and rage.

"Where are they?" she asked.

What are they; that was the question. I ought to have had the answer, but didn't. It could be she meant people—St. Ives, maybe, and Hasbro. She thought, perhaps, that they were lurking roundabout, waiting for me. It didn't sound like that's what she meant, though. I scrambled through my mind, recalling her conversation at Godall's shop.

"I can lead you to them." I was clutching at straws, hoping it wasn't as utterly obvious as it seemed to be.

She nodded. The son peered at me slyly.

"But I want some assurances," I said.

"An affidavit?" she asked, cackling with sudden laughter. "*I'll* give you assurances, Mr. High-and-mighty."

"And I'll give you *this*!" cried the son, leaping up as if spring-driven and waving his straight razor in the air like an Afghani assassin. In a sudden fit he flailed away with it at the remains of the elephant, chopping it like an onion, carving great gashes in the tabletop and banging the razor against the little gear mechanism inside the ruined toy, the several gears wobbling away to fall off the table and onto the floor. Then he cast down the razor, and, snarling and drooling, he plucked up the little jumbo trousers and tore them in half, throwing them to the carpet, alternately treading on them and spitting at them in a furious spastic dance, and meaning to say, I guess, that the torn pants would be my head if I didn't look sharp.

His mother turned around and slammed him with the paddle again, shouting "Behavior!" very loud, her face red as a zinnia. He yipped across the room and sank into the chair, sitting on his hands and glowering at me.

"Where?" asked the woman. "And no games."

"At the Crown and Apple," I said. "In my room."

"*Your* room." She squinted at me.

"That's correct. I can lead you there now. Quickly."

"You won't lead us anywhere," she said. "We'll lead ourselves. You'll stay here. There's not another living soul on this floor, Mr. Who-bloody-is-it, and everyone on the floor below has been told there's a madman spending the night, given to fits. Keep your lip shut, and if we come back with the notebooks, we'll go easy on you."

Willis Pule nodded happily. "Mummy says I can cut out your tripes," he assured me enthusiastically, "and feed them to the bats."

"The bats," I said, wondering why in the world he had chosen the definite article, and watching him pocket the razor. So it was the notebooks... Both of them donned webby-looking shawls and toddled out the door like the Bedlam Twins, she covering me all the time with the revolver. The door shut and the key clanked in the lock.

I was up and searching the place for a window, for another key, for a vent of some sort—for anything. The room was on the inside of the hallway, though, and without a window. And although both of them were lunatics, they were far too canny to leave spare keys roundabout. I sat down and thought. The Crown and Apple wasn't five minutes' walk. They'd get into my room right enough, search it in another five minutes, and then hurry back to cut my tripes out. Revolver or no revolver, they'd get a surprise when they pushed in through the door. She would make him come through first, of course, to take the blow... I studied out a plan.

What the room lacked was weapons. She had even taken the wooden paddle with her. There were a couple of chairs that would do in a pinch, but I wanted something better. I had worked myself into a bloodthirsty sort of state, and I was thinking in terms of clubbing people insensible. Chairs were too spindly and cumbersome for that.

I went to town on the bedstead—a loose-jointed wooden affair that wanted glue. Yanking the headboard loose from the side rails, I listened with satisfaction as the mattress and rails bumped to the floor, loud enough to alert anyone below that the visiting lunatic was doing his work. Then I leaned on one of the posts of the headboard itself, smashing the headboard sideways, the posts straining to tear away from the cross-members. Dowels snapped, wood groaned, and after a little bit of playing ram-it-against-the-floorboards the whole thing went to smash, leaving the turned post free in my hands. I hefted it; I would have liked it shorter, but it would do the trick.

The doorknob rattled just then. They were back, and quick, too. Either that or else maybe the landlady, noticing that the lunatic had been doing his job too well, had come round to investigate. I slid across to stand by the door, thinking that I wouldn't smash the landlady with my club, but would simply push past her instead, and away down the stairs. If it was a man, though...

Whoever it was was having a terrible time with the lock. It seemed like an eternity of metallic clicking before the door swung to. I tensed, the club over my shoulder. A man's face poked in from the dark hallway, the rest of the head following. I closed my eyes, stepped away from the wall, and pounded him one, slamming the club down against the back of his head, and knowing straight out that it wasn't Willis Pule at all, but someone perhaps even more deadly: it was Higgins, the academician-gone-to-seed, still gripping a skeleton key in his right hand.

The blow left him half senseless, knocking him onto his face on the floor. He lay writhing. I stepped across, thinking to give him another one, a sort of cricket swing to the cranium, but he was already down and I couldn't bring myself to do it—something I'm happy about today, but which took all my civilized instincts at the time.

The door lay open before me, and I was out of it quick, bolting for the stairs, throwing the post onto the floor of the hallway, and wondering about Higgins sneaking around like that. He wasn't expected; that was certain. He had seen them both go out, perhaps, and had crept in, no doubt searching for the very notebooks that they were off ransacking my room for. They weren't in league, then, but were probably deadly enemies. The Pules would take good care of him if they found him on the floor of their room.

I peered cautiously down the dark and empty stairwell, and then leaped down the stairs three at a time toward the second-floor landing, thinking to charge into the foyer at a run, knocking down anyone between me and the door and maybe shouting something clever at the landlady to regain some lost dignity. I fairly spun around the baluster and onto the bottom flight of stairs, straight into the faces of the two Pules, who puffed along like engines, coming up, she holding the revolver under her shawl and he going along before, both of them with a deadly resolve.

"Here now!" piped the son, clutching my arm in the devil's own grip.

"Hold him!" she cried. "*We'll* make him sing! Up the stairs, Bucko!"

I kicked him on the shin as hard as I could, my momentum lending it some mustard. He howled and slammed backward against the railing, nearly knocking his mother down. He didn't let go of my arm, though, but pulled me over with him, both of us flailing and rolling and me jerking free and scrabbling back up toward the landing like an anxious crab, expecting to be shot. I was on my feet and jumping up the stairs three at a time toward the third floor, listening to the curses and slaps and yips behind me as Mrs. Pule rallied her son.

There was no shot, despite the way being clear for it and the range close, but I ducked and danced down the third-floor hall anyway, trying to convince myself that she was loath to fire the gun in public and bring about the collapse of her plans. I should have thought of that an hour ago, when she collared me at the window, but I didn't, and wasn't convinced of it now.

I blasted past the room again, its door still open and Higgins on his hands and knees on the floor, ruminating. The sight of him brought the Pules up short as they came racing along behind me, and for the moment they let me go in order to attend to him. I headed straight toward a French window, grappled with the latch, pulled it open, and looked out, not onto three stories of empty air, thank heaven, but onto a little dormer balcony. There was a hooting from the open door of the room, and a grunt, and then an outright shriek, as the Pules visited the sins of Jack Owlesby onto the head of poor Higgins.

I closed the window behind me, although I couldn't latch it. In a moment they'd be through it and upon me. Without a bit of hesitation I hoisted myself over the railing, swinging myself down and in, landing on my feet on an identical balcony below and immediately crumpling up, my ankles ringing with the impact. I was up again, though, climbing across this railing too, and clutching two handfuls of ivy tendrils with the nitwit idea of clambering down through it to safety like an ape in a rain forest. I scrabbled in the vines with my feet as the ivy tore loose in a rush, and I slid along through it shouting, landing in a viney heap in a flower bed.

The window banged open upstairs, and I was on my feet and running, trailing vines, wincing at the pain in my ankles, but damned if I'd let any of it slow me down. I expected a shot, but none came—just a litany of curses cried into the night and then cut off abruptly when a voice from a window in a nearby house shouted, "Wot the hell!" and the strollers down along the street to the pier began to point. Mrs. Pule, blessedly, wasn't keen on calling attention to herself just then.

I ran straight toward the gap between the two houses that would lead me to the seawall, not slowing down until I was there, clambering over the now-damp stone and jumping to the shingle below, where I found myself slogging through ankle-deep water, the tide having come up to lap against the wall. I nearly slipped on the slick stones, and forced myself to slow down. There was no sound of pursuit, nothing at all, and the wild sense of abandon that had fueled my acrobatic leap from the top balcony drained away, leaving me cold and shaking, my shoes filled with seawater.

I climbed back over the wall and tramped along to the Crown and Apple, up the backstairs to find the door unlocked. I slipped into my room, dead tired and even more deadly thirsty. In fifteen minutes I strolled into the dining room in *dry* shoes, feeling tolerably proud of myself, and there sat St. Ives and Hasbro, stabbing at cutlets and with a bottle of Burgundy uncorked on the table. It did my heart good, as they say.

"Not with a revolver, she didn't," said St. Ives. "You were too far away for anyone to have brought off so close a shot. My guess is that it was a Winchester, and that it was your man Bowker who fired it. Clearly they and the Pules are working at cross-purposes, although both of them chase the same ends—

which have little to do, I'm convinced, with drawing ships to their doom. That's a peripheral business—quick cash to finance more elaborate operations."

St. Ives emptied the bottle into Hasbro's glass and waved at the waiter, ordering a second bottle of wine and another pint for me. I'm a beer man generally; red wine rips me up in the night. St. Ives studied his plate for a moment and then said, "It's very largely a distraction, too, the ship business, and a good one. Godall seems to think that the Crown is on the verge of paying them what they ask, in return for their solemn assurance that they'll abandon the machine where she lies. Imagine that. Those were Parsons's words, 'Their solemn assurance.' The man's gone round the bend. Now that we've found the machine, though, they'll wait on the ransom. We've accomplished that much. The Academy has the area cordoned off with ships and are going to try to haul it up out of there."

St. Ives drained his glass, then scowled into the lees, swirling them in the bottom. "If I had half a chance..." he said, not bothering to finish the sentence. I thought I knew what he meant, though; he had harbored a grim distrust of the machine ever since Lord Kelvin had set out to reverse the polarity of the earth with it. What were they keeping it for, if not to effect some other grand and improbable disaster in the name of science? I half believed St. Ives knew what it was, too—that there was far more to the machine than he was letting on and that only the principal players in the game fully understood. I was a pawn, of course, and resolved to keeping to my station. I'm certain, though, that St. Ives had contemplated on more than one occasion going into that machine works up in Holborn and taking it out of there himself. But he hadn't, and look what had come of his hesitating. That's the way *he* saw it—managing to blame himself from a fresh angle.

I tried to steer the subject away from the business of the machine. "So what *do* they want?" I asked.

"The notebooks, for the moment. The damnable notebooks. They think that they're an ace away from immortality. Narbondo very nearly had it ten years ago, back when he was stealing carp out of the aquarium and working with Willis Pule. He was close— close enough so that in Norway Higgins could revive him with the elixir and the apparatus. For my money Narbondo was pumped up with carp elixir when he went into the pond; that's what kept him alive, kept his entire cellular structure from crystallizing. Higgins's idea, as I see it, is that he would revive the doctor, and the two of them would search out the notebooks and then hammer out the fine points; together they would bottle the Fountain of Youth. How much they know about the machine I can't say.

"Higgins had been tracking them—the notebooks—and he wrote to Mrs. Pule, who he suspected might know something of their whereabouts, but his writing to her just set her off. She came around to Godall's very cleverly, knowing that to reveal to us that the notebooks existed and that Narbondo was alive would put us on the trail. She and the son merely followed us down from London."

It made sense to me. Leave it to St. Ives to put the pieces in order. "Why," I asked, "are they so keen on killing *me*, that's what I want to know. I'm the lowly worm in the whole business."

"You were available," said St. Ives. "And you were persistent, snooping around their hotel like that. These are remarkably bloodthirsty criminals. And the Pules, I'm afraid, are amateurs alongside the doctor. Higgins didn't have any idea on earth what it was he was reviving, not an inkling."

St. Ives pushed his plate away and ordered a bit of custard. It was getting along toward ten o'clock, and the evening had wound itself down. The beer was having its way with me, and I yawned and said that I would turn in, and St. Ives nodded thoughtfully and said that he'd just stroll along over to the icehouse in a bit and see what was up. I slumped. I wasn't built for it, not right then, and yet it was me who had found out about the business up in Norway. I was pretty sure that I understood the icehouse, and it didn't seem fair that I be left out. "It's early for that, isn't it?" I asked.

St. Ives shrugged. "Perhaps."

"I suggest a nap. Just a couple of hours to rest up. Let's tackle them in the middle of the night, while they sleep."

St. Ives considered, looked at his pocket watch, and said, "Fair enough. Stroke of midnight. We'll be across the hall, just in case anyone comes sneaking around."

"Knock me up with fifteen minutes to spare," I said, getting up. And with that I toddled off to my room and fell asleep in my clothes.

The night was howling cold and the sky clear and starry. There was a moon, but just enough to hang a coat on. We had slipped out the back and taken my route along the seawall, none of us speaking and with the plan already laid out. Hasbro carried a revolver and was the one among us most capable of using it.

Absolutely no one was about. Lamps flickered here and there along the streets, and a single light glowed in one of the windows of The Hoisted Pint—Willis Pule turning Higgins into an amphibian, probably. The shadowy pier stretched into the moonlit ocean, and the icehouse loomed dark and was empty in the weeds—very ominous, it seemed to me.

We wafered ourselves against the wall and waited, listening, wondering what lay within. After a moment I realized that Hasbro was gone. He had been behind me and now he wasn't; just like that. I tugged on St. Ives's coat, and he turned around and winked at me, putting a finger to his lips and then motioning me forward with a wave of his hand.

We crept along, listening to the silence and ducking beneath a bank of dirty windows, hunching a few steps farther to where St. Ives stopped outside a door. He put a finger to his lips and a hand on the latch, easing the latch down gently. There sounded the hint of a click, the door swung open slowly, and we were through, creeping along across the floor of a small room with a broken-down desk in it.

Some little bit of moonlight filtered in through the window—enough to see by now that our eyes had adjusted. Carefully, St. Ives pushed open another heavy door, just a crack, and peered through, standing as if frozen until he could make out what lay before him. He turned his head slowly and gave me a look—just a widening of the eyes—and then pushed the door open some more.

I caught the sound of snoring just then, low and labored like that of a hibernating bear, and when I followed St. Ives into the room, both of us creeping along, I looked for Captain Bowker, and sure enough there he was, asleep on a cot, his head turned to the wall. We slipped past him, through his little chamber and out into the open room beyond.

It was fearfully cold, and no wonder. Great blocks of ice lay stacked in the darkness like silvery coffins beneath the high ceiling. They were half covered with piled straw, and there was more straw littering the floor and a pair of dumpcarts and a barrow and a lot of shadowy odds and ends of tongs and tools and ice saws along the wall—none of it particularly curious, considering where we were.

St. Ives didn't hesitate. He knew what he was looking for, and I thought I did too. I was wrong, though. What St. Ives was after lay beyond the ice, through a weighted door that was pulled partly open. We stepped up to it, dropping to our hands and knees to peer beneath it. Beyond, in a square slope-ceilinged room with a double door set in the far wall, was a metal sphere, glowing dully in the moonlight and sitting on four squat legs.

It's Lord Kelvin's machine!—I said to myself, but then saw that it wasn't. It was a diving bell, a submarine explorer, built out of brass and copper and ringed with portholes. Mechanical armatures thrust out, with hinged elbows so that the device looked very jaunty, as if it might at any moment shuffle away on its piggy little legs. We rolled under the door, not wanting to push it open farther for fear of making a noise. And then all of a sudden, as we got up to dust ourselves off, there was noise to spare—the rattling and creaking of a wagon drawing up beyond the doors, out in the night.

A horse snorted and shook its head, and there was the sound of a brake clacking down against a wheel. I dropped to the ground, thinking to scramble under and into the ice room again before whoever it was in the wagon unlocked the outside doors and confronted us there. St. Ives grabbed my coat, though, and shook his head, and in a moment there was a fiddling with a lock and I stood up slowly, ready to acquit myself like a man.

The doors drew back, and between them, pulling them open, stood the remarkable Hasbro. St. Ives didn't stop to chat. He put his shoulder against one of the doors, pushing it fully open while Hasbro saw to the other one, and then as St. Ives latched on to the harness and backed the horses and dray around and through the doors, Hasbro clambered up onto the bed, yanked loose the wheel brake, and began to unlatch a clutch of chain and line from the post of a jib crane bolted to the bed.

I stood and gaped until I saw what it was we were up to, and then I hitched up my trousers and set to. Lickety-split, passing the line back and forth, looping and yanking, we tied the diving bell in a sort of basket weave. Hasbro hoisted it off the ground with the jib crane, which made the devil's own creaking and groaning, and St. Ives and I guided it by the feet as it swung around and onto the bed of the dray, clunking down solidly. Hasbro dropped down onto the plank seat, plucked up the ribands, clicked his tongue, and was gone in a whirl of moonlit dust, cantering away into the night.

It was a neat bit of work, although I had no real notion of its purpose. If the machine in the Strait was guarded by Her Majesty's navy, then our villains had no real use for the diving bell anyway; that part of their adventure, it seemed to me, had already drawn to an unsuccessful close. But who was I to question St. Ives? He was damned glad to get the bell out of there; I could see that in his face.

But we weren't done yet; I could see that too. Why hadn't we ridden out of there with Hasbro? Because St. Ives was in a sweat to see what else lay in that icehouse. Narbondo himself was in there somewhere, and St. Ives meant to find him. We bellied straightaway under the weighted door, back into the ice room, St. Ives first and me following, and stood up to peer into the grinning face of the jolly Captain Bowker, who stood two yards distant, staring at us down the sights of his rifle.

VILLAINY AT MIDNIGHT

He wouldn't miss this time. I was determined to play the part of the cooperative man, the man who doesn't want to be shot. The door slammed up and open behind us, and there stood Higgins, dressed in a lab coat, his head bandaged and him winded and puffing. Tufts of hair poked through the bandage. He smelled awful, like a dead fish in a sack.

"Leopold Higgins, I presume," said St. Ives, bowing. "I am Langdon St. Ives."

"I know who you bloody well are," he said, and then he looked at me for a cold moment, smiled, and said, "How did you like the fruit?"

Clearly he didn't know it was me who had beaned him at The Hoisted Pint when he was sneaking into the Pules' room. That was good; he wouldn't have been making jokes otherwise. Despite the gloom of the icehouse I could see that his face was bruised pretty badly. That must have been the work of the wonderful Pules.

"Catch it?" asked the captain, still training the rifle on us.

"Got away right enough," said Higgins. "What sort of watch was that you were keeping? Napping is what I call it. Sleeping like a baby while these two…"

The captain swiveled the rifle around and—blam!—fired a round past Higgins's ear. I leaped straight off my feet, but not nearly so far off them as Higgins did. He threw himself facedown into the straw on the floor, mewling like a wet cat. Captain Bowker chuckled until his eyes watered as Higgins, pale and shaken, struggled back up, fear and fury playing in his eyes.

"Who cares?" said the captain.

Higgins worked his mouth, priming his throat. "But the diving bell…"

"Who cares about the filthy bell? It ain't worth a nickel to me. *You* ain't worth a nickel to me. I'd just as leave kill the three of you and have done with it. You'll get your diving bell back when the tall one finds out we've got his friends."

This last added an optimistic flavor to the discussion. "The tall one" was clearly Hasbro, who, of course, would happily trade a dozen diving bells for the lives of dear old Jack and the professor. I didn't at all mind being held for ransom; it was being dead that bothered me.

"Or *one* of his friends, anyway." The captain shifted his gaze from one to the other of us, as if coming to a decision. There went the optimism. I was surely the most expendable of the two of us, since I knew the least. Captain Bowker sniffed the air and wrinkled up his face. "Gimme the 'lixir," he said to Higgins.

"*He* needs it," said Higgins, shaking his head. It was a brave act, considering, for the captain trained the rifle on Higgins again, dead between the eyes now, and started straight in to chuckle. Without an instant's hesitation, Higgins's hand went into the pocket of his

153

lab coat and hauled out a corked bottle, which he reached across toward the captain.

The captain grabbed for it, and St. Ives jumped—just when the rifle was midway between Higgins and us. It was the little pleasure in baiting Higgins that tripped the captain up.

"Run, Jack!" shouted St. Ives when he threw himself at the captain. In a storm of arms and legs he was flying forward, into the air, sideways into Captain Bowker's expansive stomach. The captain smashed over backward, his head banging against the floorboards and the bottle of elixir sailing away toward the stacked ice with Higgins diving after it. I was out both doors and into the night, running again toward the two houses before St. Ives's admonition had faded in my ears. He had commanded me to run, and I ran, like a spooked sheep. Live to fight another day, I told myself.

And while I ran I waited for the sound of a shot. What would I do if I heard it? Turn around? Turning around wasn't on my mind. I pounded down the little boardwalk and angled toward the seawall, leaping along like an idiot instead of slowing down to think things out. No one was after me, and I was out of sight of the icehouse, so there was no longer any chance of being shot. It was cold fear that drove me on. And it was regret at having run in the first place, at having left St. Ives alone, that finally slowed me down.

I was walking when I got to the water, breathing like an engine. Fog was blowing past in billows, and the moon was lost beyond it. In moments I couldn't see at all, except for the seawall, which I followed along up toward the Apple, moving slowly now and listening to the dripping of water off eaves and to what sounded like the slow dip of oars out on the bay. Suddenly it was the heavy silence that terrified me, an empty counterpoint, maybe, to the now-faded sound of gunfire and the moment of shouting chaos that had followed it.

Where was I bound? Back to the Apple to hide? To lie up until I learned that my friends were dead and the villains gone away? Or to confront the Pules, maybe, who were awaiting me in my room, honing their instruments? It was time for thinking all of a sudden, not for running. St. Ives had got me out of the icehouse. I couldn't believe that his heroics were meant simply to save my miserable life—they *were*, without a doubt, but I couldn't admit to it—and so what I needed was a plan, any plan, to justify my being out of danger.

I just then noticed that a lantern glowed out to sea, coming along through the fog, maybe twenty yards offshore; you couldn't really tell. The light bobbed like a will-o'-the-wisp, hanging from a pole affixed to the bow of a rowboat sculling through the mist. I stopped to finish catching my breath and to wait out my hammering heart, and I watched the foggy lantern float toward me. A sudden gust of salty wind blew the mists to tatters, and the dark ocean and its rowboat appeared on the instant, the boat driving toward shore when the man at the oars got a clear view of the seawall. The hull scrunched up onto the shingle, the stern slewing around and the oarsman clambering into shallow water. It was Hasbro. His pant legs were rolled and his shoes tied around his neck.

He looped the painter through a rusted iron ring in the wall and shook my hand as if he hadn't seen me in a month. Without a second's hesitation I told him about St. Ives held prisoner in the icehouse, about how I was just then formulating a plan to go back after him, working out the fine points so that I didn't just wade in and muck things up. Captain Bowker was a dangerous man, I said. Like old explosives, any little quiver might detonate him.

"Very good, Mr. Owlesby," Hasbro said in that stony butler's voice of his. Wild coincidence didn't perturb him. Nothing perturbed him. He listened and nodded as he sat there on the wet seawall and put on his shoes. His lean face was stoic, and he might just as well have been studying the racing form or laying out a shirt and trousers for his master to wear in the morning. Suddenly there appeared in my mind a picture of a strangely complicated and efficient clockwork mechanism—meant to be his brain, I suppose—and my spirits rose a sizable fraction. As dangerous as Captain Bowker was, I told myself, here was a man more dangerous yet. I had seen evidence of it countless times, but I had forgot it nearly as often because of the damned cool air that Hasbro has about him, the quiet efficiency.

Here he was, after all, out on the ocean rowing a boat. A half hour ago he was tearing away in a wagon, hauling a diving bell to heaven knows what destination. *That* was it—the difference between us. He was a man with destinations; it was that which confounded me. I rarely had one, unless it was some trivial momentary destination—the pub, say. Did Dorothy know that about me? Was it clear to the world as it was to me? Why on earth did she humor me day to day? Maybe because I reminded her of her father. But this was no time for getting morose and enumerating regrets. Where had Hasbro been? He didn't tell me; it was later that I found out.

At the moment, though, both of us slipped along through the fog, and suddenly I was a conspirator again. A destination had been provided for me. I wished that Dorothy could see me, bound on this dangerous mission, slouching through the shadowy fog to save St. Ives from the most desperate criminals imaginable. I tripped over a curb and sprawled on my face in the grass of the square, but was up immediately, giving the treacherous curb a hard look and glancing around like a fool to see if anyone had been a witness to my ignominious tumble. Hasbro disappeared ahead, oblivious to it—or so he would make it seem in order not to embarrass me.

But there, away toward the boardwalk and the pier, across the lawn… It was too damnably foggy now to tell, but someone had been there, watching. Heart flailing again, I leaped along to catch up with Hasbro. "We're followed," I hissed after him.

He nodded, and whispered into my ear. "Too much fog to say who it is. Maybe the mother and son."

I didn't think so. Whoever it was, was shorter than Willis Pule. Narbondo, maybe. He was somewhere about. It wasn't certain that he was on ice; that was mere conjecture. Narbondo skulking in the fog—the idea of it gave me the willies. But we were in view of the icehouse again, and the sight of it replaced the willies with a more substantial fear. The glow of lamplight filtered through a dirty window, and Hasbro and I edged along toward it, just as St. Ives and I had done an hour earlier.

I kept one eye over my shoulder, squinting into the mists, my senses sharp. I wouldn't be taken unawares; that was certain. What we saw through the window, though, took my mind off the night, and along with Hasbro I gaped at the three men within—none of whom was St. Ives.

What we were looking at wasn't a proper room, but was a little niche cut off from the ice room with a canvas drape. It was well lit, and we had a first-rate view of the entire interior, what with the utter darkness outside. The floor was clean of litter, and the whole of the room had a swabbed-out look to it, like a jury-rigged hospital room. On a wheeled table in the middle of it, lying atop a cushion and wearing what appeared to be a rubber all-together suit, was Dr. Narbondo himself, pale as a corpse with snow-white hair that had been cropped short. Frost was a more appropriate name, certainly. Narbondo *had* met his fate in that tarn; what had risen from it was something else entirely.

He lay there on his cushion, with fist-sized chunks of ice packed around him, like a jolly great fish on a buffet table. Captain Bowker sat in a chair, looking grizzled, tired, and enormous. His rifle stood tilted against the back corner of the room, always at hand. Higgins hovered over the supine body of the doctor. He meddled with chemical apparatus—a pan of yellow cataplasm or something, and a rubber bladder attached by a coiled tube to a misting nozzle. On a table along the wall sat the bottle of elixir that Higgins had apparently saved from its flying doom an hour past.

He showered the doctor with the mist, pulling open either eyelid and spraying the stuff directly in. The interior of the room was yellow with it, like a London fog. Narbondo trembled, as if from a spine-wrenching chill, and shouted something— I couldn't make out what—and then half sat up, lurching onto his elbows and staring round about him with wide, wild eyes. In seconds the passion had winked out of them, replaced by a placid know-it-all look, and he took up the bottle of elixir, uncorked it with a trembling hand, and drank off half the contents. He glanced at our window, and I nearly tumbled over backward, but he couldn't have seen us out there in the darkness and the fog.

What to do; that was the problem. Where was St. Ives? Dead? Trussed up somewhere within? More than likely. There were too many issues at stake for them to waste such a hostage as that. I nudged Hasbro with my elbow and nodded off down the dark clapboard wall of the icehouse, as if I were suggesting we head down that way—which I was. I saw no reason not to get St. Ives out of there. Hasbro was intent on the window, though, and he shook his head.

It was the doctor that he watched, Dr. Frost, or Narbondo, whichever you please. He had sat up now and was turning his head very slowly, as if his joints wanted oil; you could almost hear the creak. A startled expression, one of dread and confusion, passed across his face in waves. He was obviously troubled by something, and was making a determined effort to win through it. He slid off onto the floor and stood reeling, turning around with his back to us and with his hands on the table. I saw him pluck up a piece of ice and hold it to his chest, an artistic gesture, it seemed to me, even at the time.

Higgins hovered around like a mother hen. He put a hand on the doctor's arm, but Narbondo shook it off, nearly falling over and then grabbing the table again to steady himself. He turned slowly, letting go, and then, one step at a time, tramped toward the canvas curtain like a man built of stone, taking three short steps before pitching straight over onto his face and lying there on the floor, unmoving. Captain Bowker stood up tiredly, as a man might who didn't care a rap for fallen doctors, and he trudged over to where Higgins leaped around in a fit, shouting orders but doing nothing except getting in the way. The captain pushed him against the wall and said, "Back off!" Then he picked the doctor up and laid him back onto his bed while Higgins hovered about, gathering up the ice chunks knocked onto the floor.

"It's not working!" Higgins moaned, rubbing his forehead. "I've *got* to have the notebooks. I'm so *close!*"

"Looks like a bust to me," said the captain. "I'm for making them pay out for the machine. I'm for Paris, is what I'm saying. Your friend here can rot. Say, gimme some more of that 'lixir now. He won't be needing no more tonight."

It was then, while the captain's back was turned and Higgins was furiously snatching up the bottle of elixir to keep it away from him, that the canvas curtain lifted and into the little room slipped Willis Pule and his ghastly mother, she holding her revolver and he grinning round about him like a giddy child and carrying a black and ominous surgeon's bag.

Captain Bowker was quick; I'll give him that. He must have seen them out of the corner of his eye, for he half turned, slamming Willis on the ear with his elbow and knocking him silly, if such a thing were possible. Then he lunged for his rifle; and it's here that he moved too slowly. He would have got to it right enough if he hadn't taken the time to hit Willis first. But he had taken the time, and now Mrs. Pule lunged forward with a look of insane glee on her face, shoving the muzzle of the revolver into the captain's fleshy midsection so that the barrel entirely disappeared and the explosion was muffled when she fired. He managed to knock her away too, even as the bullet kicked him over backward in a sort of lumbering spin. He clutched at his vitals, his mouth working, and he knocked his rifle down as he caved in and sank almost like a ballerina to the floor, where he lay in a heap.

It was the most cold-blooded thing I've ever seen, and I've seen a few cold-blooded things in my day. Mrs. Pule turned her gun on Higgins, who couldn't stand it, apparently, and leaped at the canvas curtain. But Pule, who still sat on the floor, snaked out his arm and clutched Higgins's leg, and Higgins went over headforemost as if he *had* been shot. Pule climbed up onto his back and sat there astride him, giggling hysterically and shouting "Horsey! Horsey!" and poking Higgins in the small of the back with his finger, trying to tickle him, as impossible as that sounds, and then cuffing him on the back of the head with his open hand. "Take that! Take that! Take that!" he shrieked, as if the words were hiccups and he couldn't stop them.

Mrs. Pule saw her chance, and leaned in to slap Willis a good one, shouting, "Behavior!" again, except that this time the word had no effect on her son, and she was forced to box his ears, and so it went for what must have been twenty seconds or so: Willis slapping the back of Higgins's jerking head and yanking his ears and pulling his hair, and Mrs. Pule cuffing Willis on the noggin, and both of the Pules shouting so that neither of them could make themselves heard. Finally the woman grabbed a handful of her son's hair and gave it a yank, jerking him over backward with a howl, and Higgins flew to his knees and scrambled for the canvas, his bandages falling loose around his shoulders and fresh blood seeping through them.

They had him by the feet, though, just as quick as you please, and hauled him back in. They jerked him upright and slammed him into the late Captain Bowker's chair, trussing him up with the captain's own gaiters.

It was then that I saw someone right at the edge of my vision, down at the far end of the icehouse. I was certain of it. Someone was prowling around and had come out into the open, I suppose, at the sound of the gunfire and the scuffle, and then had seen us still standing by the window, doing nothing, and had darted away again, assuming, maybe, that there wasn't any immediate alarm.

By the time I nudged Hasbro there was no one there, and there was precious little reason to go snooping off in that direction, especially since whoever it was, it wasn't one of our villains; they were all present and accounted for. It's someone waiting, I thought at the time—waiting to see how things fell out before making his move, waiting for the dirty work to be done for him.

And all the while Dr. Narbondo lay there on ice, seemingly frozen. Willis seemed to see him for the first time. He crept across to peer into the doctor's face, then blanched with horror at what he saw there. Even in that deep and impossible sleep, Narbondo terrified poor Willis. And then, as if on cue, the doctor flinched in his cold slumber and mumbled something, and Pule fell back horrified. He cringed against the far wall, crossing his arms against his chest and drawing one leg up in a sort of flamingo gesture, doing as much as he could do to roll up into a ball and still stay on his feet—so that he could run, maybe, if it came to that.

His mother hunched across, goo-gooing at him, and rubbed his poor forehead, fluttering her eyelids and talking the most loathsome sort of baby talk to comfort him while still holding on to the revolver and stepping over the captain's splayed legs, straight into the blood that had pooled up on the floor. She nearly slipped, and she caught on to her son's jacket for support, giving off the baby talk in order to curse, and then wiping the bottom of her shoe very deliberately on the captain's shirt. Maybe Hasbro couldn't see this last bit from where he stood, but I could, and I can tell you it gave me the horrors, and doubly so when she went straightaway for her son again, calling him a poor lost thing and a wee birdy and all manner of pet names. I couldn't get my eyes off that horrifying bloody shoe-smear on the captain's already gruesome shirtfront. I was sick all of a sudden, and turned away to glance at Hasbro's face. He had taken the whole business in. His stoic visage was evaporated, replaced by a look of pure puzzlement and repulsion; he was human, after all.

"Let's find the professor," I whispered to him. I had no desire to watch what would surely follow; they wouldn't leave the doctor alive, and his death wouldn't be pretty. These two were living horrors—but even then, bloodthirsty and hypocritical as it sounds, somehow I didn't begrudge them their chance to even the score with Narbondo; I just didn't want to see them do it.

We stepped along through the weeds, around to the door that opened onto what had been Captain Bowker's sleeping quarters. The door was secured now, the hasp fitted with a bolt that had been slipped through it—enough merely to stop anyone's getting out. We got in, though, quick as you please, and there was St. Ives, tied up hands and feet and gagged, lying atop the bed. We got the gag out and him untied, and we indicated by gestures and whispers what sort of monkey business was going on in the room beyond. He was up and moving toward the door to the ice room, determined to stop it. It didn't matter who it was that was threatened. St. Ives wouldn't brook it; even Narbondo would have his day before the magistrate.

He tugged open the door, and you can guess who stood there—Mrs. Pule, grinning like a gibbon ape and holding the gun. I whirled around to the outside door, which still stood open, ready to leap out into the night, and thinking, of course, that one of us ought to get out in order to find the constable, to summon aid. Could I help it if it was always me who was destined for such missions? But there stood Willis, right outside, looking haggard and wearing the mask of tragedy—and training the captain's rifle on me with ominously shaking hands. I stopped where I stood and waited while Mrs. Pule took Hasbro's revolver away from him. So much for that.

They marched us back through the ice room, the floor of

which was wet and mucky with meltwater and sopping hay, and smelled like an ammoniated swamp. I was desperately cold all of a sudden, and thought about how unpleasant it was to have to face death when you were shaking with cold and dead tired and it was past three in the morning. The night had been one long round of wild escapes, followed by my striding back into various lion's dens and tipping my hat. There was no chance of another go at it now, though, with one of them in front and one behind.

St. Ives started right in, as soon as he saw Narbondo lying there on the table. He felt for a pulse, nodded, and raised one of the doctor's eyelids. Next he examined the bladder apparatus and sniffed the elixir, and then, as if it was the most natural and unpretentious thing in the world, he slipped the bottle of elixir into his coat pocket.

"Out with it!" hissed the woman, tipping the revolver against my head. My eyes shot open in order to better watch St. Ives remove the bottle.

"Wake him up," she said, removing the revolver from my temple and gesturing toward the sleeping doctor.

St. Ives shook his head. "I'd love to," he said. "But I don't know how. It would be the happiest day of my life if I could animate him in order that he be brought to justice."

She laughed out loud. "Them's my words," she said, referring to that day in Godall's shop. "Justice! We'll bring him justice, won't we, Willis?"

Willis nodded, wild with happiness now—partly, I thought, because of St. Ives's insisting that the doctor couldn't be awakened. Pule didn't want him awake. He picked up his bag of instruments and set it on the table. When he opened it, I could smell burnt rubber, and sure enough, he pulled out the hacked and charred fragments of the toy elephant and the little collection of gears, put back together now. "This is what I did to his elephant," he said, nodding at me, but looking at Higgins.

"Elephant?" Higgins said, casting me a terrified and wondering glance. This obscure reference to the elephant must have struck him as significant in some unfathomable way, largely because what Pule held in his hand no longer had anything to do with elephants. It was simply a limp bit of flayed rubber and paint.

I shrugged at Higgins and started to speak to the poor man, but Willis cut me off, shouting, "Shut up!" in a lunatic falsetto and blinking very fast and hard. He wasn't interested in hearing from me. He was caught up in his own twisted story, and he happily set about laying out an array of operating instruments—scalpels and clamps and something that looked a little like a bolt cutters and a little like a pruning shears and was meant, I guess, for clipping bone.

He made a bow in our direction, and, gesturing at Narbondo, he said, as if he were addressing a half score of students in a surgery, "I intend to affix this man's head to the fat man's body, and then to wake him up and make him look at himself in a mirror and see how ugly he is. Then I'm going to install this mechanism"—and here he plucked up the reassembled gears from the elephant—"in his heart, so that I can control him with a lever. And this man," Pule said, pointing at poor terrified and befuddled Higgins, "I'm going to cut apart and put together backward, so that he has to reach behind himself to button his shirt, and then I'm going to sell him to Mr. Happy's Circus."

Pule was madder than I thought him. What on earth did he mean by nonsense like "put him together backward"? It was clear that he could actually accomplish none of this. What real evidence was there that he had any skills in vivisection at all? None, and never had been—only his association with Narbondo, which proved nothing, of course, except that he was capable of committing vile acts. He was simply going to hack three men up—two of them alive at the moment—for the same utterly insane reasons that he had hacked up my elephant or that he chopped apart birds and hid them under the floorboards of his house. And he would do it all with relish—I was certain of it.

Poor Higgins was even more certain, it seemed, for just as soon as Pule mentioned this business about selling him to Mr. Happy's Circus, he began to utter a sort of low keening noise, a strange and mournful weeping. His eyes rolled back up into his head just as he slumped forward, tugging at the gaiters that held him to the chair, his voice rising another octave.

Mrs. Pule handed Willis the revolver, and he shifted the rifle to his left hand, not wanting to put it down. She picked up the dish of yellow chemical and advised Higgins to pipe down. But he couldn't, and so she splashed the stuff into Higgins's face, at which Higgins lurched upright, spitting and coughing, and she slapped him one, catching him mostly on the nose because of his twitching around. "Did you *hear* him?" she hissed.

"What! What! What!" cried Higgins, out of his mind now.

"You can save yourself," she said. "Or else..." She hunched over and whispered the rest of the sentence in his ear.

"Merciful Jesus! I'm what?" he shouted. "You're going to *what?* Mr. Happy!" His voice cracked. He began to gibber and moan.

They had gone too far. She had wanted to bargain with him, but she had made the mistake of driving him mad first, and now he was beyond bargaining. So she hit him again, twice—slap, slap—and he sat up straight and listened harder.

"The notebooks," she said. "Where are they?"

St. Ives cleared his throat, and very cheerfully, as if he were talking to a neighbor over the garden wall, he said, "I don't believe that the man knows..."

"Shut up!" she cried, turning on the three of us.

"Shut up!" cried her son, rapidly opening and closing his eyes and training the revolver on me, of all people; *I* hadn't said anything. I shrugged, very willing to shut up.

St. Ives was a different kettle of fish. "I mean to say, madam," he said, calmly and deliberately, "that Professor Higgins is utterly ignorant of the whereabouts of the notebooks. It was he who posted that letter to you, after he had revived the doctor. And since then he hasn't found them, although he's made a very pretty effort. Your torturing him now won't accomplish a thing, unless, as I suspect, you're torturing him for sport."

"You filthy..." she said, leaving it unfinished, and in a wild rage she snatched the revolver away from her son and pointed it at the professor. "You scum-sucking pig! You know *nothing*. I'll *start* with you, Mr. Hooknose, and then Willis will make a scarecrow of you."

She croaked out a laugh just as I lunged at her; don't ask me why I did it—making up for lost opportunities, maybe. I threw myself onto the revolver and grabbed it by the barrel, hitting her just as hard as I could on the jaw, which was plenty hard enough to knock her over backward.

Willis grappled with the rifle, but hadn't gotten it halfway up before Hasbro clipped him neatly on the side of the head, and he sank to his knees and slumped forward.

It was over, just like that. I'd had to hit a woman to accomplish it, but by heaven I would hit her once more, harder, if I had it to do again.

"Go for the constable, Jack," cried St. Ives, taking the revolver from me. "Bring him round, quick. I won't leave Narbondo's side, not until he's in a cell, sleeping or awake, I don't care."

I turned and started out, but didn't take more than a step, for the canvas pulled back, and there stood the constable himself, the one that had questioned me on the green, and Parsons stood with him, along with two sleepy-looking men who had obviously been routed out as deputies. For it had been Parsons who was lurking about, waiting for his chance. When it had got rough, and he had realized what a spot we had got ourselves into, he had himself run for the constable, and here they were, come round to save us now that we didn't want saving.

"I'll just take those weapons," said the constable, very officiously.

"Certainly," said St. Ives, handing over the revolver as if it were a snake.

Then there was a lot of talk about Narbondo, on the table, and a fetching of more ice, and a cataloging of the bits and pieces of scientific apparatus, and finally St. Ives couldn't stand it any longer and he asked Parsons, "The notebooks. You've got them, haven't you?"

Parsons shrugged.

"It was Piper, wasn't it? The oculist. He had got them from the old man, and had them all along. And when he died you came down and fetched them."

"Accurate to the last detail," said Parsons, smiling to think that at last he'd put one across St. Ives, that at last he had been in ahead of us. "What you *don't* know, my good fellow, is that I've destroyed them. They were a horror, a misapplication of scientific method, an abomination. I burned them in Dr. Piper's incinerator without bothering to read more than a snatch of them."

"Then it's my view," said St. Ives, "that Narbondo is dead, or as good as dead. How long he can last in this suspended state, I don't know, but it's clear that Higgins couldn't entirely revive him. Neither can I, and without the notebooks, thank God, neither can you."

Parsons shrugged again. "Keep him on ice," he said to the constable. "The Academy will want him. He'll make an interesting study."

The use of the word *study* had a Willis Pule ring to it that I didn't like, and I was reminded of what it was about Parsons that set the men of the Academy apart from a man like St. Ives. I was almost sorry that Narbondo at last had fallen into their hands.

St. Ives, however, didn't seem in the least sorry. "I suggest we retire to the Crown and Apple, then," he said. "I have a few bottles of ale in my room. I suggest that we sample it—toast Professor Parsons's success."

"Hear, hear," said Parsons, a little vainly, I thought, as we trooped out into the night, leaving the icehouse behind. In fact, though, a couple of bottles of ale and a few hours of sleep would settle me right out. Our adventure was over, and tomorrow, I supposed, it was back to London on the express. I patted my coat pocket, where I still had the proof of my reserving a room for me and Dorothy at The Hoisted Pint. You'd think that I would have had my fill of the place, but in fact I was determined to stay there as I'd planned, under happier circumstances, especially since whoever it was that we would find tending to the guests, it wouldn't be the woman who had hoodwinked me. The constable had already sent someone around to collect her.

* * *

o there we were, sitting in St. Ives's room, and him passing around opened bottles of ale, until he got to Parsons and said, "You're strictly a water man, aren't you?"

"You've got an admirable memory, sir. Water is the staff of life, the staff of life."

"And I've got a bottle of well water right here," said St. Ives, uncorking just such an object. Parsons was delighted. He took the glass that St. Ives gave him and swirled the water around in it, as if it were Scotch or Burgundy or some other drinkable substance. Then he threw it down heartily and smacked his lips like a connoisseur, immediately wrinkling up his face.

"Bitter," he said. "Must be French. Lucky I'm thirsty after tonight's little tussle." He held out his glass.

"Mineral water," said St. Ives, filling it up.

I was tempted to say something about "tonight's little tussle" myself, but I put a lid on it. Hasbro had fallen asleep in his chair.

Parsons winked at the professor. He was as full of himself as I've ever seen him. "About revivifying Narbondo," he said. "I've got a notion involving Lord Kelvin's machine. You've read of Sir Joseph John Thomson's work at the Cavendish Laboratory."

St. Ives's face betrayed what he was thinking, as if he had known that it would come to this, and here it was at last. "Yes," he said, "I have. Very interesting, but I don't quite see how it applies."

This made Parsons happy. To hear St. Ives admit such a thing was worth a lifetime of waiting and plotting. He had the face of a man holding four aces and looking at a table mounded with coin. "Electrons," he said, as if such a word explained everything.

"Go on," said the professor.

"Well, it's rather simple, isn't it? They spin sphere-wise around their atom. An intense electromagnetic field yanks them into a sort of oval, rather like the shifting of tides on the earth, and in animate creatures causes immediate and unrestrained cellular activity. What if Narbondo were subjected to such a force—a tremendous dose of electromagnetism? It might—how shall I put it?—'start him up,' let's say, like turning over an Otto's four-stroke engine."

"It might," said St. Ives darkly. "It might do a good deal more. I'll get directly to the point here; this isn't a matter for dalliance. The Academy undertook to start that damnable machine once, and to be straight with you, I had my man sabotage it. Do you remember?"

Of course Parsons remembered. It had been the incident of Lord Kelvin's machine that had caused the deepening of the chasm between the two men. Parsons looked almost sneery for a moment and said, "He loaded the contrivance with field mice, if I remember aright. Very effective, if a little bit—what?—primitive, maybe."

"Well," continued St. Ives, going right on, "some few of those field mice lived to tell the tale, as my friend Jack might put it. I carried on a study of them for almost two years in the fields round about the manor, until I was certain, finally, that the last of those poor creatures was dead, and what I discovered was a remarkably horrendous syndrome of mutations and cancers. It's my theory quite simply that this 'unrestrained cellular activity,' as you put it, is more likely ungovernable cellular growth. Your engine analogy may or may not apply. It doesn't matter. You simply cannot start the machine for any purpose, especially for something as frivolous as this. Leave Narbondo's fate in the hands of the Almighty, for heaven's sake."

"Frivolous!" shouted Parsons. "I don't give a rap for Narbondo's fate. Imagine, though, what this will mean. Here's poor Higgins, who has devoted a lifetime to the study of cryogenics. Here's Narbondo and a lifetime's study of chemistry. He was a monster, certainly, but so what? You must be a pitifully shortsighted scientist if you can't see the effect the sum total of their work will have on the future of the human race. And it's Lord Kelvin's machine that will usher in that future. To put it simply, my ship is putting in and I mean to board her." Parsons struck the arm of his chair with his fist to punctuate his speech. Then his eyes half closed and his head nodded forward. He shook himself awake and mumbled something about being suddenly sleepy, and then his head fell against his chest and straightaway he began to snore through his beard, having said, apparently, all he had to say.

The sight of him sleeping so profoundly put me in mind of my own bed, and I was just yawning and starting to say that I would turn in too, when St. Ives leaped to his feet, dropped an already-prepared letter into Parsons's lap and cried out, "It's time!" Then he roused Hasbro, who himself leaped up and headed straight for the door.

"Coming or not, Jacky?" asked the professor.

"Why, coming, I suppose. Where? Now?"

"To the Dover Strait. You can sleep on board."

With that he rushed into Parsons's room, coming back out with a bundle of the man's clothes, and I found myself following them through the night—out the backdoor of the inn, down along the seawall, and clambering into the tethered rowboat. Hasbro unshipped the oars and we were away, through the patchy fog, dipping along until the shadowy hull of a small steam trawler rose out of the mists ahead of us. We thunked into the side of her and clambered aboard, then winched up the rowboat after us. Up came the anchor, and I found myself saying hello to Hasbro's stalwart Aunt Edie and to the grizzled Uncle Botley, pilot of the trawler. Roped onto a little barge behind us rested the diving bell that we had stolen earlier that very night from the icehouse.

St. Ives had drugged poor Parsons. The water bottle had been doctored, and Parsons, in the joy of his victory, had swallowed enough of it to make him sleep for half a day. We would get into the Strait before him, towing the bell, and when we did...

PARSONS BIDS US ADIEU

We found the waters around the submerged machine alive with a half-dozen ships, all of them at anchor a good distance away. They had attached a buoy directly to it, to track it so as to avoid either losing it or coming too near it. We showed no hesitation at all, but steamed right up to the line. That was where I played my part, and played it tolerably well, I think.

Up onto the deck I came, wearing an enormous white beard and wig and dressed in Parsons's clothes, which St. Ives had stolen from his room at the Apple. St. Ives stayed hidden; his face would excite suspicion in any of a number of people. He coached me, though, from inside a cabin, and together we bluffed our way through that line of ships with a lot of what sounded to me like convincing talk about having learned how to "disarm" the machine and having brought along a diving bell for the purpose.

Anyway, certain that I was Parsons, they let us through right enough, and we navigated as close to the buoy as we dared, then set out in the rowboat, towing the barge with the bell standing straddle-legged atop the deck, the jib crane attached to the barge now with brass carriage bolts, its chain pulled off and replaced entirely with heavy line. We would have to be quick, though. Uncle Botley had removed as much iron from the rowboat and barge as he could manage, but there was still the chance that if we didn't look sharp, the machine would start to tug out nails and would scuttle us.

Hasbro and I manned the oars—work that I was admirably suited to from my days of punting on the Thames. They must have been surprised, though, to see old Parsons hauling away like that, given that he was upward of eighty-five years old. The idea of it amused me, and I pulled all the harder, watching over my shoulder as we drew slowly nearer to the buoy.

St. Ives was in the bell itself, making ready. His was the dangerous work. He was going down without air, because a compressor would have been pulled to pieces. But it was a shallow dive, and it wouldn't take him long. That was his claim, anyway. "Give me eight minutes by the pocket watch," he had told us, "and then pull me out of there. I can go down again if need be. And," he said darkly, "if the rowboat starts to go to pieces, or if there's trouble down below, cut the line and get away as quick as you can."

Hasbro insisted at once on going with him, as did I, neither one of us keen on getting away. But that wasn't St. Ives's method and never had been. He was still in a funk because of the time he thought we had wasted and because of the two ships that had gone down needlessly. And there was the fact of his—as he saw it—having allowed the machine to exist all these years, sitting placidly in that machine works, only to be stolen and misused. He was the responsible party, and he would brook no nonsense to the contrary. There was a certain psychological profit, then, in his going down and facing the danger alone; his face seemed to imply that if something went wrong and we had to leave him, well, so be it; it was no more than he deserved.

Then there was the business of Alice, wasn't there? It hovered over the man's head like a rain cloud, and I believe that I can say, without taking anything away from his natural courage, that St. Ives didn't care two figs whether he lived or died.

And although in truth I had no idea how much air one working man would breathe at a depth of eight fathoms, I accepted his assurances that two men would breathe twice as much and increase the dangers accordingly. The controls were meant for a single man, too, and St. Ives had been studying and manipulating them all the way out from Sterne Bay. Hasbro and I would have been nothing but dangerous baggage, trying to demonstrate our loyalty by our willingness to die along with him, if it came to that. He didn't need any such demonstrations.

Down he went, into the dark ocean. One of the handlike armatures of the bell held on to a bundle of explosives wrapped in sheet rubber and sealed with asphaltum varnish. There was a timing device affixed to it. St. Ives had never meant to "disarm" the machine at all. He had meant all along to blow it to kingdom come, and he had stolen Higgins's bell for just that purpose.

The Strait was blessedly placid—just a trace of wind and a slightly rolling ground swell. Line played slowly out through the oaken blocks, and we watched the bell hover deeper, down toward the vast black shadow below. I hadn't expected quite what I saw—a sort of acreage of shadow down there, but then I realized that what I saw wasn't merely the machine, but was a heap of derelict iron ships clustered together, the whole heap lying, I supposed, on a sandy shoal.

And that was why St. Ives hadn't done the obvious—merely

wrapped a hunk of iron into that package of explosives and tossed it over the side. It might easily have affixed itself to the hull of a downed ship and blown it up, leaving the machine alone. What the professor had to do was drop onto the machine itself, or grapple his way to it by the use of the bell's armatures, and plant the explosives just so; otherwise they were wasted. Eight minutes didn't seem like such a long time after all.

But then the line went suddenly slack and began to coil onto the top of the water. St. Ives had hooked on to something—the machine, a ship. All of us studied our pocket watches.

You'd think that the minutes would have flown by, but they didn't; they crept. The breeze blew, clouds slipped across the sky, the loose circle of ships rolled on the calm waters, no one aboard them suspecting who I really was in my beard and wig. Hasbro counted the minutes aloud, and Uncle Botley stood at the winch. At the count of eight the three of us put our backs into it. The line went quivering-taut, spraying droplets. The blocks groaned and creaked. The bell very slowly swam into view, and in a rush of ocean water it burst out into the air, St. Ives visible within, the explosive package gone. He had either succeeded or failed utterly; it didn't matter which, not at the moment.

Thunk went the bell onto the deck, and while Uncle Botley lashed it down, Hasbro and I bent to the oars and had that barge fairly skimming, if I do say so myself. There's nothing like a spot of work when you know what the devil you're doing and, of course, when there's an explosion pending.

A cheer went up from the ships waiting in a circle around us, and I took my hat off and waved it in the air, my wig nearly blowing away in the sea wind. I clapped the hat back down and gave up the histrionics, hauling us through the chop, bang up against the hull of our trawler. We clambered aboard, taking the barge in tow and setting out at once.

We didn't leave St. Ives in the bell, of course. He climbed out at the last possible minute, taking the risk now of being seen. "Let's go," he said simply, and into the cabin he went as I took up the speaking trumpet and started to shout at the nearest ship, on which a half-dozen men stood at attention along the rail, and a captain or some such thing awaited orders. In my best Parsons voice, helpfully disguised by the speaking tube, I gave him all the orders he needed—that we had set into motion the disarming of the machine, but that its excess electromagnetic energies would reach capacity just before she shut down. Move away, is what I told him, for safety's sake, or risk going to the bottom!

That drew their attention. I think they would have run for it even if my beard had been plucked off right then by a sea gull. Flags were run up; whistles blew; men scrambled across the decks of the several ships, which began to make away another quarter of a mile, just as I told them, where they would await orders. We kept right on going—steaming back toward Sterne Bay. That must have confounded them, our racing off like that. For my money, though, it didn't confound them half as much as did the explosion that followed our departure. We were well away by then, on the horizon, but we saw the plume of water, and then heard the distant whump of the concussion.

So Lord Kelvin's machine was nothing but sinking fragments, an instant neighborhood for the denizens of the sea. Dr. Narbondo would continue his cold sleep until whatever it was that animated him had played itself out. Parsons, poor man, wouldn't be at the helm of whatever grand ship he had imagined himself piloting into the harbor of scientific fame. His schemes were a ruin—blown to pieces. Even his victory over St. Ives had been a short-lived one—toasted to with drugged water.

St. Ives wasn't happy with that part. He felt guilty about Parsons, and he felt even worse that Narbondo would sleep through what ought to have been his public trial and execution. Ah well, I was happy enough. I wasn't fond of Parsons in the first place, and had rather enjoyed parading around in the beard and wig. I wish there had been some way to let him know about that, just to make him mad, but I guess there wasn't. He would hear most of it, likely enough, but he probably wouldn't guess it had been me, and that was too bad.

We landed in Sterne Bay, our business done. And we parted company with Hasbro's aunt and with Uncle Botley. At the Crown and Apple we found a note under St. Ives's door—the same note, in fact, that St. Ives had left on Parsons's lap. The old man had scrawled on it the words, "I'm on the afternoon train to London; you might have the kindness to see me off." Just that. You would have expected more—some little bit of anger or regret—given what St. Ives had revealed to him. But there was no anger, just the words of a sad man asking for company.

We hurried down to the station to do his bidding. It was the least we could do. His just giving in like that made the business doubly sorrowful, and although I was tempted for a moment to wear them, I left the beard and wig at the Apple.

The train was chuffing there on the track, the passengers already boarded. We ran along the platform. St. Ives was certain that there was some good reason for Parsons's having summoned him, and that it was his duty, our duty, after exploding Parsons's dreams, to see what it was that the old man wanted, what last tearful throwing-in-the-towel statement he would utter. Let him complain to our faces, I thought, taking the long view. He had been riding high just yesterday, astride his charger, but now, as they say, the mighty had fallen. The race was not always to the swift. Parsons could have his say; I wouldn't begrudge him.

But where was he? The cars were moving along. We trotted beside them, keeping up, out toward the empty tracks ahead, the train chugging forward and away. Then, as the last car but one rolled past, a window slid down, and there was Parsons's face grinning out at us like a winking devil. "Haw! Haw! Haw!" he shouted, apparently having run mad, the poor bastard.

Then he dangled out the window a bound notebook, tattered and old-looking. Streaked across it in faded ink was the name "John Kenyon," written in fancy-looking heavy script—the name, of course, of Mrs. Pule's derelict father. Despite what was utterly obvious, and thinking to put on a show of being interested in the old man's apparent glee, I was witless enough to yell, "What is it?" as we watched the train pick up speed and move away from us toward London.

And he had the satisfaction of leaning out even farther in order to make a rude gesture at us, shouting in a sort of satisfied whinny, "What the hell do you think it is, idiot?" Then the damned old fool drew the notebook in and slammed the window shut, clipping off the sound of his own howling laughter.

The train bore Parsons away to London, along with—if the half-frozen doctor had only been aware of his victory, of this renewed promise of resurrection—the gloating still-animate body of Ignacio Narbondo.

PART III

THE TIME TRAVELER

IN THE NORTH SEA

Air hissed through rubber tubing like the wheezing of a mechanical man. There was the odor of machine oil and metal in the air, mixed with the damp aquarium smell of seawater seeping slowly past riveted joints and rubber seals. The ocean lay silent and cold and murky beyond porthole windows, and St. Ives fought off the creeping notion that he had been encased in a metal tomb.

One of the bathyscaphe's jointed arms clanked against the brass hull with a dull echo, a sound from a distant world. St. Ives felt it in his teeth. He smeared cold sweat from his forehead and focused his mind on his task—recovering Lord Kelvin's machine from the debris-covered sandbar forty feet beneath the Dover Strait. The hulks of three ships lay roundabout, one of them blown apart by the dynamite bomb that St. Ives had dropped into its hold six months past.

He pulled a lever in the floor, feeling and hearing the metallic ratchet of the pair of retractable feet that thrust out from the base of the bathyscaphe. Laboriously, inch by inch, the spherical device hopped across the ocean floor. Fine sand swirled up, obscuring the portholes, and for the space of a minute St. Ives could see nothing at all. He shut his eyes and pressed his hands to his temples, aware again of the swish of air through tubing and of the sound of blood pounding in his head. He felt a great pressure, all imaginary, but nonetheless real for that, and he began to breathe rapidly and shallowly, fighting down a surge of panic. The portholes cleared, and a school of John Dory lazied past, gaping in at him, studying him as if he were a textbook case on the extravagances of human folly...

"Stop it!" he said out loud. His voice rang off the brass walls, and he peered forward, trying to work the looped end of line around the far side of the machine.

"Pardon me, sir?" The stalwart voice of Hasbro sounded through the speaking tube.

"Nothing. It's close down here."

"Perhaps if I had a go at it, sir?"

"No. It's nothing. I'm at the end of it."

"Very well," the voice said doubtfully.

He let go of the line, and it slowly sank across the copper shell of the machine, drifting off the far edge and settling uselessly on the ocean floor. Failure—he would have to try again. He closed his eyes and sat for a moment, thinking that he could easily fall asleep. Then the idea of sleep frightened him, and he looked around himself, taking particular note of the dials and levers and gauges. He needed something solid to use as ballast for his mind— something outside, something comfortable and homely.

Abruptly he thought of food, of cottage pie and a bottle of beer. With effort, he began to think through the recipe for cottage pie, reciting it to himself. It wouldn't do to talk out loud. Hasbro would haul him straight out of the water. He pictured the pie in his head—the mashed potatoes whipped with cream and butter, the farmer's cheese melted across the top. He poured a mental beer into a glass, watching it foam up over the top and spill down the sides. Keeping the image fresh, he pulled in the line again, working diligently until he gripped the noose once more. Then, slowly, he carried it back out with the mechanical hand. He dropped it carefully, and this time it floated down to encircle a solid piece of outthrust metal.

"Cottage pie," he muttered.

"I'm sorry, sir?"

"Got its… eye," he said weakly, realizing that this sounded even more lunatic than what he *had* said. It didn't matter, though. He was almost through. Already the feeling of desperation and confinement was starting to lift. Carefully, he clamped on to the line again, pulling it tight inch by inch, working steadily to close the loop. If he could attend to his work he would be on the surface in ten minutes. Five minutes.

"Up we go," he said, loud this time, like a sea captain, and in a matter of seconds there was a jolt, and the bathyscaphe tilted just a little, lifting off the ocean floor. It rose surfaceward in little jerks, and the school of John Dory followed it up, nosing against the portholes. St. Ives was struck suddenly by how friendly the fish were, nosing against the glass like that. God bless a fish, he thought, keeping a man company. The water brightened around him, and the feeling of entombment began to dissipate. He breathed deeply, watching bubbles rush past now and the fish turn in a school and dart away. Suddenly the wave-lapped surface of the gray ocean tossed across the porthole, and then the sea gave way to swirling fog, illuminated by a morning sun and enlivened by the muffled sound of water streaming off the sides of the bathyscaphe. Then there was the solid clunk of metal feet settling on a wooden deck.

St. Ives opened the hatch and climbed out, and immediately he and Hasbro swung the dripping bathyscaphe across the deck so as to make room for Lord Kelvin's machine. They unfastened it from the jib crane and lashed it down solidly, hiding it beneath oiled canvas, working frenziedly while the sun threatened to burn off the fog and to reveal their efforts to the light of day. Hurrying, they fixed the line that grappled Lord Kelvin's machine to the jib crane and set about hauling it out of the water, too, afterward hiding it beneath more tied down canvas.

In another twenty minutes the steam trawler, piloted by the man that St. Ives knew as Uncle Botley, made off northward. St. Ives remained on deck for a time, watching through the mist. Soon they would be far enough from the site that they could almost pretend to be innocent—to have been out after fish.

It had been six months since anyone from the Royal Academy had been lurking in the area. So they ought to have been safe; the issue of the machine was officially closed. Yet St. Ives was possessed with the notion that he would be discovered anyway, that there was something he had missed, that his plans to save Alice would fail if he wasn't vigilant night and day. Fears kept revealing themselves to him, like cards turned up in a deck. He kept watch for another hour while the fog dissipated on the sea wind. The horizon, when he could see it, was empty of ships in every direction.

Exhausted, he went below deck and fell into a bunk as the trawler steamed toward Grimsby, bound, finally, up the Humber to Goole. In three days he would be home again, such as it was, in Harrogate. Then the real work would start. Secrecy now was worth—what? His life, pretty literally. Alice's life. They would transport the machine overland from Goole, after disguising it as a piece of farm machinery. Even so, they would keep it hidden beneath canvas. No one could be trusted. Even the most innocent bumpkin could be a spy for the Royal Academy.

When they reached the environs of Harrogate they would wait for nightfall, sending Kraken ahead to scout out the road. That's when the danger would be greatest, when they got to within hailing distance of the manor. If the Academy was laying for St. Ives, that's where they would hide, waiting to claim what was theirs. How desperate would they be? More to the point, how far would St. Ives go to circumvent them?

He knew that there were no steps that Parsons wouldn't take in order to retrieve the machine. If Parsons knew, that is, that the machine was retrievable. For the fiftieth time St. Ives calculated the possibility of that, ending up, as usual, awash with doubts. Parsons was a doddering cipher. He had out-tricked St. Ives badly in Sterne Bay, and the only high card left to St. Ives now was the machine itself. Parsons hadn't expected St. Ives to destroy it, and he certainly couldn't have expected St. Ives to *pretend* to destroy it. Perhaps he should pretend to destroy it again, and so confuse the issue utterly. He could spend the remainder of his life pretending to have destroyed and recovered the machine. They could scuttle Uncle Botley's trawler after transferring the machine to some other vessel, making Parsons believe that it was still on board. Of course, Parsons didn't know it was on board in the first place; they would have to find a way to reveal that. Then they could pretend to pretend to scuttle the ship, maybe not move the machine off at all, but only pretend to…

He tossed in his bunk, his mind aswirl with nonsense. Finally the sea rocked him to sleep, settling his mind. Water swished and slapped against the hull, and the ship creaked as it rose and fell on the ground swell. The noises became part of a dream—the sounds of a coach being driven hard along a black and muddy street.

He was alone on a rainy night in the Seven Dials, three years past. At first he thought his friends were with him, but around him now lay nothing but darkness and the sound of rain. There was something—he squinted into the night. A shop window. He could see his own reflection, frightened and helpless, and behind him the street, rain pelting down. The rainy curtain drew back as if across a darkened theater stage, and a picture formed in the dusty window glass: a cabriolet overturned in the mud, one spoked wheel spinning round and round past the upturned face of a dead woman...

He jerked up out of his bunk, fighting for breath. "Cottage pie," he said out loud. Damn anyone who might hear him. What did they know? He was a man alone. In the end, that was what had proved to be true. It wasn't anybody's fault; it was the way of the world. He lay down again, feeling the ship rise on the swell. He thought hard about the pie, about the smell of thyme and rosemary and sage simmering in a beef broth, about the herb garden that Alice had started and that was now up in weeds. He hadn't given much of a damn about food before he knew Alice, but she had got him used to it. He had kept the herb garden flourishing for a month or so, in her memory. But keeping the memory was somehow worse than fleeing from it. Moles were living in the garden now—a whole village of them.

He drifted off to sleep again, dreaming that he watched the moles through the parlor window. One of them had the face and spectacles of old Parsons. It pretended to be busy with mole activities, but it regarded him furtively over the top of its spectacles. Away across the grounds lay the River Nidd, fringed with willows.

Through them, his beard wagging, stepped Lord Kelvin himself, striding along toward the manor with the broad ever-approaching gait of a man in a dream. He wasn't in a jolly mood, clearly not coming round to chat about the theory of elasticity or the constitution of matter. He carried a stick, which he beat against the palm of his hand.

Willing to take his medicine, St. Ives stepped out into the garden to meet him, nearly treading on the mole that looked like Parsons. Weeds crackled underfoot and the day was dreary and dim, almost as if the whole world were dilapidated. This wasn't going to be pretty. Lord Kelvin wasn't a big man, and he was getting on in years, but there was a fierce look in his eyes that seemed to say, in a Glasgow brogue, "You've blown my machine to pieces. Now I'm going to beat the dust out of you."

What he said was, "I spent twenty-odd years on that engine, lad. I'm too old to start again." His face was saddened, full of loss.

St. Ives nodded. One day, maybe, he would give it back to the man. But he couldn't tell him that now.

"I'm truly sorry…" he began.

"Ye can't imagine what it was, man." He gestured with the stick, which had turned into a length of braided copper wire.

On the contrary, St. Ives had imagined what it was on the day that he walked into Lord Kelvin's barn, looking to ruin it. He took the braided wire from the old man, but it fell apart in his hands, dropping in strands across his shoes.

"We might have gone anywhere in it," the old man said wistfully. "The two of us. Traveled across time…" He could be open and honest now that he thought the machine was blasted to pieces. There was nothing to hide anymore. St. Ives let him talk. It was making them both feel better, filling St. Ives with remorse and happiness at the same time: the two of them, traveling together, side by side, back to the Age of Reptiles, forward to a day when men would sail among the stars. St. Ives had worked too long in obscurity, shunned by the Academy and so pretending to despise it—but all the time pounding on the door, crying to be let in. That was the sad truth, wasn't it? Here was its foremost member, Lord Kelvin himself, talking like an old and trusted colleague.

Lord Kelvin nodded his head, which turned into a quadrant electrometer. In his hand he held a mariner's compass of his own invention. The needle pointed east with awful, mystifying significance.

"I knew what it... what it was," St. Ives said remorsefully. "But I wanted the machine for myself, to work my own ends, not yours. I've given up science for personal gain." He couldn't help being truthful.

"You'll never be raised to the peerage with that attitude, lad."

St. Ives noticed suddenly that the mole with Parsons's face was studying him out of its squinty little eyes. Hurriedly, it turned around and scampered away across the meadow, carrying a suitcase. Lord Kelvin looked at his pocket watch, which swung on the end of a length of transatlantic cable. "If he hurries he can catch the 2:30 train to London. He'll arrive in time."

He showed the pocket watch to St. Ives. The crystal was enormous, nearly as big as the sky, filling the landscape, distorting the images behind it like a fishbowl. St. Ives squinted to make things out. The hands of the watch jerked around their course, ticking loudly. Behind them, on the watch face, a figure moved through the darkness of a rainy night. It was St. Ives himself, wading through ankle-deep water. It was fearsomely slow going. Like quicksand, the water clutched his ankles. Going round and round in his head was a hailstorm of regrets—if only the ships hadn't gone down, if he hadn't missed his train, if he hadn't come to ruin on the North Road, if he could tear himself loose now from the grip of this damnable river... He wiped rainwater out of his eyes. Crouched before him in the street was Ignacio Narbondo, a smoking pistol in his hand and a look of insane triumph on his face.

St. Ives jackknifed awake again. The air of the cabin was cold and wet, and for a moment he imagined he was once more in the bathyscaphe, on the bottom of the sea. But then he heard Uncle Botley shout and then laugh, and the voice, especially the laughter, seemed to St. Ives to be a wonderful fragment of the living world— something he could get a grip on, like a cottage pie.

St. Ives studied his face in the mirror on the wall. He was thin and sallow. He felt a quick surge of terror without an object, and he realized abruptly that he had gotten old. He seemed to have the face of his father. "Time and chance happeneth to them all," he muttered, and he went out on deck in the gathering night, where the lights of Grimsby slipped past off the starboard bow, and the waters of the Humber lost themselves in the North Sea.

THE SAVING OF BINGER'S DOG

St. Ives sat in the chair in his study. It was a dim and wintry day outside, with rain pending and the sky a uniform gray. He had been at work on the machine for nearly six months, and success loomed on the horizon now like a slowly approaching ship. There had been too little sleep and too many missed or hastily eaten meals. His friends had rallied around him, full of concern, and he had gone on in the midst of all that concern, implacably, like a rickety millwheel. Jack and Dorothy were on the Continent now, though, and Bill Kraken was off to the north, paying a visit to his old mother. There was a fair chance that he wouldn't see any of them again. The thought didn't distress him. He was resigned to it.

A fly circled lazily over the clutter on the desk, and St. Ives whacked at it suddenly with a book, knocking it to the floor. The fly staggered around as if drunk. In a fit of remorse, St. Ives scooped it up on a sheet of paper, walked across and opened the French window, and then dumped the fly out into the bushes. "Go," he said hopefully to the fly, which buzzed around aimlessly, somewhere down in the bushes.

St. Ives stood breathing the wet air and staring out onto the meadow at the brick silo that rose there crumbling and lonely, full to the top with scientific aspirations and pretensions. It looked to him like a sorry replica of the Tower of Babel. Inside it lay Lord Kelvin's machine, along with Higgins's bathyscaphe. St. Ives had removed and discarded most of the shell of the machine, hauling the useless telltale debris away by night. What was left was nearly ready; he had only to wheedle what might be called fine points out of the gracious Lord Kelvin who would abandon Harrogate for Glasgow tomorrow morning.

St. Ives hadn't slept in two days. Dreaming had very nearly cured him of sleep. There would be time enough for sleep, though. Either that, or there wouldn't be. On impulse, he left the window open, thinking to show other flies that he harbored no ill will toward them, and then he slumped back across to the chair and sat down heavily, sinking so that he rested on his tailbone. A shock of hair fell across his eyes, obscuring his vision. He harrowed it backward with his fingers, then nibbled at a grown-out nail, tearing it off short and taking a fragment of skin with it. "Ouch," he said, shaking his hand, but then losing interest in it almost at once. For a long time he sat there, thinking about nothing.

Coming to himself, finally, he surveyed the desktop. It was a clutter of stuff—tiny coils and braids of wire, miniature gauges, pages torn out of books, many of which torn pages now marked places in other books. There was an army of tiny clockwork toys littering the desktop, built out of tin by William Keeble. Half of them were a rusted ruin, the victims of an experiment he had performed three weeks past. St. Ives looked at them suspiciously, trying to remember what he had meant to prove by spraying them with brine and then leaving them on the roof.

He had waked up in the middle of the night with a notion involving the alteration of matter, and had spent an hour meddling with the toys, leaving them, finally, on the roof before going back to bed, exhausted. In the morning, somehow, he had forgotten about them. And then, days later, he had seen them from out on the meadow, still lying on the roof, and although he remembered having put them there, and having been possessed with the certainty that putting them there was good and right and useful, he couldn't for the life of him recall why.

That sort of thing was bothersome—periods of awful lucidity followed by short bursts of rage or by wild enthusiasm for some theoretical notion having to do with utter nonsense. Moodily, he poked at the windup duck, which whirred momentarily to life, and then fell over onto its side. There were ceramic figures, too, sitting among comical Toby mugs and glass gewgaws, some few of which had belonged to Alice. Balls of crumpled paper lay everywhere, along with broken pens and graphite crumbs and fragments of India-rubber erasers. A lake of spilled ink had long ago dried beneath it all, staining the brown oak of the desktop a rich purple.

Filled with a sudden sense of purpose, he reached out and swept half the desk clear, the books and papers and tin toys tumbling off onto the floor. Carefully, he straightened the glass and ceramic figurines, setting a little blue-faced doggy alongside a Humpty Dumpty with a ruff collar. He stood a tiptoeing ballerina behind them, and then, in the foreground, he lay a tiny glass shoe full of sugar crystals. He sat back and looked at the collection, studying it. There was something in it that wasn't quite satisfying, that wasn't—what? Proportionate, maybe. He turned the toe of the glass shoe just a bit. Almost… He rotated the Humpty Dumpty so that it seemed to be regarding the ballerina, then slid the dog forward so that its head rested on the toe of the shoe.

That was it. On the instant, meaning had evolved out of simple structure. Something in the little collection reminded him of something else. What? Domestic tranquillity. Order. He smiled and shook his head nostalgically, yearning for something he couldn't recall. The comfortable feeling evaporated into the air. The nostalgia, poignant as it had been for that one moment, wasn't connected to anything at all, and was just so much vapor, an abstraction with no concrete object. It was gone now, and he couldn't retrieve it. Maybe later he would see it again, when he wasn't trying so hard.

Frowning, he returned to the window where he worked his fingers through his hair again. There was a broken limb on the bush where he had dropped the fly, as if someone had stepped into it clumsily. For a moment he was puzzled. There hadn't been any broken limb a half hour ago.

A surge of worried excitement welled up in him, and he stepped out through the window, looking up and down along the wall of the house. Here he is again! he said to himself. No one was visible, though.

He sprinted to the corner, bursting quickly past it to catch anyone who might still be lurking. He looked about himself wildly for a moment and then ran straight toward the carriage house and circled entirely around it. The door was locked, so he didn't bother going in, but headed out onto the meadow instead straightaway toward the silo. He realized that he should have fetched Hasbro along with him, or at any rate brought a weapon.

He had left the silo doors double-locked, though. They were

visible from the house, too—both from the study and from St. Ives's bedroom upstairs. Hasbro's quarters also looked out onto the meadow, and Mrs. Langley could see the silo from the kitchen window. St. Ives had been too vigilant for anyone to have... And no one had. The doors were still locked, the locks untouched. Carefully, he inspected the ground finding stray shoeprints here and there. He stepped into them, realizing only then that he was in his stocking feet. Still, there was one set of prints that were smaller even than his unshod foot. They wouldn't belong to Hasbro, then. Possibly they were Bill Kraken's, except that Kraken was up in Edinburgh and these prints were fresh. Parsons! It had to be Parsons, snooping around again. Who else could it be? No one.

Finally he jogged off toward his study window, pounding his fist over and over into his hand in a fit of nervous energy. His mind was a turmoil of conflict. He *had* to sort things out... The ground outside the French windows was soft, kept wet by water falling off the overhanging eaves. A line of shoeprints paralleled the wall, as if someone had come sneaking along it, stepping onto the bush in order to sandwich himself in toward the window without being seen. In his excitement St. Ives hadn't seen the prints, but he stooped to examine them now. The toes were pressed deeply into the dirt, so whoever it was had been hunched over forward, keeping low, moving slowly and heavily. Small shoeprints again, though. Certainly not his own.

St. Ives hurried back into the study. He opened a desk drawer and rooted through it, pulling out papers and books until he found a cloth-wrapped parcel. He pulled the cloth away, revealing four white plaster-of-Paris shoeprint casts. He turned them over, and, on the bottom, printed neatly in ink, were dates and place-names. The first set was dated six months past, taken in Sterne Bay from the dirt outside the icehouse. The second pair were taken a week past, down along the River Nidd. They were from different pairs of shoes of the same size.

He put the first pair back into the drawer and carried the second outside, laying them into appropriate prints. They settled in perfectly. On his hands and knees he squinted closely at one of the heel prints in the dirt. The back outside corner of the heel was gone, worn away, so that the heel print looked like someone's family crest, but with a quarter of the shield lopped away. An image leaped into his mind of Parsons walking along in his usual bandy-legged gait, scuffing the leather off the corners of his heels. The heels on the plaster casts were worn out absolutely identically. There couldn't be any doubt, or almost none. Parsons had come snooping around. He couldn't have been entirely positive that the man he had seen skulking along the river had been Parsons. It had been late evening, and drizzling. Whoever it had been, though, it was the same man who, within the last half hour or so, had sneaked along the wall of the house, stepped into the bush and broke off the limb, and then, no doubt, peered in at the window.

He climbed back into the room, rewrapping the plaster casts and closing them up in the drawer. Then, pulling on his coat, he strode out across the meadow once again like a man with a will, noticing only when he was halfway to the River Nidd that he still wasn't wearing any shoes.

He returned late that afternoon in an improved mood, although he felt agitated and anxious. He had spent three hours with Lord Kelvin. The great scientist had come to understand that tragedy had turned St. Ives into a natural fool. He had even patted St. Ives on the head once, which had been humiliating, but to some little extent St. Ives had been grateful for it—a sign, he realized, of how dangerously low his spirits had fallen. But things were looking up now. His efforts weren't doomed after all, although he was certain that he was running a footrace with Parsons and the Royal Academy. When they were sure of themselves, they would merely break down the silo door—come out with a dozen soldiers and checkmate him. The game would be at an end.

The idea of it once again darkened his thoughts. His elation at having swindled Lord Kelvin out of certain tidbits of information suddenly lapsed, and he slumped into his chair feeling fatigued and beaten. He seemed to swing between two extremes—doom and utter confidence. Middle ground had become the rarest sort of real estate. What he needed, desperately, was to be levelheaded, and here he was atilt again, staggering off course.

Tomorrow, though, or the next day, he would set out. Right now he would rest. Lord Kelvin had taken pity on him this afternoon. That was the long and the short of it. One look at St. Ives's face, at his disheveled clothes, and Lord Kelvin had been ready to discuss anything at all, as if he were talking to the village idiot. The man had a heart like a hay wagon, to be sure. St. Ives's wandering over without any shoes on had probably done the trick. Kelvin had finally warmed to the subject of time travel, and St. Ives had led him through a discussion of the workings of the machine itself as if he were a trained ape.

That was clever, he told himself, going out shoeless was. He half believed it for a moment. Then he knew that it hadn't been clever at all; he had gone out shoeless without meaning to, and in late autumn, yet. He would have to watch that sort of thing. They'd have him tied down in Colney Hatch if he wasn't careful. He was too close to success. He couldn't chance a strait-waistcoat. Seeing things clearly for the moment, he looked at himself in the cheval glass on the desk. A haircut wouldn't be a bad idea, either. Perhaps if a man affected sanity carefully enough…

Almost happy again, he stepped into his slippers and lit a pipe, sitting back and puffing on it. Failure—that's what had squirreled him up. Too much failure made a hash of a man's mind… He thought for a moment about his manifold failures, and suddenly and inexplicably he was awash with fear, with common homegrown panic. He found that he could barely keep his hands still.

Immediately, he tried to recite the cottage-pie recipe, finding that he couldn't remember it. He pulled a scrap of paper from his shirt pocket and studied the writing on it. There it was—sage and sweet basil. Not sweetbread. He could feel his heart flutter like a bird's wings, and he felt faint and light-headed. Desperately, he breathed for a moment into a sack until the light-headedness began to abate. Sweetbread? Why had he thought of sweetbread? That was some kind of gland, wasn't it? Something the French ate, probably out of buckets and without the benefit of forks.

With an unpleasant shock, he noticed just then that someone had cleaned up his desk. The debris on the floor was separated into tidy piles against the wall. The papers were shuffled, and the books stacked. The glass and ceramic figurines were dusted and lined up together. The neatened desk baffled him for a moment. Then, slowly, a dark rage began to rise in him, and the whole business of an orderly desk became an affront.

He bent down and tossed together the stuff on the floor, mixing it into a sort of salad. Then he kicked through it, sending it flying, winding himself up. He turned to the desk itself, methodically picking up books and shaking out the loose leaves so that they fluttered down higgledy-piggledy. He picked up a heavy iron elephant paperweight and one by one smashed his quill pens, accidentally catching the squared-off edge of the crystal ink bottle and smashing it too, so that ink spewed out across his shirtfront. The shock of smashing the glass made him bite down hard on the stem of his pipe. He heard and felt the stem crack, and quickly let up on it. The pipe fell neatly into two pieces, though, so that the stem stayed in his mouth and the bowl fell down onto the desktop, wobbling around in the ink and broken glass like a drunkard. Furious, he picked up the elephant again and smashed the pipe, over and over and over, until he noticed with a deep rush of demoralizing embarrassment that Mrs. Langley stood in the open door of the room, her eyes wide open with horror and disbelief.

Coldly he put the elephant down and turned to her, realizing without knowing why that she had become an obstruction to him. Somehow, his rage had been transferred en masse to the housekeeper, to Mrs. Langley. He had no need for a housekeeper. He saw that clearly. What he had a need for was to be left alone. His desk, his books, his things, wanted to be left alone. Soon he would be gone altogether, perhaps never to return. A page in his life was folding back, a chapter coming to a close. The world was rife with change.

And this wasn't the first time that she had cut this sort of caper. He had spoken to her about it before. Well, the woman had been warned, hadn't she? There wouldn't be any need to speak to her about it again. "As of this moment, Mrs. Langley," he said to her flatly, "you are relieved of your duties. You'll have three months' severance pay."

She put her hand to her mouth, and he realized that his eye

was twitching badly and that every muscle in his body was stiff with tension, his hands opening and closing spasmodically. He gestured toward the window, the open road. "*Must* you stare so?" he demanded of her.

"He's gone stark," she muttered through her fingers.

He clenched his teeth. "I have *not* gone stark," he said. "Understand that! I have *not* gone stark!" Even as he said it, there flickered across his mind a vague understanding of what it meant—that he *had* gone mad, utterly. He wasn't quite sane enough to admit it, though, to hold on to the notion. He was too far around the bend to see it anymore, but could merely glimpse its shadow. He knew only that he couldn't have Mrs. Langley meddling with his things, chasing after him with a dust mop as if he wanted a keeper. He watched her leave, very proudly, with her head up. She wasn't the sort to forgive easily. She would be gone, up to her sisters. Well… For a moment he nearly called her back, but was having difficulty breathing again. He put his head into the sack.

After a moment he sat back down in his chair and contrived to rearrange the four objects amid the clutter on the desktop. His hand shook violently, though, and he accidentally uncorked the glass shoe, spilling out half the sugar crystals. Then he knocked the Humpty Dumpty over twice. He concentrated, making himself breathe evenly, placing the objects just so. Surely, if he could get them right, he would regain that moment of indefinable satisfaction that he had felt a few hours past. It would settle him down, restore a sense of proportion. It wouldn't work, though. He couldn't manage it.

He forced himself to concentrate on the desktop again. There was something in the arrangement that was subtly wrong. The figurines stood there as ever, the dog with his head on the shoe, the

Humpty Dumpty gazing longingly at the ballerina. But there was no pattern any longer, no art to it. It was as if the earth had turned farther along its axis and the shadows were different.

He found his shoes, putting them on this time before going out. Work was the only mainstay. He would let Mrs. Langley stew for a while and then would commute her sentence. She must learn not to treat him like a child. Meanwhile he would concentrate on something that would yield a concrete result. With effort, with self-control, he would have what he wanted within twenty-four hours. Where the machine would take him was an utter mystery. Probably he would be blown to fragments. Or worse yet, the machine would turn out to be so much junk, sitting there in the silo with him at the controls, making noises out of his throat like a child driving a locomotive built out of packing crates. He stood by the window, focusing his mind. There wasn't time to regret this business with Mrs. Langley. There wasn't time to regret anything at all. There was only time for action, for movement.

His hands had stopped shaking. As an exercise, he coldly and evenly forced himself to recite the metals in the order of their specific gravities. The cottage-pie recipe was well and good when a man needed a simple mental bracer. But what he wanted now was honing. He needed his edges sharpened. With that in mind, he worked through the metals again, listing them in the order of their fusibility this time, then again backward through both lists, practicing a kind of dutiful self-mesmerization.

Halfway through, he realized that something was wrong with him. He was light-headed, woozy. He held on to the edge of the desk, thinking to wait it out. He watched his hand curiously. It seemed to be growing transparent, as if he had the flesh of a jelly-fish. It was happening to him again—the business on the North

Road, the ghostly visitation. His vision was clouded, as if he were under water. He slid to the floor and began to crawl toward the window. Maybe fresh air would revive him. Each foot, though, was a journey, and all at once his arms and legs gave way beneath him and he slumped to the floor, giving up and lying there unhappily in front of the open window, thinking black thoughts until suddenly and without warning he thought no more at all.

And then he awakened. His head reeled, but he was solid again. He stood up and studied his hand. Rock steady. Opaque. How long had he been away? He couldn't say. He was confused for a moment, trying to make sense of something that didn't want sense to be made of it. Either that or it already made sense, and he was looking for something that was now plain to him.

Suddenly full of purpose, he straightened his collar and went out into the deepening twilight, having already forgotten about Mrs. Langley but this time wearing his shoes.

His cod had got cold, and the restaurant, the Crow's Nest in Harrogate, had emptied out. Lunch was over, and only a couple of people lingered at their tables. St. Ives sat in the rear corner, his back to the window, doodling on a pad of paper, making calculations.

He felt suddenly woozy, light-headed. Lack of sleep, he told himself, and bad eating habits. He decided to ignore it, but it was suddenly worse, and he had to shove his feet out in order to brace himself. Damn, he thought. Here it was again—another seizure. This time he would fight it.

He heard muffled laughter from across the room and looked up to see someone staring back at him, someone he didn't recognize. The man looked away, but his companion sneaked a glance in St. Ives's direction, his eyes full of furtive curiosity. Nettled, St. Ives nodded at the man and was suddenly aware of his own slept-in clothes, of his frightful unshaven face. His fork, along with a piece of cod, fell from his hand, dropping onto his trousers, and he stared at it helplessly, knowing without trying that his hand would refuse to pick it back up.

In a moment he would pass out. Better to simply climb down onto the floor and be done with it. He didn't want to, though, not in public, not in the condition he was in. He pressed his eyes shut. Slowly and methodically he began to recite the cottage-pie recipe, forcing himself to consider each ingredient, to picture it, to smell it in his mind. He felt himself recover momentarily, as if he were grounding himself somehow, holding on to things anchored in the world.

Hearing a noise, he slumped around in his chair, looking behind himself at the window. Weirdly, a man's face stared back in at him, past the corner of the building. He was struck at first with the thought that he was looking at his own reflection—the disheveled hair, the slept-in clothes. But it wasn't that. It was himself again, just like on the North Road, his coat streaked with muck, as if he had crawled through every muddy gutter between Harrogate and London. The ghost of himself waved once and was gone, and simultaneously St. Ives fell to the floor of the restaurant and knew no more until he awoke, lying in a tangle among the table legs.

The two men who had been staring were endeavoring to yank on him, to pull him free of the table. "Here now," one of them said. "That's it. You'll be fine now."

St. Ives sat up, mumbling his thanks. It was all right, he said. He wasn't sick. His head was clear again, and he wanted nothing more than to be on his way. The two men nodded at him and moved off, back to their table, one of them advising him to go home and both of them looking at him strangely. "I tell you he bloody well disappeared," one man said to the other, staring once more at St. Ives. His companion waved the comment away.

"Disappeared behind the table, you mean." They went back to their fish, talking between themselves in low voices.

St. Ives was suddenly desperate to reach the sidewalk. These spells were happening too often, and he believed that he understood what they meant, finally. What could he have seen but his future-time self, coming and going, hard at work? He had seen the dominoes falling, catching glimpses of them far down the line. The machine would be a success. That must be the truth. He was filled with optimism, and was itching to be away, to topple that first domino, to set the future into motion.

He left three shillings on the table and nodded his thanks at the two men as he strode toward the door. They looked at him skeptically. He burst out into the sunlight, nearly knocking straight into Parsons, who retreated two steps away, a wild and startled look on his face, as if he had been caught out. Parsons yanked himself together, though, and reached out a hand toward St. Ives. For a moment St. Ives was damned if he would shake it. But then he saw that such a course was unwise. Better to keep up the charade.

"Parsons!" he said, forcing animation into his voice.

"Professor St. Ives. *What* an unbelievable surprise."

"Not terribly surprising," St. Ives said. "I live right up the road. What about you, up on holiday?" He realized that his voice was pitched too high and that he sounded fearful and edgy. Parsons by now was the picture of cheerful serenity.

"Fishing holiday, actually. Lot of trout in the Nidd this time of year. Fly-fishing. Come into town to buy supplies, have you? Going somewhere yourself?" He squinted at St. Ives, taking in the down-at-heels look of him. Parsons couldn't keep an element of discomfort out of his face, as if he regretted encountering a man who was so obviously out humiliating himself. "You look... tired," he said. "Keeping late hours?"

"No," St. Ives said, answering all of Parsons's questions at once. Actually, he *had* been keeping late hours. Where he was going, though, he couldn't rightly say. He knew just where he wanted to go. He had the coordinates fined down to a hair. His mind clouded over just then, and he again felt momentarily dizzy, just as he had the other three times. Some sort of residual effect, perhaps. He couldn't attend to what Parsons was saying, but was compelled suddenly to concentrate merely on staying on his feet. Basil, potatoes, cheese... he said to himself. It was happening again— the abysmal and confusing light-headedness, as if he would at any moment float straight up into the sky.

Parsons stared at him, and St. Ives shook his head, trying to clear it, realizing that the man was waiting for him to say something more. Then, abruptly, as if a trapdoor had opened under him, St. Ives sat down hard on the sidewalk.

He was deathly cold and faint. There could be no doubt now. Here he was again—his future-time self—the damned nitwit. He had better have a damned good excuse. His brain seemed to be a puddle of soft gelatin. He pictured the pie in his head, straight out of the oven, the cheese melting. Sometimes he made it with butter rather than cheese. Never mind that. Better to concentrate on one thing at a time.

There was a terrible barking noise. Some great beast... He looked around vaguely, still sitting on the sidewalk, holding on to his mind with a flimsy grasp. A dog ran past him just then, a droopy-eyed dog, white and brown and black, its tongue lolling out of its mouth. Even in his fuddled state he recognized the dog, and for one strange moment he was filled with joy at seeing it. It was Furry, old Binger's dog, the kind of devoted animal that would come round to see you, anxious to be petted, to be spoken to. A friend in all kinds of weather... Another dog burst past, nearly knocking Parsons over backward. This one was some sort of mastiff, growling and snarling and snapping and chasing Binger's dog. Weakly, St. Ives tried to throw himself at the mastiff, nearly getting hold of its collar, but the dog ran straight on, as if St. Ives's fingers were as insubstantial as smoke.

Through half-focused eyes, St. Ives saw Binger's poor dog running straight down the middle of the road, into the path of a loaded dray. The air was full of noise, of clattering hooves and the grinding of steel-shod wheels. And just then a man came running from the alley behind the Crow's Nest. He waved curtly to Parsons as he leaped off the curb, hurtling forward into the street, his arms outstretched. St. Ives screwed his eyes half-shut, trying to focus them, the truth dawning on him in a rush. He recognized the tattered muddy coat, the uncombed hair. It was the same man whose reflection he had seen in the glass. It was himself, his future-time self. Parsons saw it too. St. Ives raised a hand to his face, covering his eyes, and yet he could see the street through his hand as if through a fog.

The running man threw himself on the sheepdog. The driver of the dray hauled back on the reins, pulling at the wheel brake. A woman screamed. The horses lunged. The dog and its savior leaped clear, and then the street and everything in it disappeared from view, winking out of existence like a departing hallucination.

* * *

Suddenly he could see again. And the first thing he noticed was Parsons, hurrying away up the sidewalk in the direction taken by the St. Ives that had saved the dog. There's your mistake, St. Ives said to himself as he struggled to his hands and knees. You're already too late. He felt shaky, almost hung over. He staggered off toward the corner, in the opposite direction to that taken by Parsons. The man would discover nothing. The time machine had gone, and his future-time self with it. St. Ives laughed out loud, abruptly cutting off the laughter when he heard the sound of his own voice.

Mr. Binger's dog loped up behind him, wagging its tail, and St. Ives scratched its head as the two of them trotted along. At the corner, coming up fast, was old Binger himself. "Furry!" he shouted at the dog, half mad and half happy to see it. "Why, Professor," he said, and looked skeptically at St. Ives.

"Have you got your cart?" St. Ives asked him hastily.

"Aye," said Binger. "I was just coming along into town, when old Furry here jumped off the back. Saw some kind of damned mastiff and thought he'd play with it, didn't he?" Binger shook his head. "Trusts anybody. Last week…"

"Drive me up to the manor," St. Ives said, interrupting him. "Quick as you can. There's trouble."

Binger's face dropped. He didn't like the idea of trouble. In that way he resembled his dog. "I don't take any stock in trouble," he had told St. Ives once, and now the look on his face seemed to echo that phrase.

"Cow in calf," St. Ives lied, defining things more carefully. He patted his coat, as if somehow there was something vital in his pocket, something a cow would want. "Terrible rush," he said, "but we might save it yet."

Mr. Binger hurried toward his cart, and the dog Furry jumped on behind. Here was trouble of a sort that Mr. Binger understood, and in moments they were rollicking away up the road, St. Ives calculating how long it would take for Parsons to discover that the man he was chasing was long gone, off into the aether aboard the machine. He was filled with a deep sense of success, transmitted backward to him from the saving of old Furry. It was partly the sight of himself dashing out there, sweeping up the dog. But more than that, it was the certainty that he was moments away from becoming a time traveler, that he could hurry or not hurry, just as he chose. It didn't matter, did it?

The truth was that he was safe from Parsons. The saving of the dog meant exactly that, and nothing less. He was destined to succeed that far, at least. He laughed out loud, but then noticed Mr. Binger giving him a look, and so he pretended to be coughing rather than laughing, and he nodded seriously at the man, patting his coat again.

The manor hove into view as Mr. Binger drove steadily up the road, smoking his pipe like a chimney. There, on the meadow, grazed a half-dozen jersey cows. A calf, easily two months old, stood alongside its mother, who ruminated like a philosopher. "Well, I'll be damned," St. Ives said, jerking his thumb in the direction of the calf. "Looks like everything's fine after all." He smiled broadly at Mr. Binger, in order to demonstrate his deep delight and relief.

"That ain't..." Mr. Binger started to say.

St. Ives interrupted him. "Pull up, will you? I'll just get off here and walk the rest of the way. Thanks awfully." Mr. Binger slowed and stopped the horses, and St. Ives gave him a pound note. "Don't know what I'd do without you, Mr. Binger. I'm in your debt."

Mr. Binger blinked at the money and scratched his head,

staring out at the two-month-old calf on the field. He was only mystified for a moment, though. The look on his face seemed to suggest that he was used to this kind of thing, that there was no telling what sorts of shenanigans the professor might not be up to when you saw him next. He shrugged, tipped his hat, turned the wagon around, and drove off.

St. Ives started out toward the manor, whistling merrily. It was too damned bad that Mrs. Langley had gone off to her sister's yesterday without having waited for morning. St. Ives hadn't had time to put things right with her. What had he been thinking of, talking to her in that tone? The thought of his having run mad like that depressed him. He would fetch her back. He had tackled the business of Binger's dog; he could see to Mrs. Langley, too. With the machine he would make everything all right.

Then he began to wonder how on earth he had known about Binger's dog. In some other historical manifestation he must have witnessed the whole incident, and it must have fallen out badly— Binger's dog dead, perhaps, smashed on the street. Via the machine, then, St. Ives must have come back around, stepping in out of time and snatching the dog from the jaws of certain death. Now he couldn't remember any of that other manifestation of time. The first version of things had ceased to exist for him, perhaps now had never existed at all. There was no other explanation for it, though. He, himself, must have purposefully and effectively altered history, *even after history had already been established*, and in so doing had obliterated another incarnation of himself along with it. Nothing is set in stone, he realized, and the thought of it was dizzying— troubling too. What else might he have changed? Who and what else might he have obliterated?

He would have to go easy with this time-traveling business.

The risks were clearly enormous. The whole thing might mean salvation, and it might as easily mean utter ruin. Well, one way or another he was going to find out. He no longer had any choice, had he? There he had been, after all, peeking in at the window, saving the dog in the road. There was no gainsaying it now. What would happen, would happen—unless, of course, St. Ives himself came back and made it happen in some other way altogether.

His head reeled, and it occurred to him that there would be nothing wrong, at the moment, with opening a bottle of port—a vintage, something laid down for years. Best taste it now, he thought, the future wasn't half as secure as he had supposed it to be even twenty minutes past. He set out for the manor in a more determined way, thinking happily that if a man were to hop ten years into the future, that same bottle of port would have that many more years on it, and could be fetched back and…

Something made him turn his head and look behind him, though, before he had taken another half-dozen steps. There, coming up the road, was a carriage, banging along wildly, careering back and forth as if it meant to overtake him or know the reason why. Mrs. Langley? he wondered stupidly, and then he knew it wasn't.

Fumbling in his pocket for the padlock key, he set out across the meadow at a dead run, angling toward the silo now. For better or worse, the past beckoned to him. The bottle of port would have to wait.

THE TIME TRAVELER

Even as he was climbing into the machine he could hear them outside, through the brick wall of the silo: the carriage rattling up, the shouted orders, then a terrible banging on the barred wooden doors. He shut the hatch, and the sounds of banging and bashing were muffled. In moments they would knock the doors off their hinges and be inside—Parsons and his ruffians, swarming over the machine. They would have to work on getting in, though, since it was unlikely that they'd brought any sort of battering ram. St. Ives prayed silently that Hasbro wouldn't try to stop them. He could only be brought to grief by tangling with them. They meant business this time, doubly so, since Parsons knew, or at least feared, that he was already too late, and that fear would drive him to desperation. And St. Ives's salvation lay in the machine now, not in his stalwart friend Hasbro, as it had so many times in the past.

He settled himself into the leather seat of what had once been Leopold Higgins's bathyscaphe. It made a crude and ungainly time machine, and most of the interior space had been consumed by Lord

Kelvin's magnetic engine, stripped of all the nonsense that had been affixed to it as modification during the days of the comet. There was barely room for St. Ives to maneuver, what with the seat moved forward until his nose was very nearly pressed against a porthole. An elaborate system of mirrors allowed him to see around the device behind him, out through the other porthole windows.

He glanced into the mirrors once, making out the dim floor of the silo: the tumbled machinery and scrap metal, the black forge with its enormous bellows, the long workbench that was a chaos of debris and tools. What a pathetic mess. The sight of it reminded St. Ives of how far he had sunk in the last couple of years—the last few months, really. His mental energy had been spent entirely, to its last farthing, on building the machine; he hadn't enough left over to hang up a hammer. He remembered a dim past day when he had been the king of regimentation and order. Now he was the pawn of desperation.

It was then that he saw the message, scrawled in chalk on the silo wall. "Hurry," it read. "Try to put things right on the North Road. If at first you fail…" The message ended there, unfinished, as if someone—he himself—had abandoned the effort and fled. And just as well. It was a useless note, anyway. He would remember that in the future. Time was short; there was none left over for wasted words and ready-made phrases.

He concentrated on the dials in front of him, listening with half an ear to the muffled bashing of the doors straining against the bar. He knew just exactly where he wanted to go, but harmonizing the instrumentation wanted minutes, not seconds. Measure twice, cut once, as the carpenter said. Well, the carpenter would have to trust to his eye, here; there was no time to fiddle with tape measures. Hastily, he made a final calculation and delicately turned the longitudinal dial, tracking a route along the Great North Road, into London. He set the minutes and the seconds and then went after the latitudinal dial.

There was a sound of wood splintering, and the murky light of the silo brightened. They were in. St. Ives reeled through the time setting, hearing the delicate insect hum of the spinning flywheel. The machine shook just then, with the weight of someone climbing up the side. Parsons's face appeared in front of the porthole. He was red and sweating, and his beard wagged with the effort of his shouting. St. Ives winked at him, and glanced into the mirrors again. The silo door was swung wide open, framing a picture of Hasbro, carrying a rifle, running across the meadow. Mrs. Langley followed him, a rolling pin in her hand.

Mrs. Langley! God bless her. She had gone away miffed, but had come back, loyal woman that she was. And now she was ready to hammer his foes with a rolling pin. St. Ives very nearly gave it up then and there. She would sacrifice herself for him, even after his shabby treatment of her. He couldn't let her do that, or Hasbro either.

For a moment he hesitated. Then, stoically and calmly, he set his mind again to his instruments. By God, he *wouldn't* let them do it. He was a time traveler now. He would save them all before he was through, whatever it took. If he stayed, if he abandoned the machine to Parsons, he would be a gibbering wreck for ever and ever. If he lived that long. He'd be of no use to anyone at all.

He heard the sound of someone fiddling with the hatch. The moment had come. "Hurry," the message on the wall had said. He threw the lever that activated the electromagnetic properties of Lord Kelvin's machine. The ground seemed suddenly to shake beneath him, and there was a high-pitched whine that rose within a second to the point of disappearing. Parsons pitched over backward as the bathyscaphe bucked on its splayed legs. Simultaneously, there was a shouting from overhead, and a pair of legs and feet swung down across the porthole. Parsons scrambled upright, latching on to the dangling man and pulling him free.

And then, abruptly, absolute darkness prevailed, and St. Ives felt himself falling, spinning round and round as he fell, as if down a dark and very deep well. His first impulse was to clutch at something, but there was nothing to clutch, and he seemed to have no hands. He was simply a mind, spiraling downward through itself, seeming already to have traveled vast distances along endless centuries and yet struck with the notion that he had merely blinked his eyes.

Then he stopped falling, and sat as ever in the bathyscaphe. He realized now that his hands shook treacherously. They had been calm and cooperative when the danger was greatest, but now they were letting themselves go. He was still in darkness. But where? Suspended somewhere in the void, neither here nor there?

He saw then that the darkness outside was of a different quality than it had been. It was merely nighttime, and it was raining. He was in the country somewhere. Slowly, his eyes accustomed themselves to the darkness. A muddy road stretched away in front of him. He was in an open field, beside the North Road.

From out of the darkness, cantering along at a good pace, came a carriage. St. Ives—his past-time self—was driving it. The horses steamed in the rain, and muddy water flew from the wheels. Bill Kraken and Hasbro sat inside. Somewhere ahead of them, Ignacio Narbondo fled in terror, carrying Alice with him. They were nearly upon him…

Shrugging with fatalistic abandon, the St. Ives in the machine scribbled a note to himself. He knew that it was possible that he could deliver the note, if he hurried. He knew equally well what attempting to deliver it might mean. He had experienced this fiasco once before, seeing it through the eyes of the man who drove the wagon. He was filled suddenly with feelings of self-betrayal.

Still, he reminded himself, he *could* change the past: witness the saving of Binger's dog. And in any event, what would he sacrifice by being timid here? His failing to act would *necessarily* alter the past, and with what consequences? It wouldn't serve to be stupid and timid both; one mistake was enough.

He read hastily through the finished note. "N. will shoot Alice on the street in the Seven Dials," the note read, "unless you shoot him first. Act. Don't hesitate." As a lark he nearly wrote, "Yrs. sincerely," and signed it. But he didn't. There was no time for that. Already the man driving the horses would be losing his grip on the reins. St. Ives had waited long enough, maybe too long. He tripped the lever on the hatch and thrust himself through, into the rainy night, sliding down the side of the bathyscaphe onto his knees in ditch water. Rain beat into his face, the fierce roar of it mixing with the creaking and banging of the carriage.

He cursed, slogging to his feet and up the muddy bank, reeling out onto the road. The carriage hurtled toward him, driven now by a man who was nearly a ghost. There was a look of pure astonishment in its eyes. He had recognized himself, but it was too late. His past-time self was already becoming incorporeal. St. Ives reached the note up, hoping to hand it to himself, hoping that there was some little bit of substance left to his hands. His past-time self spoke, but no sounds issued from his mouth. He bent down and flailed at the note, but hadn't the means to grasp it.

St. Ives let go of it then, although he knew it was too late. "Take it!" he screamed, but already the carriage was driverless. His past-time self had simply disappeared from the carriage seat, reduced to atoms floating now in the aether. The note blew away into the rainy darkness like a kite battered by a hurricane, and for one desperate moment St. Ives started to follow it, as if he would chase it forever across the countryside. He let it go and turned momentarily back to the road, watching the reins flop across the horses' backs as they hauled the carriage away, bashing across deep ruts, smashing along toward certain ruin.

St. Ives couldn't stand to watch. They'll survive, he told himself. They'll struggle on into Crick where a doctor will attend to Kraken's shoulder, and then they'll be off again for London, with Narbondo almost hopelessly far ahead. Kraken would search him out in Limehouse, surprising him in the middle of one of his abominable meals, and they would pursue him to the Seven Dials, losing him again until early morning when…

There it was, laid out before him, the grim future, or, rather, the grim past, depending on one's perspective. The time machine was a grand success, and his bid to alter the past a grand failure. It was spilled milk, though. What he had to do now was get out fast. Just as the note had said. Hurry, always hurry. Still he didn't move, but stood in the rain, buffeted by wind. He couldn't see far enough up the dark road to make anything out.

"Where to?" he said out loud. Back to the silo, possibly to confront Parsons? Surely not. Back to the silo day before yesterday, perhaps? He could avoid insulting Mrs. Langley that way. But what then? He would be taking the chance of making a hash of everything, wouldn't he? There was no profit in reliving random periods in his life. Only one event was worth reliving. Only one thing had to be obliterated utterly. Suddenly, he was struck dumb with fear at the very idea of it.

Like a bolt of lightning it struck him: who was to say that his time traveling wouldn't merely change things for the worse? What if he had managed to give himself that note, and had gotten away in the machine in time? Quite likely they would have overtaken Narbondo within the hour. There would have been no wreck on the North Road, no lost day in Crick, no confrontation in the Seven Dials. The note would then have meant nothing. It would have been turned into senseless gibberish. And the ghastly irony of the business, he shuddered to realize, was that his time traveling, his desperate effort to avert Alice's death, had been the very instrument that set into motion the sequence of events that would bring about her death. He had killed her, hadn't he?

Suddenly he began to laugh out loud. The rain pounded down, washing across his face and down his coat collar as he hooted and shrieked in the mud, beating his fists against the brass wall of the time-traveling bathyscaphe until he was breathless, his energy spent. The night was black and awful, and his shoes were sodden lumps of muck and mud from the ditch. His chest heaved and his head spun. Slowly, implacably, he forced himself to crawl back up the rungs to the hatch, shuddering with little spurts of uncontrollable laughter. "Cottage pie," he said, fumbling with the latch. "Basil, sage, potatoes…" The list meant nothing to him, but he recited it anyway, until, weary and shivering, he sat once again looking out through the porthole at the night, his laughter finally spent. "Cheese," he said.

He set the dials and at once activated the machine. There was the familiar bucking and shuddering and the abruptly silenced whine, and then once again he was adrift in the well. It wasn't night when he materialized, though. There was sunlight filtering through murky water. He was on the bottom of Lake Windermere. He had got the location right. The time ought to have been fifty years past, before he had been born. So there would be no hapless past-time St. Ives in the process of disappearing. He could take his time now, safe from Parsons, safe from himself, invisible to anybody but fish. What he wanted was practice—less hurry, not more of it.

He cast about in his mind, looking for an adequate test. He had the entirety of history to peek in at—almost too much choice. He studied the lake bed outside the porthole. There was nothing but mud and waterweeds. Carefully he manipulated the dials, then threw the lever. There was an instant of black night, then water-filtered sunlight again. He was still on the lake bottom, but in shallow water now, only partly submerged. A slice of sky shone at the top of the porthole.

Cautiously, he pushed up the hatch and peered out, satisfied with where he had found himself. Across twenty yards of reeds lay a grassy bank. Sheep grazed placidly on it, with not a human being in sight. He shut the hatch, fiddled with the controls, and jumped again, into full sunlight this time. The machine sat on the meadow now, among the startled sheep, which fled away on every side. He raised the hatch cover once more and looked around him. He could see now that there was a house some little way distant, farther along the edge of the lake. Two women stood in the garden, picking flowers. One turned suddenly and pointed, shading her eyes. She had seen him. The other one looked, then threw her hand to her mouth. Both of them turned to run, back toward the house, and St. Ives in a sudden panic retreated through the hatch, slamming it behind him, and then once again set the dials, leaping back down into the bottom of the lake, five years hence, safe from the eyes of humankind.

Nimbly, he bounced forward once more, and then back another

sixty years, up onto the meadow again. The house was gone, the fields empty of sheep. He crept forward, a year at a time. Sheep came and went. There was the house, half-built. A gang of men labored at lifting a great long roof beam into place. St. Ives crept forward another hour. The beam was supported now by vertical timbers. The sound of pounding hammers filled the otherwise silent morning.

He was ready at last. He was bound for the future, for Harrogate and an encounter with Mr. Binger's dog. That would be the test. Or would it? He thought for a moment. Perhaps a better test would consist of his *not* saving Mr. Binger's dog. That might answer his questions more adequately. But what then? Then the dog would die. The answer to that particular question was evident. Old Furry would run under the wheels of that carriage. St. Ives had no choice.

He alighted in a yard off Bow Street, around the corner from the Crow's Nest. This time there was no hesitation. He climbed out through the hatch and sprinted down the sidewalk, slowing as he approached the corner. He could picture himself bursting out, snatching up the dog, thumbing his nose at Parsons.

Something was wrong, though. He knew that. There was no barking. And no dray, either. He was early. Seeing his mistake he stopped abruptly, swung around, and started back, running toward the machine. How early was he? He thought he knew, but he couldn't take any chances. He must know for certain. Abruptly, he angled into the weedy back lot behind the Crow's Nest, slowing down and sneaking along the wall. Carefully he peered around the corner, looking in the rear window of the almost-empty restaurant. There he sat, his past-time self, just then dropping his fork onto his trousers. Slowly the St. Ives inside the restaurant turned around to face the window, and for a split second he looked himself straight in the eye, holding his own gaze long enough for both of him to understand how haggard and drawn and cockeyed he appeared.

Then with that lesson in mind, he was off and running again, leaving his past-time self to grapple with the mystery. He climbed in at the hatch, bumped the time dial forward, and skipped ahead five minutes. When he opened the hatch it was to the sound of barking dogs. He climbed hastily down the side, looking up toward the street corner where he could see the dray already coming along. Christ! Was he too late? He slid to the ground and started out at a run, but the barking abruptly turned to a single cut-off yelp, then silence. The driver shouted, and one of the horses bucked.

Already St. Ives was clambering back into the machine, sweating now, panicked. He backed the dial off slightly, giving himself twenty seconds. Again he leaped backward, rematerializing in an instant and leaping without hesitation at the hatch. He was down and running wildly toward the corner. He could hear the dray again, but this time he couldn't yet see it. The barking of old Furry, though, seemed to fill the air along with the snarling of the mastiff.

He leaped straight down off the curb, looking back at where a stupefied Parsons stared at him in wide-eyed alarm. Reaching down, he snatched up the dog, nearly slamming into the horses himself. He threw himself backward, turning, holding the struggling dog, and staggered toward the curb, where he let the creature go. Then he took one last precious second to shout like a lunatic at the snarling mastiff, which turned and fled, howling away down the street to disappear behind a milliner's shop.

"Run," St. Ives said, half out loud. And he was away up Bow Street again, pursued by Parsons, who huffed along with his hand on his hat. Full of wild energy, St. Ives easily outdistanced the old man, climbing into the machine and closing the hatch. He knew where he was going, where he *had* to go. He had done all the necessary calculations at the bottom of Lake Windermere.

As he adjusted the dials, he half expected Parsons to clamber up onto the bathyscaphe or to peer into the porthole and shake his fist. But Parsons didn't appear.

Of course he won't, St. Ives thought suddenly. Parsons was too shrewd for that. He was right then searching out a constable, commandeering a carriage in order to race up to the manor and beat the silo door in. St. Ives tripped the lever to activate Lord Kelvin's machine, and once again he felt himself falling, downward and downward through the creeping years, until he came to rest once again, in London now, in Limehouse, sometime in 1835.

⌾ LIMEHOUSE ⌾

A cold autumn fog was settling over Limehouse, and St. Ives counted this as a piece of luck, a sign, perhaps, that his fortunes were turning. The mist would hide his movements on the rooftop, anyway, although it would also make it tolerably hard to see. There was a moon, which helped, but which also would expose his skulking around if he didn't keep low and out of sight. For the moment, though, he was fascinated with the scene round about him. He looked down onto Pennyfields and away up West India Dock Road and watched the flickering of lights in windows and the movements of people below him—the streets were crowded despite the hour—sailors mostly, got up in strange costumes. There were Lascars and Africans and Dutchmen and heaven knew what-all sorts of foreigners, mingling with coal-backers and ballast-heavers and lumpers and costermongers and the thousands of destitute rag-bedraggled poor who slept in the streets in fair weather and under the bridges in foul.

The roof beams beneath his feet sagged under the weight

of the bathyscaphe, but the machine was safe enough for the moment, and St. Ives intended to stay no longer than he had to. Had to—he wondered what that meant. He had been compelled, somehow, to travel to Limehouse, but he found that he couldn't say why that was, not in so many words. Beneath his feet, in a garret room over a general shop, lay Ignacio Narbondo, probably asleep. What was he?—three or four years old? St. Ives couldn't be certain. Nor could he be certain what emotions had carried him here. He could, without any difficulty at all, murder Narbondo while he slept, ridding the world of one of its most foul and dangerous criminal minds... But the idea of that was immediately repellent, and he half despised himself for admitting it into his mind. Then he thought of Alice, and he despised himself less. Still, murder wasn't in him. What he wanted was to study his nemesis close at hand, to discover what forces in the broad universe had conspired to turn him into what he had become.

The rest of Limehouse didn't sleep. The tide was rising and the harbors navigable, so ships were loading and unloading, with no regard for the sun or for the lateness of the hour. Directly below him, from the open door of the shop, light shone out into the foggy street, illuminating a debris of broken iron, soiled overcoats, dirty bottles and crockery and linens and every other sort of household refuse that might conceivably find a use for itself, although it was an effort for St. Ives to imagine how destitute a man might be before he saw such trash as useful. He was filled, suddenly, with horror and melancholy and hopelessness, and he realized that his head ached awfully, and that he couldn't remember entirely when he'd last slept. He had always had a penchant for confused philosophy when he was tired. He recognized it as one of the sure signs of mental fatigue.

"Hurry," he muttered, as if speaking to the woman who sat below, guarding the detritus that spilled out of the shop as if it were a treasure. He looked down onto the tattered bonnet on her head and into the bowl of the short pipe that she smoked, and tried to fathom what it would be like to have one's life circumscribed and defined by a couple of filthy streets and a glass of bad gin.

Giving it up as a dead loss, he backed away from the edge of the roof, turning toward a tall garret window that stood behind him, its glass streaked and dirty and cracked and looking out on the fog and chimney pots like an occluded eye. He crept toward it across the slates, hoping that it wasn't latched, but prepared to open it by force if it was. He had a pocket full of silver, and he wondered what they would make of a strangely clothed gentleman creeping in at the window in the middle of the night for no other purpose, apparently, than to give them money—which is exactly what he intended to do if they caught him coming in at the window. He liked the idea: tiptoeing around the rooftops of Pennyfields, bestowing shillings on mystified paupers. The notion became abruptly despicable, though, a matter more of vanity than virtue. More likely he would have to use the silver to buy his freedom before the night was through.

There was no latch on the window at all, which was jammed shut with a folded-up bunch of paper torn out of a book. Without hesitation he wiggled it open and bent quietly down into the dark interior, wishing he had brought along a lantern and nearly recoiling from the fetid smell of sickness in the close air of the room. He held on to the window frame and felt around for the floor with his foot, kicking something soft, which shifted and let out a faint moan. Abruptly he pulled his foot back, perching on the sill like an animal ready to bolt. Slowly his eyes adjusted to the darkness, which, despite the thickening fog, was still lit by pale moonlight.

The room was almost empty of furniture. There was an old bed against one wall, a couple of wooden chairs, and a palsied table. Against another wall was a broken-down sideboard, almost empty of plates and glasses, as if it had no more day-to-day reason to exist than did the two sleeping humans who inhabited the room. A book lay open on the table, and more books were scattered and piled on the floor, looking altogether like superfluous wealth, an exotic treasure heaped up in a dark and musty pirates' cavern. The rags beneath his feet moved again and groaned, and then shook as the child covered by them was convulsed with coughing. On the bed someone lay sleeping heavily, unperturbed by the coughing.

Carefully now, St. Ives reached his foot past the sleeping form on the floor and pushed himself into the room, swinging the window shut behind him. He stepped across to the table to examine one of the books, which was moderately new. He was only half surprised to find that it was a volume of the *Illustrated Experiments with Gilled Beasts*, compiled by Ignacio Narbondo senior. St. Ives shook his head, calculating how long ago it must have been that Narbondo senior had been transported for the crime of vivisection. Not long—a matter of a couple of years. This collection of books seemed to be the only thing he had left to his abandoned family, except for his taste for corrupt knowledge. And now the son, young as he was, already followed in the father's bloody footsteps.

The little boy sleeping on the floor began to breathe loudly— the labored, hoarse wet breathing of someone with congested lungs. St. Ives bent over the convulsed form, gently pulling back the dirty blanket that covered it. He lay stiffly on his side, neck straight, as if he were endeavoring to keep his throat open. His arms were sticklike, and his pallid cheeks sagging. St. Ives ran his hand lightly down the child's spine, looking for the bow that would develop one day into a pronounced hump.

Strangely, there was no bow; the back was ramrod stiff, the flesh feverish. Through the thin blanket he could feel the air gurgling in and out of the child's lungs. St. Ives stood up, looking around the room again, and then immediately stepped across and fetched a glass tumbler from the sideboard. He stooped again and pressed the open end to the child's back, then listened hard to the closed end. The lungs sounded like a troubled cesspool.

The boy was taken with another coughing fit, hacking up bloodstained froth as St. Ives jerked away and stood up again. Clearly, he was far gone in pneumonia. There could be no doubt about it. He had been nauseated, too. In his weakened condition the child would die. The sudden knowledge of that washed over St. Ives like a dam breaking. Murder wasn't in the cards at all. Even if such a thing had appealed to St. Ives, it would be a redundant task. Nature and circumstance and the poverty of a filthy and overcrowded city would kill Narbondo just as surely as a bullet to the brain. St. Ives had only to crouch back out through the window and lose himself in the future.

And yet the idea of it ran counter to what he knew to be the truth. How could Narbondo die without St. Ives's helping him to do it? A man might alter the future, but how could the future alter itself? He examined the child's face, thinking things through. He needed light. Hurrying to the sideboard again, he carefully opened cupboard doors until he found candles and sulphur matches. The woman on the bed wouldn't awaken. She was lost in gin, snoring loudly now, her head covered with blankets. He struck a match and lit the candle, bending over the child and studying his face, looking for a telltale rash. There was nothing, only the sweating pale skin of an undernourished sick child.

Surely it hadn't a chance of survival. The boy would be dead tomorrow. Two days, maybe. Pneumococcal meningitis—that was his guess. It was a hasty candlelight-and-glass-tumbler diagnosis, but the pneumonia was certain, and alone was enough to kill him. He stood for a moment thinking. Meningitis could explain the hump. If Narbondo lived, the spinal damage might easily pull him into a stoop that would become permanent over the years.

It really didn't matter how accurately he understood the child's condition. The boy was doomed; of that St. Ives was certain. He pulled the blanket back up, taking off his coat and laying that too over the sleeping child, who exhaled now like a panting dog, desperately short of breath. St. Ives couldn't bring himself to equate the suffering little human with the monster he had shot in the Seven Dials. They simply were not the same creature. "Time and chance…" he thought, then remembered that he'd said the same thing not six months back—about himself and what he had become, and the feelings of melancholy and futility washed over him again.

He had a vision of all of humanity struggling like small and frightened animals in a vast black morass. It was easy to forget that there had ever been a time when he was happy. Surely this dying child couldn't remember any such happiness. St. Ives sighed, rubbing his forehead to drive out the fatigue and doom. That sort of thinking accomplished nothing. It was better to leave it to the philosophers, who generally had the advantage of having a bottle of brandy nearby. Right now all abstractions were meaningless alongside the fact of the dying child. Abruptly, he made up his mind.

He left his three silver coins on the table and stepped out

through the window, pulling it shut, leaving his coat behind. If he failed to return, they could have the coat and the silver both; if he did return, they could have it anyway. He shivered on the rooftop, hurrying across toward the bathyscaphe, no longer interested in the early morning bustle below.

As he stepped into the study through the open French window— all still very much as he remembered it—he half expected to see himself as an old man, disappearing into the atmosphere. But by now he would already have vanished. It had taken that long to get out through the window of the silo and sneak across to the manor. He might be long ago dead, of course. It was 1927, a date he had struck upon randomly. The manor might have a new owner, perhaps a man with a rifle loaded with bird shot. The interior of the silo, however, argued otherwise. It was full of faintly mystifying apparatus now, but it was the sort of apparatus that only a scientist like St. Ives would possess, and it wasn't rusty and scattered, either; instead it was orderly, not the ghastly mess that he had let it decline to back... when? For a moment he was disoriented, unable to recall the date.

The study was neatened up, too—no books scattered around, no jumbled papers. He thought guiltily of Mrs. Langley, and then quickly pushed the thought from his mind. Muddling himself up wouldn't serve. Mrs. Langley would wait. There were interesting and suggestive changes in the room around him. From the study ceiling hung the wired-together skeleton of a winged saurian, and leaning against one wall, braced by a couple of wooden pegs, was the femur of a monstrous reptile, something the size of a brontosaurus. So he had followed his whims, had he? He had taken up paleontology. How so? Had he utilized the time machine? Traveled back to the Age of Reptiles? A thrill of anticipation surged through him along with the knowledge, once again, that things, ultimately, must have fallen out for the best. Here was evidence of it—the well-apportioned room of a man in possession of his faculties.

Then it struck him like a blow. He wasn't any such man yet. There was no use being smug. He had to go back, to return to the past, to drop like a chunk of iron into the machinery of time, maybe fouling it utterly. This was one manifestation of time, no more solid than a soap bubble. He caught sight of himself in the mirror just then, recoiling in surprise. A haunted, gaunt, unshaven face stared out at him, and involuntarily he touched his cheek, forgetting his newfound optimism.

A note lay on the cleaned-off desk. He picked it up, noticing only then that a bottle of port and a glass stood at the back corner. He smiled despite himself, remembering suddenly all his blathering foolishness about fetching back bottles of port from the future. To hell with fetching anything back; he would have a taste of it now. "Cheers," he said out loud.

He settled himself into a chair in order to read the note. "I cleared out the silo," it read. "You would have materialized in the center of a motorcar if I hadn't, and caused who-knows-what kind of explosion. Quit being so proud of yourself. You look like hell. Talk to Professor Fleming at Oxford. He can be a bumbling idiot, but he possesses what you need. We're friends, after a fashion, Fleming and I. Go straightaway, and then get the hell out and don't come back. You're avoiding what you know you have to do. You're purposefully searching out obstacles. Look at you, for God's sake. You should make yourself sick."

Frowning, St. Ives laid the note onto the desk, drinking off the last of his glass of port. He was in a foul mood now. The note had done that. How dare he take that tone? Didn't he know whom he was talking to? He had half a mind to… what? He looked around, sensing that the atoms of his incorporeal self were hovering roundabout somewhere, grinning at him. Maybe they inhabited the bones of the pterodactyl hanging overhead. The thing regarded him from out of ridiculously small, empty eye sockets, reminding him suddenly of a beak-nosed schoolteacher from his childhood.

He searched in the drawer for a pen, thinking to write himself a note in return. What should he say? Something insulting? Something incredibly knowledgeable? Something weary and timeworn? But what did his present-time self know that his future-time self didn't know? In fact, wouldn't his future-time self know even the contents of the insulting note? He would simply rematerialize, see the note, and laugh at it without having to read it. St. Ives put down the pen dejectedly, nearly despising himself for his helplessness.

The door opened and Hasbro stepped in. "Good morning, sir," he said, in no way surprised to see St. Ives and laying out a suit of clothes on the divan.

"Hasbro!" St. Ives shouted, leaping up to embrace the man. He was considerably older. Of course he would be. He still wasn't in any way feeble, though. Seeing him so trim and fit despite his white hair caused St. Ives to lament his own fallen state. "I'm not who you think I am," he said.

"Of course you're not, sir. None of us are. This should fit, though."

"It's good to see you," St. Ives said. "You can't imagine…"

"Very good, sir. I've been instructed to trim your hair." He looked St. Ives up and down, squinting just a little, as if what he saw amounted to something less than he'd anticipated. He went out again, saying nothing more, but leaving St. Ives open-mouthed. In a moment he returned, carrying a pitcher of water and a bowl. "The ablutions will have to be hasty and primitive," he said. "I'm afraid you're not to visit any other room in the house for any reason whatever. I've been given very precise instructions. We're to go straightaway to Oxford, returning as soon as possible and keeping conversation to a minimum. I have a pair of train tickets. We board at the station in fifty-four minutes precisely."

"Yes," said St. Ives. "You would know, wouldn't you?" He hastily removed his shirt, scrubbing his face in the bowl, dunking the top of his head into the water and soaping his hair. Within moments he sat again in the chair, Hasbro shaving his overgrown beard. "Tell me, then," St. Ives said. "What happens? Alice, is she all right? Is she alive? Did I succeed? I must have. I can see it written all over this room. Tell me what fell out."

"I'm instructed to tell you nothing, sir. Tilt your head back."

Soapy water ran down into St. Ives's shirtfront. "Surely a little hint…" he said.

"Not a word, I'm afraid. The professor has informed me that the entire fabric of time is a delicate material, like old silk, and that the very sound of my voice might rip it to shreds. Very poetic of him, I think."

"He talks like a fool, if I'm any judge," St. Ives said angrily. "And you can tell him that from me. Poetic…!"

"Of course, sir. Just as you say. We'll need to powder your hair."

"Powder my hair? Why on earth…?"

"Professor Fleming, sir, up at Oxford. He knows you as a considerably older man. Due to your fatigued and malnourished state, of course, you appear to *be* an older man. But we mustn't assume anything at all, mustn't take any unnecessary risks. You can appreciate that."

"Older?" said St. Ives, looking skeptically at himself in the mirror again. It was true. He seemed to have aged ten years in the last two or three. His face was a depressing sight.

"You'll be young again, sir," Hasbro said reassuringly, and suddenly St. Ives wanted to weep. It seemed to him that he was caught up in an interminable web of comings and goings in which every action necessitated some previous action and would promote some future action and so on infinitely. And what's more, no outcome could be certain. Like old silk, even the past was a delicate thing…

"What does this Fleming have, exactly?" asked St. Ives, pulling himself together.

"I really must insist that we forego any discussion at all, sir. I've been instructed that you are to be left entirely to your own devices."

St. Ives sat back in the chair, regarding himself in the mirror once more. The stubble beard was gone, and his hair was clipped and combed. He felt worlds better, although the clothes that Hasbro fitted him with were utterly idiotic. Who was he to complain, though? If Hasbro had been instructed that it was absolutely necessary to hose him down with pig swill, he would have to stand for it. His future-self held all the cards and could make him dance any sort of inconceivable jig.

Together they went back out through the window, Hasbro insisting that St. Ives not see anything of the rest of the house. A long sleek motorcar sat on the drive. St. Ives had seen motorized carriages, had even toyed with the idea of building one, but this was something beyond his dreams, something—something from the future. He climbed into it happily. "Fueled by what?" he asked as they roared away toward Harrogate. "Alcohol? Steam? Let me guess." He listened closely. "Advanced Giffard injector and a simple Pelton wheel?"

"I'm terribly sorry, sir."

"Of course it's not. I was testing you. Tell me, though, how fast will she go on the open road?"

"I'm afraid I'm constrained from discussing it."

"Is the queen dead?"

"Lamentably so, sir. In 1901. God bless her. Royalty hasn't amounted to as much since, I'm afraid. A trifle too frivolous these days, if you'll pardon my saying so."

St. Ives discovered that he didn't have any real interest in what royalty was up to these days. He admitted to himself that there was a good deal that he didn't want to know. The last thing on earth that appealed to him was to return to the past with a head full of grim futuristic knowledge that he could do damn-all about. It was enough, perhaps, that Hasbro was hale and hearty and that he himself—if the interior of the silo was any indication—was still hard at it. Suddenly he wanted very badly just to be back in his own day, his business finished. And although it grated on him to have to admit it, his future-time self was absolutely correct. Silence was the safest route back to his destination. Still, that didn't make up for the hard tone of the man's note.

Oxford, thank heaven, was still Oxford. St. Ives let Hasbro lead him along beneath the leafless trees, toward the pathology laboratory, feeling just a little like a tattooed savage hauled into civilization for the first time. His clothes still felt ridiculous to him, despite his harmonizing nicely with the rest of the populace. Their clothes looked ridiculous too. There wasn't so much shame in looking like a fool if everyone looked like a fool. His face itched under the powder that Hasbro had touched him up with in a careful effort to make him appear to be an old man.

Professor Fleming blinked at him when they peeked in at the door of the laboratory. They found him hovering over a beaker set on a long littered tabletop. His hair hung in a thatch over his forehead, and he gazed at them through thick glasses, as if he didn't quite recognize St. Ives at all for a moment. Then he smiled, stepping across to slap St. Ives on the back. "Well, well, well," he said, his brogue making him sound a little like Lord Kelvin. "You're looking... somehow..." He gave that line up abruptly, as if he couldn't say anything more without being insulting. He grinned suddenly and cocked his head. "No hard feelings, then?"

"None at all," St. Ives said, wondering what on earth the man was talking about. Hard feelings? Of all the confounded things...

"My information was honest. No tip. Nothing. You've got to admit you lost fair and square."

"I'm certain of it," St. Ives said, looking at Hasbro.

"That's two pounds six, then, that you owe me." He stood silently, regarding St. Ives with a self-satisfied smile. Then he turned away to adjust the flame coming out of a burner.

"For God's sake!" St. Ives whispered to Hasbro, appealing to him for an explanation.

Past the back of his hand, Hasbro whispered, "You've taken to betting on cricket matches. You most often lose. I'd keep that in mind for future reference." He shook his head darkly, as if waging sums was a habit he couldn't countenance.

St. Ives was dumbstruck. Fleming wanted his money right

now. But two and six? He rummaged in his pocket, counting out what he had. He could cover it, but he would be utterly wiped out. He would go home penniless after paying off the stupid gambling debt run up by his apparently frivolous future-self.

"This is an outrage," he whispered to Hasbro while he counted out the money in his hand.

"I beg your pardon," Fleming said.

"I say that I'm outraged that these men can't play a better game of cricket." He was suddenly certain that the cricket bet had been waged merely as a lark—to tweak the nose of his past-time self. The very idea of it infuriated him. What kind of monster had he become, playing about at a time like this? Perhaps there was some sort of revenge he could take before fleeing back into the past.

Fleming shrugged, taking the money happily and putting it away in his pocket without looking at it. "Care to wager anything further?"

St. Ives blinked at him, hesitating. "Give me just a moment. Let me consult." He moved off toward the door, motioning at Hasbro to follow him. "Who is it that I lost money on?" he whispered.

"The Harrogate Harriers, sir. I really can't recommend placing another wager on them."

"Dead loss, are they?"

"Pitiful, sir."

St. Ives smiled broadly at Fleming and wiped his hands together enthusiastically. "I'm a patriot, Professor," he said, striding across to where Fleming filled a pipette with amber liquid. "I'll wager the same sum on the Harriers. Next game."

"Saturday night, then, against the Wolverines? You can't be serious."

"To show you how serious I am, I'll give you five to one odds."

"I couldn't begin to…"

"Ten to one, then. I'm filled with optimism."

Fleming narrowed his eyes, as if he thought that something was fishy, perhaps St. Ives had got a tip of some sort. Then he shrugged in theatrical resignation. Clearly he felt he was being subtle. "I normally wouldn't make a wager of that magnitude," he said. "But this smells very much like money in the savings bank. Ten to one it is, then." They shook hands, and St. Ives nearly did a jig in the center of the floor.

"Well," Fleming said, "down to work, eh?"

St. Ives nodded as Professor Fleming held out to him a big two-liter Mason jar full of clear brown liquid.

"A beef broth infusion of penicillium mold," he was saying.

"Ah," St. Ives said. "Of course." Mold? What the hell did the man mean by that? He looked at Hasbro again, hoping to learn something from him.

"I've been constrained..." Hasbro started to say, but St. Ives ignored him. He didn't want to hear the rest.

"I'm not certain of the result of an oral dosage," Fleming said. "I'm a conservative man, and I hesitate to recommend this even to a scientist such as yourself. It needs time yet—months of study..."

"I appreciate that," St. Ives said. "It's a case of life and death, though. Literally—the life of a child who, for the sake of history, mustn't be allowed to die." He realized suddenly that this must sound like the statement of a lunatic, but Professor Fleming didn't seem confused by it. What had his future-time self told the man? Did Fleming know? He couldn't know; otherwise Hasbro wouldn't have gone through the rigamarole with the powder. "Can you give me a rough dosage, then?"

"Pint a day, taken in two doses until it's used up. Keep it cold, mind you."

"Cold," said St. Ives, suddenly worried. He would have to have a word with the mother. They could keep the stuff outside, on the roof. The London autumn would keep it cold. He hoped that the woman wasn't too far gone in gin to comprehend. But how *could* she comprehend? Here he was, a gentleman with a jar of beef broth, stepping in out of the future. He could claim to be the Angel of Mercy, perhaps show her the bathyscaphe in order to prove it. Better yet, he would show her a purse full of money, promising to come back with more if she carried out his instructions. Damn it, though; he didn't have any money. He would have to go back after some. Suddenly he was fiercely hungry, and he realized that he hadn't eaten in—how long? About eighty-odd years as the crow flies.

He took the jar from Fleming. He had what he came for, but this was too good an opportunity. Here he was in 1927, in the pathology lab of a man who was apparently one of the great minds in the field. Now that he looked about him, St. Ives could see that the laboratory was filled with unidentifiable odds and ends. He must at least know more about this beef broth elixir. "I'm still confused on a couple of issues," he said to Fleming. "Tell me how it was that you came across this penicillium."

Fleming clasped his hands together, stretching his fingers back as if he were loosening up, warming to the idea of telling the tale thoroughly. "Well," he began, "it was almost entirely by accident…" At which point Hasbro pulled out a pocket watch, contorting his face with a look of dismay.

"Our train," Hasbro said, interrupting.

"Oh, damn our train, man." St. Ives cast him a look of thinly veiled disgust.

"I'm afraid I must insist, sir." He put a hand into his coat, as if he had something in there to enforce his insistence.

St. Ives was filled with black thoughts. Here was an opportunity gone straight to hell. They had him on a leash, and they weren't going to reel out any slack line. Hasbro was deadly serious; that was the only thing that kept St. Ives in check. He knew too well that one didn't argue with Hasbro when the man was serious. Hasbro would prevail. You could chisel that legend in stone without any risk. And when Hasbro was in a prevailing mood, he generally had reason to be. It wouldn't do to argue.

The two of them left, proceeding directly to the station, and then, after no more than five minutes' wait, back to Harrogate where they drove once again out to the manor, St. Ives holding on to the jar of beef broth all the way home.

At last they stood awkwardly on the meadow, near the silo door. Hasbro held the keys in his hand. It was clear that they weren't going back into the manor. St. Ives would have liked another small glass of port before toddling off to the past again, but there he wasn't about to ask for it. Like as not, Hasbro would have complied, but there was still such a thing as dignity. Best to do what the note had instructed, leave straightaway. He had what he came for. "I'll be setting out now," he said.

"Best of luck, sir."

"I'll see you, then, when this is through."

"That you will, sir. I'd like to buy you a drink when the time comes."

"You can buy me two," St. Ives said, striding away through the weeds toward the silo. "And then I'll buy you two," he shouted, turning to wave one last time. Hasbro stood on the lonely meadow, watching him depart, the picture of an old and trusted friend saddened at this dangerous but necessary leave-taking. Either that or he was hanging about to make damn well certain that St. Ives wouldn't cut any last-moment capers.

Seated in the bathyscaphe at last, he wrapped the jar in his new coat and secured it beneath the seat, then turned his attention to the instruments. He had the wide world to travel through, but ultimately he left the spatial coordinates alone, returning simply to his own time, some two hours after his first departure so that he wouldn't run into an astonished Parsons still snooping around the silo.

He was filled with relief at being back in his own time at last, and he sat back with a sigh, regarding his surroundings. Grinning, he thought all of a sudden of the bet he'd made with Fleming. All the hindsight in the world hadn't been worth a farthing to his future-self, had it? He still couldn't believe that he had taken to betting on cricket matches. He simply wouldn't. He was warned now. Who the hell had that been? The Harrogate Haberdashers? He laughed out loud. What a lark! His future-self would be hearing the news from Hasbro about now: "I what…!"

He climbed out of the machine, weary as a coal miner but still smiling. There was no sign of Parsons, nothing but silence round about him. The silo was dim, but even in the gray twilight he could see clearly enough to know that something had changed—something subtle. Terror coursed through him. This wasn't good. This was what he had feared. It was exactly what his future-time self had been desperate to avoid.

He couldn't at first determine what it was, though. His tools lay scattered as ever… Then he saw it suddenly—the chalk marks on the wall. The message was different now. In clean block letters a new message was written out: "Harriers 6, Wolverines 2."

≈ MRS. LANGLEY'S ADVICE ≈

There was too much danger in staying. St. Ives would have liked to sleep, to eat, to sit in his study and look at the wall. The beef broth, though, wouldn't allow for it. Time—that commodity that he ought to have had plenty of—wouldn't allow for it. It would insist on going on without him, piling up complications, altering everything. Never had he been so aware of the ticking of the clock.

He sneaked into the manor by way of the study window, remaining long enough to fetch out a purse containing twenty pounds in silver, and then, without so much as a parting glance, he loped back out to the silo, climbed into the machine, and sailed away in the direction of midcentury Limehouse.

He arrived a week earlier than he had on his previous visit. The child wouldn't be so far gone this time around. It was just after midnight, and to St. Ives, looking down over Pennyfields, it seemed as if nothing had changed. There was no fog, and the moon was high in the sky. But the old woman sat as ever, smoking her pipe amid the scattered junk slopping out of the door of the general shop. Sailors came and went from public houses. The seething Limehouse night was oblivious to the tiny tragedy unfolding in the attic room above.

He pulled the garret window open and stepped in carefully, setting the jar beneath the sill. The child slept on the floor, although not under the window now. He breathed heavily, obviously already congested, lying on his back with the ragged blanket pulled to his chin. But for the sleeping child, the room was empty.

"Damn it to hell," St. Ives muttered. He *must* talk to the mother. He couldn't be popping back in twice a day to feed the child the beef broth. He could think of nothing to do except leave, climb back into the bathyscaphe and reset the coordinates, maybe arrive three hours from now, or maybe yesterday. What a tiresome thing. He would make the child drink the broth now, though, just to get it started up. Trusting to the future was a dangerous thing. A bird in the hand... he told himself.

There was a noise outside the door just then, a woman's high-pitched laughter followed by a man's voice muttering something low, then the sound of laughter again. A key scraped in the lock, and St. Ives hurried across toward the window, thinking to get out onto the roof before he was discovered. The door swung open, though, and he stopped abruptly, turning around with a look of official dissatisfaction on his face. He would have to brass it out, pretend to be—what? Merely looking grave might do the trick. Thank heaven he had shaved and cut his hair.

In the open doorway stood the woman who must have been the child's mother. She was young, and would have been almost pretty but for the hardness of her face and her general air of shabbiness. She was half drunk, too, and she stood there swaying like a sapling in a breeze, looking confusedly at St. Ives. Sobering suddenly, she peered around the room, as if to ascertain that she hadn't opened the wrong door by mistake. Then, as her countenance changed from confusion to anger, she said, "What are you doing here?"

The man behind her gaped stupidly at St. Ives. He was drunk, too—drunker than she was. A look of skepticism came into his eyes, and he took a step backward.

"Who's this?" asked St. Ives, nodding at the man. He pitched it just as hard and mean as he could, as if it meant something, and the man turned around abruptly, caromed off the hallway wall, and scuttled for the stairs. There was the sound of pounding feet and a door slamming, then silence.

"There goes half a crown," she said steadily. "I'm not any kind of bunter, so if you've been sent round by the landlord, tell him I pay my rent on time, and that there wouldn't be half so many bunters if they didn't gouge your eyes out for the price of a room."

"Not at all, my good woman," St. Ives said, surprised at first that she was moderately well-spoken. Then he realized that it wasn't particularly surprising at all. She had been the wife of a famous, or at least notorious, scientist. The notion saddened him. She had fallen a long way. She was still youthful, and there was something in her face of the onetime country girl who had fallen in love with a man she admired. Now she was a prostitute in a lodging house.

She stood yet in the doorway, waiting for him to explain himself, and St. Ives realized almost shamefully that she held out some little bit of hope—of what? That she wouldn't have lost her half crown after all? St. Ives, her eyes seemed to say, was the sort of man she would expect to find in the West End, not your common sailor rutting his way through Pennyfields before his ship set sail.

"I'm a doctor, ma'am."

"Really," she said, stepping into the room now and closing the door. "You wouldn't have brought a drain of gin, would you? A *doctor*, is it? Brandy more like it." She gave him what was no doubt meant to be a coy look, but it disfigured her face awfully, as if it weren't built for that sort of theatrics, and it struck him that a great deal had been taken away from her. He could hear the emptiness in her voice and see it in her face. The country girl who had fallen in love with the scientist was very nearly gone from her eyes, and there would come a day when gin and life on the Limehouse streets would sweep it clean away.

"I'm afraid I haven't any brandy. Or gin, either. I've brought this jar of beef broth, though." He pointed at the jar where it sat beneath the window.

"What is it?" She looked at him doubtfully, as if she couldn't have heard what she thought she heard.

"Beef broth. It's an elixir, actually, for the child." He nodded at the sleeping boy, who had turned over now and had his face against the floor molding. "Your son is very sick."

Vaguely, she looked in the child's direction. "Not so sick as all that."

"Far sicker than you realize. In two weeks he'll be dead unless we do something for him."

"Who the devil *are* you?" she asked, finally closing the door and lighting a lantern on the sideboard. The room was suddenly illuminated with a yellow glow, and a curl of dirty smoke rose toward a black smudge on the ceiling. "Dead?"

"I'm a friend of your husband's," he lied, the notion coming to him out of the blue. "I promised him I'd come round now and then to check on the boy. Three times I've been here, and each time there was no one to answer my knock, so this time I let myself in by the window. I'm a doctor, ma'am, and I tell you the boy will die."

At the mention of her husband, the woman slumped into a chair at the table, burying her face in her hands. She remained so for a moment, then steeled herself and looked up at him, some of the old anger rekindled in her eyes. "What is it that you want?" she asked. "Have your say and get out."

"This elixir," he said, setting to work on the child, "is our only hope of curing him." The boy awoke just then, recoiling in surprise when he saw St. Ives huddled over him.

"It's all right, lamby," his mother said, kneeling beside him and petting his lank hair. "This man is a doctor and a friend of your father's."

At the mention of this, the child cast St. Ives such a glance of loathing and repugnance that St. Ives nearly toppled over backward from the force of it. The complications of human misery were more than he could fathom. "Do you have a cup?" he asked the mother, who fetched down the tumbler from the sideboard—the same tumbler that St. Ives, a week from now, would use to...

What? He reeled momentarily from a vertigo that was the result of sudden mental confusion.

"Careful!" the woman said to him, taking the half-filled tumbler away.

"Yes," he said. "Have him drink it down. All of it."

"What about the rest of it?" she asked. "A horse couldn't drink the whole jar."

"Two of these glasses full a day until the entire lot's drunk off. It *must* be done this way if you want the boy to live."

She looked at him curiously, hesitating for a moment, as if to say that life wasn't worth so much, perhaps, as St. Ives thought it was. "Right you are," she said finally, returning the glass to the sideboard. "Go back to sleep now, lamby," she said to the boy, who pulled the blanket over his head and faced the wall again. She patted her hair, as if waiting now for St. Ives to suggest something further, as if she still held out hope that he might be worth something more to her than the half crown she had lost along with the sailor.

"Well," he said awkwardly, stepping toward the window. "I'll just…" He looked down at the jar again. In his haste to leave he had nearly forgotten it. Now he was relieved to see it, if only to have something to say. "This has to be kept cold. My advice is to leave it on the roof, outside the window."

In truth, the room itself was nearly cold enough to have done the trick. It was a good excuse to swing the window open and step through it, though. Hurrying, he nearly fell out onto the slates. He stood up, brushing at his knees, and leaned in at the window.

"Leaving by way of the roof?" she asked, making it sound as if she had been insulted. It was clear to her now that this was just what St. Ives was doing. He wasn't interested in what she had to sell. He had chased off the sailor, and to what end? Now she would have to go down into the street again… "Stairs aren't good enough for you?" she asked, raising her voice. "Don't want to be seen coming down from the room of a *whore*? Precious bloody doctor…"

He nodded weakly, then checked himself and shook his head instead. "My… carriage."

"On the roof, is it?"

"Yes. I mean to say…" He hesitated, stammering. "What I meant to say was that there was the matter of the money."

"To hell with your filthy money. I wouldn't take it if I were dying. Lord it over someone else. If the boy gets well, I'll thank you for it. But you can bloody damn well leave and take your money with you."

"It's not *my* money, madam, I assure you. Your husband and

I wagered a small sum four years back. I've owed him this, with interest." St. Ives pulled out the purse he'd taken from his study in Harrogate, full of money that would no doubt mystify her. She would make use of it, though. Here goes another twenty, he thought, handing it in to her. She paused just a moment before snatching it out of his hand. It would buy a lot of gin, anyway... Ah well, he would win it back from Fleming someday in the hazy future. Time and chance, after all...

He tipped his hat and walked away across the roof, having nothing further to say. He would trust to fate. He climbed in through the hatch and calibrated the instruments, his head nearly empty of thought. Then he realized that during the entire exchange in the room he had never once associated the sick child with Dr. Ignacio Narbondo. There seemed to be no earthly connection between the two. Even the look on the child's face at the mention of his father—a shadow so deep and dark that it belied the child's age. Well... it didn't bear thinking about, did it?

As he switched on Lord Kelvin's machine, he glanced out one last time through the porthole. There was the woman, holding the purse, staring out through the open window with a look of absolute and utter amazement on her face. Then, along with the rest of the world, she vanished, and he found himself hurtling up the dark well of time, her face merely an afterimage on the back of his eyelids.

There was one more task ahead of him before the end. He would pay a visit to Mrs. Langley. Into his head came the vision of her stumping across the grass toward the silo, ready, on his behalf, to beat men into puddings with her rolling pin. He wondered suddenly how it was that virtues seemed to come so easily to chosen people, while other people had to work like dogs just to hold on to the few little scraps they had.

He reappeared directly outside his study this time, on the lawn, and he sat for a moment in the time machine, giving himself a rest. The silo, right now, contained its own past-time version of the bathyscaphe, which would right at that moment be in the process of itself becoming incorporeal. As his future-self had pointed out in the nastily written note, it wouldn't do to drop straight into the middle of it.

He sat for a moment orienting himself in time. Soon, within the next couple of hours, his past-time self would wander shoeless over to Lord Kelvin's summerhouse and would hit upon the final bit of information he would need to make the machine work. But right now, his past-time self was disintegrating into atoms, crawling unhappily toward the window. Well, it couldn't be helped. If his past-time self was irritated at this little visit, then he was a numbskull. It was his own damned fault, treating Mrs. Langley as if she were a serf.

After another few moments, he climbed out onto the ground, nervously keeping an eye open for Parsons even though he knew from experience that he would easily accomplish his task and be gone before Parsons came snooping around. He checked his pocket watch, calculating the minutes he had to spare, then climbed in through the window. He couldn't bring himself to look at the desk. It was a mess of broken stuff from when he'd hammered everything with the elephant.

Suddenly he staggered and nearly fell. A wave of vertigo passed over him, and he braced himself against the back of a chair, waiting for it to subside. For a moment he was certain what it meant—that one of his future-time selves was paying him a visit, that in a moment there would be *two* invisible St. Iveses lying about the room. The time machine would sit on the lawn unguarded, except that it, too, would disappear. The whole idea of it enraged him. Of all the stupid…

But that wasn't it. The vertigo passed. His skin remained opaque. He didn't disappear at all. This was something else. Something was wrong with his mind, as if bits of it were being effaced. It struck him suddenly that his memory was faulty. Expanses of it were dissipating like steam. Vaguely, he remembered having gone to Limehouse twice, but he couldn't remember why. The events of the last few hours—the trip to Oxford, then back to Limehouse to dose the child—those were clear to him. But what did he even mean by thinking, "*back* to Limehouse"? *Had* he been there twice?

Now for an instant it seemed as if he had, except that one of his visits had the confused quality of a half-forgotten dream that was fading even as he tried desperately to hold on to it. Fragments of it came to him—the smell of the sick child's room, the sensation of treading on the sleeping form, the cold tumbler pressed against his ear.

All this, though, was swept away again by an ocean of memories that were at once new to him and yet seemed always to have been part of him. These new memories were roiled up and stormy, half-hidden by the spindrift of competing, but fading, recollections that floated and bobbed on this ocean like pieces of disconnected flotsam going out with the tide: the tumbler, the candle, his stepping across to open a heavy volume lying on a decrepit table. Beyond, bobbing on the horizon, were a million more odds and ends of memory, already too distant to recognize. For a moment he was neither here nor there, neither past nor present, and the storm tossed in his head. Then the sea began to calm and authentic memory took shape, shuffling itself into order, solid and real and full.

Those bits of old flotsam still floated atop it, though, half submerged; he could still make a few of them out, and he knew that soon they would sink forever. Frantically, he searched the desk for a pen and ink. Then, finding them, he began to write. He forced himself to recall the hard, cold base of the tumbler against his ear. And with that, the memory of his first past-time trip to Limehouse ghosted up once again like a feebly collapsing wave, a confused smattering of images and half-dismantled thoughts. The pen scratched across the paper. He barely breathed.

Then, abruptly, it was gone again, whirled away. The very idea of the tumbler against his ear vanished from his head. Weirdly, he could recall that the image of a tumbler had meant something to him only seconds ago; he even knew what tumbler it was that his mind still grappled with. He could picture it clearly. But now it was half full of beef broth, and the mother was feeding it to her sick child, calling him pet names.

Hurriedly, he read over the notes he had scrawled onto the paper—fragments of memory written out in half sentences. "Woman in bed, snoring. Stepping on child. Child nauseated, feverish. Pneumococcal meningitis diagnosed. Child near death. Inflamed meninges cause spinal deformity; hence Narbondo the hunchback? Left coat, money on table. Watch for Parsons snooping along the window..." There was more of the same, then the writing died out. What did it all mean? He no longer knew. It was all fiction to him. It had no reality at all. What coat? He was wearing his coat—or what would *become* his coat, anyway. Hunchback? Narbondo a hunchback? He cast around in his mind, trying to make sense of it all. Narbondo was not a hunchback. And why would Parsons come snooping along the window? Parsons was no stranger at the manor, not since Lord Kelvin had discovered that St. Ives possessed the machine. Parsons was petitioning him daily to give it up.

Just then he saw something out of the corner of his eye, near the window, but when he turned his head, it was gone. It had looked for all the world like a body, lying crumpled on the floor. His heart raced, and he half stood up, wondering, squinting his eyes. There was nothing, though, only the meadow with the machine sitting among wildflowers like an overgrown child's toy. St. Ives looked away, but when he did, he saw the thing again, peripherally. He held his gaze steady, focusing on nothing. The thing lay by the window; he must have stepped on it when he came in. It was his past-time self, lying where he had fallen by the window—or rather it was the ghost of his past-time self, unshaven and with wild hair—waiting for his future-time self to leave.

Ghosts—it all had to do with ghosts, with the fading of one world and the solidifying of the next. Just as concrete objects— he, the machine, any damned thing at all—began to fade when a copy of that object appeared from another point in time, so did memory. Two conflicting memories could not coexist. One would supplant the other. Whatever Narbondo had been, or would have become if St. Ives had left him alone, he wasn't that anymore. St. Ives had dosed him with Fleming's potion, and he had got well. And the result was that he hadn't become a hunchback at all, which is what he must have become in that other history that St. Ives had managed to efface. Which meant, if St. Ives read this right, that the sickly child *would not have died at all*, but must ultimately have recovered, although deformed by the disease.

Fear swarmed over him again. He had gone and done it this time. He was a victim of his own compassion. He had meddled with the past, and the result was that he had come back to a different world than he had left. How much it was different, he couldn't say. He had forgotten. And it didn't matter now, anyway; there was no recalling that lost fragment of history. All of that had simply ceased to exist.

What a fool he had been, jaunting around through time as if he were out for a Sunday ramble. Why in heaven's name hadn't his future-time self warned him against this? The damned old fool. Perhaps he could go back and unchange what he had changed. Except, of course, that he had made the change over fifty years ago. He would have to return to Limehouse and convince himself not to leave Fleming's elixir with the mother, but to dump it off the roof instead. Let the child suffer… Well…

Going back would make a bad matter worse. He could see that. He sighed, getting a grip, finally. What else might all this mean? Anything might have changed, maybe for the better. Mightn't Alice be alive? Why not? He was filled with a surge of hope, which died out almost at once. Of course she wasn't alive. That much hadn't changed. His mind worked furiously, trying to make sense of it. Here was his littered desk and his ghostly unshaven self lying in a heap by the window. What was all that but a bit of obscure proof that this world must be in most ways similar to the one he had buggered up?

And more than that, he *remembered* it, didn't he?—the business of his going out barefoot, of his finally putting the machine right, of his saving Binger's dog, of Alice murdered in the Seven Dials.

Where was Mrs. Langley? He *must* talk to her. At once. Speak to her and get out. He was only a day away from his own rightful time. Minimize the damage, he told himself, and then go home.

He went out into the kitchen. There she was, the good woman, putting a few things into a carpetbag, packing her belongings. She was going to her sister's house. Her face was full of determination, but her eyes were red. This hadn't been easy for her. St. Ives hated himself all of a sudden. He would have fallen to his knees to beg her forgiveness, except that she disliked that sort of indignity almost as much as he did.

"Mrs. Langley," he said.

She turned to look at him, affecting a huff, her mouth set in a thin line. She wasn't about to give in. By damn, she was bound for her sister's house, and soon, too. This had gone on entirely long enough, and she wouldn't tolerate that sort of tone, not any longer. Never in all her born years, her face seemed to say.

Still, St. Ives thought happily, ultimately she *wouldn't* go, would she? She would be there to take on Parsons with a rolling pin. St. Ives would succeed, at least in this one little thing. She was regarding him strangely, though, as if he were wearing an inconceivable hat. "I've come to my senses," he said.

She nodded. Her eyes contradicted him, though. She looked at him as if he had lost his senses entirely this time, down a well. Inadvertently he brushed at his face, fearing that something… Wait. Of course. He wasn't the man that he had been a half hour ago. He was clean-shaven now, his hair cut. He wore a suit of clothes with idiotic lapels, woven out of the wool of sheep that didn't yet exist. He was a man altered by the future, although there would be nothing but trouble in telling her that.

"What I mean to say is that I'm sorry for that stupid display of temper. You were absolutely right, Mrs. Langley. I *was* stark raving mad when I confronted you on the issue of cleaning my desk. I

know it wasn't the first time, either. I… I regret all of it. I've been…
It's been hard for me, what with Alice and all. I'm trying to put that
right, but I've made a botch of it so far, and…"

He found himself stammering and was unable to continue.
Dignity abandoned him altogether, and he began to cry shamelessly,
covering his face with his forearm. He felt her hand on his shoulder,
giving him a sympathetic squeeze. Finally he managed to stop, and
he stood there sniffling and hiccuping, feeling like a fool.

She brought him a glass of water, which he drank happily.
"It's not every man," she said to him, "who can eat crow without
the feathers sticking to his chin." She nodded heavily and slowly.
"Nothing wrong with a good cry now and then. It's like rain—
washes things clean."

"God bless you, Mrs. Langley," he said. "You're a saint."

"Not by a considerable sight, I'm not. You come closer, to my
mind. But I'm going to be bold enough to tell you that you're not cut
out for saint work. You've got the instinct, but you haven't got the
constitution for it. And if I was you I'd find a new situation just as
quick as I might. Go back to science, Professor, where you belong."

"Thank you," he said, in control of his emotions once more.
"That's just where I intend to go, just as you advise. There's one
little bit of business to attend to first, though, and by heaven, if
there were one person on earth I could bring along to help me see
it through, you would be that person, Mrs. Langley."

"I'm good with a ball of dough, sir, but not much else."

"You're a philosopher, my good woman, whether you know it
or not. And from now on your salary is doubled."

She started to protest, but he cut her off with a gesture. "I've
got to hurry," he said. "Carry on here."

With that he left her, returning to the study and going out

through the window, stepping carefully over that bit of floor where his ghost lay invisible. He clambered straight into the bathyscaphe and left. His past-time self would materialize again and set to work on the machine, never knowing that the Mrs. Langley problem had been solved. It occurred to him too late that he might have written himself a note, explaining that he had come back around to patch things up with her. But to hell with that. His past-time self was a fool—more of a fool, maybe, than his future-time self was—and would probably contrive to muck things up in some new lunatic way, threatening everything. Better to let him go about his business in ignorance.

In the time machine, he returned to the now-empty silo, some couple of hours past the time when he had fled from Parsons and the constable. It occurred to him, unhappily, that there had been no Langdon St. Ives existing in the world during the last two hours, and that the world didn't give a rotten damn. The world had teetered along without him, utterly indifferent to his absence. It was a chilling thought, and was somehow related to what Mrs. Langley had been telling him. For the moment, though, he put it out of his mind.

There were more immediate things to occupy him. It mightn't be safe to leave the machine in the silo yet, but he couldn't just plunk down on the meadow every time he reappeared. Parsons had petitioned him, as one scientist to another, to give it up. It belongs to the Crown, he had said. Parsons hadn't known until that very afternoon in Harrogate, though, that the time machine was workable, that St. Ives had got the bugs out of it at long last. Well, he knew now. There wouldn't be any more petitions. And next time Parsons wouldn't just bring the local constable along to help.

St. Ives climbed out wearily, looking around him at the sad

mess of tools and debris. He had half a mind to set in on it now—neaten it up, stow it away as if it was himself he was putting right. He couldn't afford the time, though.

Then he saw the chalk markings—changed again. Lord help us, he thought, feeling again a surge of distaste for his future-self. This was no lark, though. It was a warning: "Parsons looming," the message read. "Obliterate this and take the machine out to Binger's."

~~ THE RETURN OF DR. NARBONDO ~~

Smoking very slowly on his pipe, Mr. Binger stood staring at St. Ives, who smiled cheerfully at him from halfway out of the bathyscaphe hatch. St. Ives had just arrived from out of the aether, surprising Mr. Binger in the pasture. "Good afternoon, Mr. Binger," St. Ives said.

Furry hopped around, happy to see St. Ives and not caring a rap that he had appeared out of nowhere. Binger looked up and down the road, as if expecting to see a dust cloud. There was nothing, though, which seemed to perplex him. Finally, he removed his pipe and said, nodding at the bathyscaphe, "No wheels, then?"

"Spacecraft," St. Ives said, and he pointed at the sky. "You remember that problem with the space alien some few years back?"

"Ah!" Binger said, nodding shrewdly. That would explain it. Perhaps it would suffice to explain everything—St. Ives's sudden arrival, his strange clothes, his being clean-shaven and his hair trimmed. Just a little over two hours ago St. Ives had been in town, disheveled, hunted, looking like the Wild Man of Borneo. He had been babbling about cows and seemed to be in a terrible hurry. Now the mysteries were solved. It was spacemen again.

St. Ives climbed down onto the ground and petted Furry on the back of the head. "Can you help me, Mr. Binger?" he asked.

"Aye," the man said. "They say it was you that saved old Furry up to town today."

"Do they?"

"They do. They say you come near to killing yourself over the dog, nearly struck by a wagon. Chased off that bloody mastiff, too. That's what they say."

"Well." St. Ives was at a momentary loss. "They exaggerate. Old Furry's a good pup. Anyone would have done the same."

"Anyone didn't do it, lad. You did, and I thank you for it."

Anyone didn't *know* to do it, St. Ives thought, feeling like a fraud. He hadn't so much chosen to save the dog as he had been *destined* to save the dog. Well, that wasn't quite true, either. The past few hours had made a hash of the destiny notion—unless there were infinite destinies waiting in the wings, all of them in different costumes. One destiny at a time, he told himself, and with the help of Binger and his sons, St. Ives hauled the time machine to the barn, in among the cows, and then Mr. Binger drove him most of the way back to the manor. He walked the last half mile, thinking that if Parsons was lurking about, it would be better not to reveal that Binger was an accomplice.

It was dark when he bent through the French window again and lay down on the divan, telling himself that he ought not to risk waiting, that he ought to be off at once and finish what he had meant to finish. But he was dog-tired, and what he meant to do wouldn't allow for that. Surely an hour's sleep...

The street in the Seven Dials came unbidden into his mind—the rain, the mud, the darkness, the shadowy rooftops and entryways and alleys—but this time he let himself go, and he wandered into his dream with a growing sense of purpose rather than horror.

Hasbro shook him awake in the morning. The sun was high and the wind blowing, animating the ponderous branches of the oaks out on the meadow. "Kippers, sir?" Hasbro asked.

"Yes," said St. Ives, sitting up and rubbing his face blearily.

"Secretary Parsons called again, sir, early this morning. And Dr. Frost, too, some little time later."

"Yes," said St. Ives. "Did you tell them to return?"

"At noon, sir. An hour from now."

"Right. I'll…" He stood up slowly, wondering what it was he would do. Eat first. Mrs. Langley came in just then, carrying the plate of kippers and toast and a pot of tea. She handed him a newspaper along with it, just come up from London. The front page was full of Dr. Frost, lately risen from his long and icy sleep. He had got the ear of the Archbishop of Canterbury, it said, who had taken a fancy to Frost's ideas regarding the rumored time-travel device sought after by the Royal Academy.

The journalist went on to describe the fanciful device in sarcastic terms, implying that the whole thing was quite likely a hoax perpetrated for the sake of publicity by Mr. H. G. Wells, the fabulist. Frost already had a large following, though, and considered himself a sort of lay clergyman. He had taken to wearing white robes, and his followers had no difficulty believing that his rising from an icy sleep held some great mystical import. Accordingly, there was widespread popular support for Frost's own claim to the alleged time-travel device. What Frost had proposed that had won the heart of the Archbishop yesterday afternoon was that a journey be undertaken to the very dawn of human time, to the Garden itself, where Frost would pluck that treacherous apple out of Eve's hand by main force and beat the serpent with a stick...

The article carried on in suchlike terms, the journalist sneering openly at the whole notion and lecturing his readers on the perils of gullibility. St. Ives didn't sneer, though. Frost's, or Narbondo's, capacity for generating mayhem and human misery didn't allow for sneering. The journalist was right, but really he knew nothing at all. Frost would take the machine if he could; but he jolly well wouldn't travel back to eat lunch with Adam and Eve.

St. Ives scraped up the last of the kippers and watched the meadow grasses blow in the wind. Parsons, too. He intended to make careful scientific journeys, he and his cronies. They knew St. Ives had the machine. The evidence was all circumstantial, but it was sufficient. Two days ago they had finished their search of the sea bottom off Dover. There was no trace of the machine, no wreckage beyond that of the sunken ships. And Parsons had made it very clear to St. Ives that Lord Kelvin, just yesterday afternoon, had recorded strange electromagnetic activity in the immediate area of Harrogate.

Parsons had been diplomatic. St. Ives, he had said, was always the most formidable scientist of them all—far deeper than they had supposed. His interest in the machine, his pursuit of it, could not have culminated in his destroying it. Parsons admired this, and because he admired it, he had come to appeal to St. Ives to give the thing up peaceably. There was no profit in coming to blows over it. The law was all on the side of the Academy.

Well, today it would come to blows. His future-time self knew that, and had returned to warn him with the chalk markings in the silo. And Parsons was right. The device *did* belong to the Academy, or at least to Lord Kelvin. When had Kelvin deduced that St. Ives had it? It was conceivable that he suspected it all along, and that he had let St. Ives fiddle away on it, thinking to confiscate it later, after the dog's work was done.

Hasbro appeared just then. "Secretary Parsons," he announced.

"Tell him to give me five minutes. Pour him a cup of tea."

"Very good, sir."

St. Ives stood up, straightened his clothes, ran his hands through his hair, and went out again at the window, heading at a dead run for the little stable behind the carriage house. Sitting in the parlor, Parsons wouldn't see him, and given a five-minute head start, St. Ives didn't care a damn what Parsons saw. Across the meadow the silo stood as ever, but now with the door ajar. They had broken into it, thinking simply to take the machine, but finding it gone. So much for being peaceable. He laughed out loud.

Hurriedly, he threw a saddle onto the back of old Ben, the coach horse, and old Ben immediately inflated his chest so that St. Ives couldn't cinch the girth tight. "None of your tricks, Ben," St. Ives warned, but the horse just looked at him, pretending not to understand. There was no time to argue. St. Ives had to get across the river before he was seen. He swung himself into the saddle and walked the horse out through the open stall gate, heading for the river. The saddle was sloppy, and immediately slid to the side, and St. Ives wasted a few precious moments by swinging down and tugging on the girth, trying to cinch it tighter. Old Ben reinflated, though, and St. Ives gave up. There was no time to match wits with a horse, and so he remounted, hunkering over to the left and trotting out toward the willows along the river.

They crossed the bridge and cantered along the river path, emerging through the shrubbery on the opposite bank. Now the manor was completely hidden from view, and so St. Ives kicked old Ben into the semblance of a run. They skirted the back of Lord Kelvin's garden and angled toward the highroad, St. Ives yanking at the saddle to keep it on top of the horse. On the road he headed east at a gallop, leaning hard to the left to compensate and keeping his head down along Ben's neck, like a jockey. Old Ben seemed to recall younger and more romantic days, and he galloped away without any encouragement at all, his mane blowing back in St. Ives's face.

St. Ives smiled suddenly with the exhilaration of it, thinking of Parsons unwittingly drinking tea back at the manor, wondering aloud of Hasbro whether St. Ives wasn't ready to see him yet. Suspicions would be blooming like flowers. The man was a simpleton, a bumpkin.

The saddle inched downward again, and St. Ives stood up in the stirrups and yanked it hard, but all the yanking in the world seemed to be useless. Gravity was against him. The right stirrup was nearly dragging on the ground now. There was nothing for it but to rein up and cinch the saddle tight. He pulled back on the reins, shouting, "Whoa! Whoa!" but it wasn't until old Ben had stopped and begun munching grasses along the road, that St. Ives, still sitting awkwardly in the saddle, heard the commotion behind him. He turned to look, and there was a coach and four, kicking up God's own dust cloud, rounding a bend two hundred yards back.

"Go!" he shouted, whipping at the reins now. "Get!"

The horse looked up at him as if determined to go on with its meal of roadside grass, but St. Ives booted it in the flanks, throwing himself forward in the teetering saddle, and old Ben leaped ahead like a charger, nearly catapulting St. Ives to the road. They were off again, pursued now by the approaching coach. The saddle slipped farther, and St. Ives held on to the pommel, pulling himself farther up onto the horse's neck. His hat flew off, and his coat billowed out around him like a sail.

He turned to look, and with a vast relief he saw that they would outdistance the coach, except that just then the saddle slewed downward and St. Ives with it, and for a long moment he grappled himself to the horse's flank, yanking himself back up finally with a handful of mane. He snatched wildly at the girth, trying to unfasten the buckle as old Ben galloped up a little rise. St. Ives cursed himself for having bothered with the saddle in the first place, of all the damned treacherous things. Somehow the girth was as tight as it could be now, wedged around sideways like it was. And it was behind his thigh, too, where he couldn't see it, and old Ben didn't seem to care a damn about any of it, but galloped straight on up the middle of the road.

They crested the rise, and there before them, coming along peaceably, was another coach, very elegant and driven by a man in bright red livery. The driver shouted at St. Ives, drawing hard on the reins and driving the coach very nearly into the ditch.

A white-haired head appeared through the coach window just then—Dr. Frost himself, his eyes flying open in surprise when he saw who it was that galloped past him on a horse that was saddled sideways. Frost shouted, but what he said was lost on the wind. St. Ives tugged hard on the girth, feeling it give at last, and then with a sliding rush, the saddle fell straight down onto the road, and old Ben tripped right over it, stumbling and nearly going down. St. Ives clutched the horse's neck, his eyes shut. And then the horse was up again, and flying toward Binger's like a thoroughbred.

When St. Ives looked back, Frost's coach had blocked the road. It was turning around, coming after him. Parsons's coach was reining up behind it. Good, let them get into each other's way. He could imagine that Parsons was apoplectic over the delay, and once again he laughed out loud as he thundered along, hugging old Ben's neck, straight through Binger's gate and up the drive toward the barn.

"They're after me, Mr. Binger!" St. Ives yelled, leaping down off the horse.

"Would it be men from the stars again?" Binger asked, smoking his pipe with the air of a farmer inquiring about sheep.

"No, Mr. Binger. This time it's scientists, I'm afraid."

Binger nodded, scowling. "I don't much hold with science," he said, taking his pipe out of his mouth. "Begging your honor's pardon. You're not like these others, though. The way I see it, Professor, there's this kind of scientist, and then there's that other kind." He shook his head darkly.

"This is that other kind, Mr. Binger." And right then St. Ives was interrupted by a clattering out on the road—both the coaches drawing up and turning in at the gate. St. Ives strode straight into the barn, followed by Binger, who still smoked his pipe placidly. One of his sons was mucking out a pen, and old Binger called him over. "Bring the hayfork," he said. The dog Furry wandered out of the pen along with him, happy to see St. Ives again.

At the mention of the hayfork, St. Ives paused. "We mustn't cause these men any trouble, Mr. Binger," he said. "They're very powerful…" But now there was a commotion outside—Parsons and Frost arguing between themselves. St. Ives would have liked to stop and listen, but there wasn't time. He climbed aboard the bathyscaphe, pulling the hatch shut behind him. Settling himself in the seat, he began to fiddle with the dials, his heart pounding, distracted by what he saw through the porthole.

Seeing the hatch close down, Frost and Parsons gave off their bickering and hurried along, followed by the driver in livery and two other men who had accompanied Parsons. Binger pointed and must have said something to Furry, because as Parsons and one of the other men made a rush forward, the dog bounded in among them, catching hold of Parsons's trousers and ripping off a long swatch of material. Parsons stumbled, and the other man leaped aside, swiping at the dog with his hand.

Binger's son shoved the end of the hayfork into the dirt directly in front of the man's shoe, and he ran into the handle chin-first, recoiling in surprise and then pushing past it toward the machine as Furry raced in, nipping at his shoe, finally getting hold of his cuff and worrying it back and forth.

Parsons was up and moving again and Frost along with him. Together they rushed at the machine, pushing and shoving at each other, both of them understanding that they had come too late. Furry let loose of his man's cuff and followed the two of them, growling and snapping so that they were forced to do a sort of jug dance there in front of the porthole while they implored St. Ives with wild gestures to leave off and see reason.

But what St. Ives saw just then was darkness, and he heard the by-then-familiar buzzing and felt himself falling down and down and down, leaving that far-flung island of history behind him, maybe never to return. And good riddance—Narbondo, somehow, wasn't born to be a man of the cloth. He looked cramped and uncomfortable in his new clothing. And Parsons— well, Parsons was Parsons. You could take a brickbat to history six-dozen times, and somehow Parsons would stride into every altered picture wearing the same overgrown beard.

Just then there was darkness of a different caliber again, nighttime darkness and rain falling. St. Ives came to himself. He patted his coat pocket, feeling the cold bulk of the revolver. He had come too far now to be squeamish about anything, but it occurred to him that there was something ironic about setting out to kill the man whose life you had recently worked so hard to save. But kill him he would, if it took that.

He climbed out into the wind-whipped rain, looking around him, and realized with a surge of horror that he was on the wrong street. He could see it straight off. He had dreamed that line of storefronts and lodging houses too many times to make any mistake now. What he saw before him was utterly unfamiliar. He had been rushed by the imbroglio in Binger's barn and had miscalibrated the instruments. But how? Panicked, he ran straight up the street, slogging through the flood, listening hard to the sounds of the night.

Lancing suddenly through his head came the confused thought that it might be worse than a mere miscalculation. It was conceivable that anything and everything might have changed by now. He had wanted the same street, but what did the notion of sameness mean to him anymore? He slowed to a stop, rain falling on him in torrents.

Then he heard it—the clatter of a coach. Gunfire!

He ran toward the sound, wiping the water out of his eyes, breathing hard. Another gunshot rang out and then a shriek and, through the sound of the rain, the tearing and banging of the cabriolet going over in the street. He could picture it in his mind—his past-time self running forward, hesitating to shoot until it was too late, and...

He rounded the corner now, his pistol drawn, and nearly ran Narbondo down as he crouched over Alice, whose leg was pinned under the overturned cabriolet. Narbondo pointed his pistol at her head, staring at the rainy street where Langdon St. Ives ought to have been, but wasn't. Hasbro and Kraken stared at the street, too, but there was nothing at all there save the empty coach, and although St. Ives alone knew why that was, he didn't give it a moment's thought, but lashed out with the gun butt and hammered Narbondo across the back of the head.

St. Ives's hand was in the way, though, and he managed only to hit Narbondo heavily with his fist. Narbondo's head jerked down, and his hands flew outward as he tumbled away from Alice. He rolled forward, still holding his pistol, struggling to one knee and looking back wild-eyed at St. Ives, then immediately aiming the pistol and shooting it wildly, without an instant's hesitation.

Already St. Ives was lunging toward him, though, and the shot went wide. Three years of pent-up energy and fear and loathing drove St. Ives forward, unthinking. Narbondo staggered backward, sprawling through the water, starting to run even before he was fully on his feet. St. Ives ran him down in three steps. Too wild to shoot him, St. Ives grabbed the back of Narbondo's coat and clubbed him again with the pistol butt, behind the ear this time, and Narbondo's head jerked sideways as he brought his pistol up, firing it pointlessly in the air. St. Ives hammered him again, still clutching his jacket as Narbondo slumped to his knees, his pistol falling into the street. A hand seized St. Ives's wrist as he raised his gun yet again, and St. Ives turned savagely, ready to strike. It was Hasbro, though, and the look on his face made St. Ives drop his own pistol into the water.

"He shot her," St. Ives mumbled. "I mean…" But he didn't right then know what he meant. He was vastly tired and confused, and he remembered the child drinking medicinal beef broth in Limehouse. He looked back down the street. Alice wasn't shot—of course she wasn't shot. Kraken bent over her, lifting off the top end of the cabriolet and then stooping to untie her. St. Ives walked toward them, as old suppressed memories freshened and grew young again in his mind. Mercifully, the rain let off just then, and the moon shone through the clouds, lightening the street.

"That were a neat trick, sir," Kraken said to him enthusiastically, standing up and making way for him. "I could have sworn you was in the coach. Why, I even seen you stepping out through the open door. Then you was gone, and then here your honor was again, smashing your man in back of the head." He looked at St. Ives with evident pride, and St. Ives kneeled in the flooded street, feeling for a pulse, fearing suddenly that it was too late after all. The crash alone might have... Then Alice opened her eyes, rubbed the back of her head with her hand, winced, and smiled at St. Ives. She struggled to sit up.

"I'm all right," she said.

Kraken let out a whoop, and Hasbro, who had dragged Narbondo to the roadside, helped both St. Ives and Alice to their feet, pulling them into a doorway out of the rain.

"Tie Narbondo up with something," St. Ives said to Kraken.

Kraken looked disappointed. "Begging your honor's pardon," he said, taking St. Ives aside, "but hadn't we ought to kill him? I should think that would be recommended, seeing as who he is. You know he would have shot her. A life don't mean nothing to the likes of him. Give me the word, sir, and I'll make it quick and quiet."

St. Ives hesitated, then shook his head tiredly. "No, he's got too much to do yet. All of us do. Heaven alone knows what will come of the world if we don't all play our parts—heroes, villains, spectators, and fools. Perhaps it's already too late," he said, half to himself. "Perhaps this changes the script utterly. So tie him up, if you will. He'll spend some time in Newgate before he escapes."

Kraken nodded, although he looked confused, like a man who understood nothing. St. Ives left him to it and faced Alice again. He sighed deeply. She was safe. Thank God for that. "I'll have to go," he said to her.

"What?" Alice looked at him in disbelief. "Why? Aren't I going with you? We'll all go, the sooner the better."

St. Ives was swept with a wave of passion and love. He kissed her on the mouth, and although she was surprised by the suddenness of it, she kissed him back with equal passion.

Hasbro cleared his throat and went off abruptly toward where Kraken was tying up Narbondo with the reins from the wrecked cabriolet.

I *will* stay, St. Ives thought suddenly. Why not? His past-time self—now nothing but a ghost—wouldn't be any the wiser. He was already gone, flitted away, into the mists of abandoned time. Why not start anew, right now? They would take a room in the West End, make it a sort of holiday—nothing but eating and the theater and lounging about all day long. He suddenly felt like Atlas, having at last shrugged off the world, ending what had turned out to be merely a lengthy nightmare.

Alice was regarding him strangely, though. "You look awful," she said, squinting at him as if she realized something was wrong but had no notion how to explain it. He knew what she had meant to say. She had meant to say that he looked old, worn-out, thin, but she had caught herself and had said something more temporary so as to preserve his feelings. "What's wrong?" she asked suddenly, and his heart sank.

He looked out into the street, where his past-time self lay invisible in the water and muck of the road. You fool, he said in his mind. I *earned* this, but I've got to give it to you, when all you would have done is botch it utterly. But even as he thought this, he knew the truth—that he wasn't the man now that he had been then. The ghost in the road was in many ways the better of the two of them. Alice didn't deserve the declined copy; what she wanted was the genuine article.

And maybe he could become that article—but not by staying here. He had to go home again, to the future, in order to catch up with himself once more.

"I won't be gone but a moment," he said, glancing back toward where he had left the machine. "And when I appear again, I might be confused for a time. It'll pass, though. When you see me next, tell me that I'm a mortal idiot, and I'll feel better about it all."

"What on *earth* are you talking about?" she asked, looking at him fearfully, as if he had lost his mind.

He almost started to explain, but it was too much for him. Now that he had made up his mind to leave, the future was calling to him, and the shortest route back to it sat in the middle of the street a block away. "Trust me," he said. "I won't be gone a moment." He kissed her again, and then stepped out of the doorway, turned, and loped off, not looking back, his heart full of gladness and regret.

EPILOGUE

He landed on the meadow, half expecting heaven knew what. There was no telling what was what anymore. Maybe Parsons would leap out of the bushes and claim the machine. Maybe Narbondo, or Frost, or whatever he called himself now, would menace him with a revolver. Maybe anything at all—he didn't care. They could have the machine. He didn't want it anymore. His work was done, and he was ready to confront the results, whatever they were, and then to give up his chasing around through time. At least for the moment.

What he couldn't do, though, was face himself. There were two present-time copies of him now, and he was determined to let the other one depart gracefully and, he hoped, privately. What sort of man had he become? A happy man, perhaps, who wouldn't relish the idea of this copycat St. Ives popping in at the window to replace him? Or, just as easily, a miserable man, who might gladly hand over the reins and disappear forever.

Fragments of his memory were even now starting to wink out

like candle flames in a breeze. His nightmares about the Seven Dials, the very fact of his returning there, his whole tiresome rigamarole life during the past three years—all of it would become vapor.

And good riddance, too. He would welcome new memories, whatever they were. He realized that this was bluff, though. He thought one last time of the child Narbondo, huddled in dirty rags in Limehouse, and of his mother and the sailor in the doorway. There were memories worse than his own. That's partly why he was still sitting there in the machine, wasn't it? He had no idea what he would find inside the manor—who he would discover himself to be.

He climbed through the hatch into the wind. It was sunny and fine with just the hint of a smoky autumn chill in the air. He pulled his coat straight and fiddled with his tie, realizing that he was a wet and dirty mess. But he felt fit, somehow, as if a great weight had fallen away from him, and then, in a confused shudder of memory, it occurred to him that he couldn't bear eating eggplant again. Not once more.

His head reeled, and he nearly fell over. Eggplant? It was starting. His memories would depart like rats from a ship. Disconcerted, he hurried through the window, into the study, and there stood Hasbro, staring at him strangely.

"We'll have to move the time machine into the silo," St. Ives said to him. "I wasn't sure whether it was empty or not."

"I beg your pardon, sir?"

"The machine on the meadow," St. Ives said. "We'll want to get it into the silo, out of the weather."

"I'm sorry, sir. I wasn't aware that Dr. Frost had returned it. This comes as a surprise. I was under the impression that he had stolen it from Secretary Parsons. He's brought it here, has he?"

"Stolen it?" St. Ives was gripped by vertigo just then. His

memory shifted. He fought to hold on to it, afraid to let pieces of it go completely. "Of course," he said. "It's a mystery to me, too, but there it sits." He gestured out the window, where the machine glinted in the sunlight.

Narbondo had taken it! That was funny, hilarious. Now St. Ives had reappeared with it, and that meant that Narbondo's copy was in the process of disappearing, out from under his nose, and stranding him, St. Ives hoped, in some distant land. Either that or the villain was gone somewhere in time, and would someday perhaps return, and then St. Ives's machine would disappear. Time and chance, he reminded himself.

And then new memories, like wraiths, drifted into his mind, shifting old memories aside. "Alice!" he cried. "Is she here then?"

"She's still in the parlor, sir," Hasbro said, looking skeptical again. "Where you left her moments ago. I really must advise you against that suit, by the way. The tailor is certifiable. Perhaps if I laid something else out…"

"Yes," St. Ives said, hurrying through the door. "Lay something out."

He was dizzy, foggy with memories, drunk on them. And as if he were literally drunk, he felt free of the depressing guilt and worry that had plagued him… for how long? And why? He couldn't entirely remember. It seemed so long ago. His mind was a confusion of images now, stolen from the man whose ghost was where? Blowing away on the wind, across the meadow? Would he remain to haunt the manor, exercising a ghostly grudge against his other-time self for having returned to supplant him?

Mrs. Langley loomed out of the kitchen, her hands white with baking flour.

"I've taken your advice, Mrs. Langley," he said.

"Beg pardon, sir? What advice?"

"I…" What advice, indeed? He didn't know. He pulled at the collar of his shirt, which was too tight for him. "Nothing," he said. "Never mind. I was thinking out loud." She nodded, baffled, and he forced himself along, walking toward the parlor. Steady on, he told himself. Keep your mouth closed. There's too much you don't know yet, and too much of what you do know is nonsense.

And then there sat Alice, reading a book. He was astonished by the sight of her. She hasn't aged a day, he thought joyfully, and then he wondered why on earth he thought any such thing, and a garden of memories, like someone else's anecdotes, sprung fully bloomed in his mind. His head swam, and he sat down hard on a chair. Maybe he ought to have waited, to have grappled with the business of memory before wading in like this. But he hadn't, and now that he got a good look at Alice, with her dark hair done up in a ribbon, he was happy that he hadn't wasted another moment.

"I'm sorry about the eggplant," she said to him, just then glancing up from her book. She squinted at the sight of him, looking unhappily surprised, and he grinned back at her like a drunken man. "That awful suit of clothes," she said. "You look rather like a dirty sausage in them, don't you? I've seen those before…"

"I'm just getting set to burn them," St. Ives said hurriedly. "They're a relic, from the future. A sort of… costume."

"Well," she said. "The trousers might look better if you hadn't waded across the river in them. But I *am* sorry about the eggplant. I don't mean to make you eat it every night, but Janet's cook, Pierre, is apparently fixing it for us this evening. Will you be ready to leave in a half hour? You looked wonderful just moments ago."

"Eggplant? Janet?" His mind fumbled with the words. Then through the parlor window he saw Alice's garden, laid out in neat rows. Purple-green eggplants hung like lunar eggs from a half-dozen plants.

"Oh, *Janet*," he said, nodding broadly. "From the Harrogate Women's Literary League!"

"What on earth is wrong with you? Of course that Janet, unless you've got another one hidden somewhere. And don't go on about the eggplant this time, will you?"

Suddenly he could taste the horrible sour stuff. He had eaten it last night mixed up with ground lamb. And the night before, too, stewed up with Middle Eastern spices. He had been on a sort of eggplant diet, a slave to the vegetable garden.

"You could use a bath, too, couldn't you? At least a wash up. And your hair looks as if you've been out in the wind for three days. What *have* you been up to?"

"I... old Ben," he began. "Mud. Up to his blinkers."

But then he was interrupted by a sort of banshee wail from somewhere off in the house. It rose to a crescendo and then turned into a series of squalling hoots.

He stood up, looking down at Alice in alarm. "What..."

"It's not all that bad," she said, nearly laughing. "Look at you! Anyone would think you hadn't ever changed his nappies before. They can't be a tremendous lot dirtier than your trouser cuffs, can they?"

The baby's crying had very nearly inundated him with fresh memories. Little Eddie, his son. He smiled broadly. *It was his turn to change the nappies.* They had agreed against a nanny, were bringing up the child themselves, spoon-feeding it with stuff mashed up out of the garden. Eddie wouldn't eat eggplant either, wouldn't touch it on a bet. "Good old Eddie!" he said out loud.

"That's the right attitude," Alice said.

And now in the shuffle of the old being washed out by the new, he saw it all clearly for one last long moment. His fears for the future had come to nothing. Alice was safe. They had a son. The garden was growing again. They were happy now. *He* was happy, nearly delirious. He found that he couldn't think in terms of future-time selves and past-time selves any longer. None of his other selves mattered to him at all.

There was only he and Alice and Eddie and... rows and rows of eggplant. He nearly started to whistle, but then the baby squalled again and Alice widened her eyes, inviting him to do something about it.

"I've changed my mind," he said, heading for the stairs. "I love eggplant." And he very nearly meant it, too.

ABOUT THE AUTHOR

James Paul Blaylock was born in Long Beach, California in 1950, and attended California State University, where he received an MA. He was befriended and mentored by Philip K. Dick, along with his contemporaries K.W. Jeter and Tim Powers, and is regarded as one of the founding fathers of the steampunk movement. Winner of two World Fantasy Awards and a Philip K. Dick Award, he is currently director of the Creative Writing Conservatory at the Orange County School of the Arts, where Tim Powers is Writer in Residence. He is also a professor at Chapman University, where he has taught for twenty years. Blaylock lives in Orange CA with his wife, they have two sons.

THE AYLESFORD SKULL
James P. Blaylock

It is the summer of 1883 and Professor Langdon St. Ives, brilliant but eccentric scientist and explorer, is at home in Aylesford with his family. A few miles to the north a steam launch has been taken by pirates above Egypt Bay, the crew murdered and pitched overboard.

In Aylesford itself a grave is opened and possibly robbed of the skull. The suspected grave robber, the infamous Dr. Ignacio Narbondo, is an old nemesis of Langdon St. Ives. When Dr. Narbondo returns to kidnap his four-year-old son Eddie and then vanishes into the night, St. Ives and his factotum Hasbro race into London in pursuit...

Also available as a limited edition.

HOMUNCULUS
James P. Blaylock

It is the late 19th century and a mysterious airship orbits through the foggy skies. Its terrible secrets are sought by many, including the Royal Society, a fraudulent evangelist, a fiendish vivisectionist, an evil millionaire and an assorted group led by the scientist and explorer Professor Langdon St. Ives.

Can St. Ives keep the alien homunculus out of the claws of the villainous Ignacio Narbondo?

"The fastest, funniest, most colorful and grotesquely horrifying novel that could ever be written about Victorian London." — Tim Powers, author of *On Stranger Tides*